THE FUGITIVE SNARE

Matt & Michelle Book 3

HENRY VOGEL

Published in the United States of America by Rampant Loon Press, an imprint of Rampant Loon Media LLC, P.O. Box 111, Lake Elmo, Minnesota 55042. "Rampant Loon Press" and the Rampant Loon colophon are trademarks of Rampant Loon Media LLC.

www.rampantloonmedia.com

Cover design by goonwrite.com

ISBN: 978-1-938834-76-9 (ebook)

ISBN: 978-1-938834-00-4 (print)

First publication: May 2017

For Barry, Chris, Ellen, Jana, and Stephen.
Thank you for making my books better.

PARTY CRASHERS

"You know, Mom, it might not be a good idea throwing a surprise party for our first anniversary." Sitting across the dinner table from me, Mom shook her head in mock irritation at me. Grinning, I jerked a thumb at Michelle, "She might shoot someone before she realized what was going on."

"It wouldn't be that bad, babe." Michelle affected a tone of wounded pride. "You *know* I keep my blaster set to stun."

"Told you Matt would find out," Cassie, my adopted sister, said to Mom.

"So you did," Mom sighed. "May we still throw a party for you?"

"That would be lovely, Angela." Michelle looped her arm through mine. "Can we keep it low-key? Dinner at our house with family and close friends?"

Mom and Michelle immediately began planning, only to be interrupted by Cassie. "Do you want me to tell you what you decide to do and who you're going to invite?"

Mom heaved a theatrical sigh. "Precogs take all the fun out of planning parties."

I gave Dad a sidelong look. "*That* is Mom's idea of fun?"

"You have no idea, son." Mom arched an eyebrow at Dad, prompting him to add, "For which I am forever grateful."

By the time Michelle and I headed home, she and Mom had everything arranged.

Before we left, I asked, "May I add one thing to the party plan?"

I felt Mom's surprise and pleasure that I was taking some interest in it. "Of course, dear."

"Don't bring gifts." I put an arm around Michelle and pulled her close. "We already have everything we'll ever need."

Of course, everyone brought gifts, anyway.

Mom and Dad gave us a big plot of land outside of Landingtown. The settlements on Ark's Landing are sparse and land is essentially free, so the real gift was an open budget with the best construction firm on the planet.

"Build the house of your dreams," Mom told us. "And make sure to include separate rooms for those two daughters you're going to have. By the time they're teenagers, you'll thank us."

Michelle's parents gave us his and hers blasters with all of the latest tech—including grips that molded to the user's hand, ultra-high capacity battery packs, and advanced targeting systems. Unable to contain his excitement over the new weapons, Jonas immediately fell into a technical discussion with my equally-excited wife.

Michelle's mother, Magda, finally intervened, gently prying the blaster from Jonas's hands. "Dear heart, why don't you wait until *after* the party to show Michelle new and exciting ways to shoot people?"

Jonas let his wife pull him away, but said, "I assumed she and Matt would have other things on their minds by then."

Michelle kissed her father on the cheek. "Don't worry, Daddy, you've explained enough for me to use it in an emergency. You can show me more tomorrow."

Nancy Martin presented us with one of the data pads from the *Ark 2*, the generation ship she had liberated years before we ever met her. Knowing her history with the ship and the rarity of artifacts from it, the gift was particularly special. Lilla and Raal, the couple who helped her defeat the insane AI controlling the ship, gave us a hand-made quilt.

"It's a traditional wedding gift in our village. Since we didn't know you when you got married, we decided it was appropriate for an anniversary gift." Lilla grinned as we admired the quilt. "For winter weddings, the couple gets under the quilt and it keeps the groom's back warm during the wedding night. For summer weddings, you spend your wedding night on top of it, so its padding protects the bride's back and the groom's knees."

As everyone laughed, my adopted sister Cassie and my long-time friend, Rob, presented us with one last gift. The two of them stood by shyly as Michelle and I gently removed wrapping paper from a framed painting.

"I drew it and Rob did the colors." Cassie smiled up at Rob. "I think he did really good!"

"We both selected the frame." Rob gave us a nervous smile. "I hope you like it."

Michelle and I gazed in wonder at the painting. It showed our family, but not our present family. I guessed the Matt and Michelle in the painting were in our late twenties. Standing next to them were two absolutely adorable blonde-haired little girls—the daughters Cassie already told us we would have—but there was a new addition to the family. Michelle held a boy who couldn't have been more than a year old.

As our family crowded around to look at the painting, Michelle wiped at her eyes and asked, "We're going to have a son?"

"Yeah," Rob said, the nervousness fading from his smile.

Cassie nodded, but added, "Unless Psi Corps grabs Matt, or something else bad happens, you are."

Kristin—Cassie called the older girl her psychic sister since the pair of them, along with Gene, Mark, and their mentor Zav, went on the run together—glared at Cassie. "Can't you precogs just let those of us stuck in the present enjoy the future even once without ruining it?"

Cassie wasn't fazed by the glare. "It's just a *possible* future,

Kristin. It's a really nice one and I hope, hope, hope it comes true. But Matt and Michelle need to remember nothing in the future is certain. Just because Rob or I see something, that doesn't mean it's going to happen."

I pulled Cassie and Rob into a hug. "Well, I love it and am going to do everything in my power to make sure the painting comes true."

Raal stood. "That sounds like a subtle hint for us to clear out so the happy couple can try out their new quilt!"

It hadn't been, but then Michelle gave me a seductive look over the top of the painting. Suddenly, I couldn't wait for our friends and family to clear out. Fortunately, everyone took Raal's suggestion to heart. We hugged and kissed them all as they left.

Lilla whispered something in Michelle's ear, causing both women to glance at me and laugh. I gave Raal a questioning glance.

He shrugged. "Who knows what runs through the minds of women? But from that look they gave you, I'd say you're in for a very good time, tonight."

As the door closed behind the last of our guests, I smiled at Michelle. "Our life sure is a lot more interesting with a pair of precognitive psychics hanging around."

"Yeah. I thought my life was exciting enough with just an empath in it." Her gaze slid from me to the painting. A bright smile lit her face. "But, oh Matt, we're going to have a *son*!"

"And don't forget two beautiful daughters," I said. Throwing the quilt over my shoulder, I asked, "Would you like your anniversary present now?"

My wife smiled in anticipation. "Absolutely. I'll give you yours in a few minutes."

I took a couple of deep breaths and cleared my mind of everything except thoughts of Michelle and my love for her. Carefully, I wrapped all of it in my power and gently pulled it from my mind and guided it toward Michelle.

She was watching me, an expectant look on her face. I saw her expression change as I guided my wrapped gift of love into her mind. Michelle is very used to the feeling of my mind merging with hers, though it always surprises her when I do it from a distance.

"What's this you're sending to me, babe?"

I was concentrating so hard on holding my power wrapped around the gift, I could only manage a one-word reply. "Everything."

I released my gift into Michelle's mind, hoping and praying it worked as intended. A look of pure wonder spread over Michelle's face, making her even more beautiful than ever. Without conscious thought, she dropped into a chair and just basked in the inner glow from my love. I kept my power hovering around her mind, doing my best to hold the emotions in her mind as long as possible. No matter how hard I try, though, the effect is short-lived. Less than a minute later, the last of it slipped past my ability and away from Michelle's mind.

I stopped concentrating and took my first good look at Michelle since that first expression of wonder. I was shocked to see tears flowing down her cheeks. I rushed to her and looked into her eyes.

"Oh God, did I hurt you?" I felt my own eyes well up at the thought of hurting the woman sitting before me. "I didn't mean-"

"Shhh," Michelle said. Then she made sure I couldn't say anything else by kissing me. It was long and tender and sensuous and deeply loving and went on and on. When we finally broke apart, Michelle rested her forehead against mine. "I thought feeling your emotions when we made love was amazing. But *that*... My God, Matt, *that*... Babe, I don't have any words to describe just how wonderful that felt."

Her blue eyes sparkled, mesmerizing me.

"But maybe I can show you."

She took the quilt and spread it out on the living room floor. "You know how Zav has been teaching me to shield my thoughts?" When I nodded, Michelle continued, "I convinced him to teach me how to open my mind, too. So you can feel everything I feel. I only hope my gift is half as fantastic as yours."

It was all of that and more. For the next couple of hours, Michelle and I shared ourselves with an intimacy we'd never achieved, before. We never did make it to the bedroom.

That's why Psi Corps didn't get us the minute their team crashed through our bedroom windows.

Michelle, trained almost from birth by her security-specialist father, reacted even before the first shot sounded from our bedroom. Already draped over me, she tightened her grip on me and rolled us behind the cover of our sofa. As I came fully awake, Michelle grabbed our new blasters from the coffee table. Soft shots sounded from the bedroom as she handed my blaster to me.

Michelle thumbed on her new gun and toggled the power level switch. "Take no chances, babe! Set it for kill!"

Low cursing came from our bedroom as the intruders discovered we weren't lying in the bed. As I followed Michelle's instructions, I reached out with my empathic ability. At the least, I could find out how many attackers we faced and their locations. Once I knew that, I could delve into my ever-increasing bag of psychic tricks and probably rout them without firing a shot.

Michelle, knowing I would automatically do a psychic scan, asked, "How many of them are there, Matt?"

"I...don't know." Saying that, I felt my first twinge of real worry.

"Crap. Someone did their homework and sent a bunch of psychic nulls after us." Even as she said that, Michelle tapped a flat section on the end of the gun. The image of our bookcase appeared and I remembered Jonas showing Michelle the targeting sights. A message flashed on the small screen, prompting an excited grin from Michelle. "Oh sweet—it's got infrared!"

From our bedroom, we heard one voice speaking too quietly for us to understand. As the voice fell silent, Michelle reached over and tapped controls on my gun. The screen came to life, showing the strangely distorted colors you get from the infrared spectrum.

"Scan the rest of the house, babe. I'll check the bedroom."

With my back against the sofa, I simply pointed my gun at the wall in front of me and swept it in an arch. At the same time, I was aware of Michelle rising into a crouch and leveling her gun over the sofa. Two completely irrational thoughts flitted through my mind as she did that—concern that I didn't want the attackers ogling my naked wife and the realization that Michelle made a really hot naked Amazon warrior.

Michelle snapped off two shots. I heard the first shot hit a wall. A scream followed the second. At the same time, my gun splashed two red, man-shaped blobs onto my targeting screen. Taking a cue from my wife, I snapped off four quick shots.

It hurt to watch some of our books blow apart and others begin burning, but it cleared the way to the wall. My second shot blew through the wall, leaving a clear line of fire into the next room for the final two. Having heard my first two shots, the men in the other room were already diving for cover. My third shot grazed one of them, and the fourth missed, entirely.

"Two were in the foyer, hon. I winged one and they dove into the kitchen. I haven't reacquired them yet."

"Three in our bedroom, babe. One is down, two took cover behind our bed."

I heard a creak from above and immediately swung my gun to the ceiling. I picked up another red blob on the roof and started firing. It took three shots to punch through the ceiling and the roof above. By that time, the blob was retreating.

A shot blazed between Michelle and me. We both turned and opened up on the doorway between the living room and the kitchen. Our two attackers ducked out of sight behind something very big and very solid.

"Keep them pinned. And, when we build our new house, remind me to make sure the butcher block isn't freestanding," Michelle said, spinning back toward the bedroom. She sprayed half a dozen quick shots through the walls. This time, return shots came through our rapidly disappearing bedroom wall. Michelle ducked down behind the sofa as the shots flew wide.

"We can hold you off all night if we have to," Michelle called. "But help will be here in less than a minute."

A deep, man's voice said, "We took out your security team first thing. There's no one left to help you."

Michelle raised her blaster over the sofa and fired several blind shots. "If you think that, you have made a *serious* mistake."

I saw a blaster poke around the butcher block and opened up with a stream of shots. Michelle, meanwhile, turned her gun to the ceiling. Her infrared sight must have picked up the same guy I shot at earlier because she peppered the ceiling with a string of shots. I immediately pointed my gun over the sofa and fired into our bedroom.

Return fire was sparse. Since the attackers were using the stun setting, they couldn't simply blast through walls and furniture like we could. They were showing good fire discipline, though, not wasting their shots unless there was a chance they could hit us.

At least, that's how they *had* been fighting. Either they got tired of taking fire with no real chance to get us or their orders allowed for killing us if they couldn't capture us. Whatever the reason, the fire from the bedroom suddenly intensified and began ripping through the sofa. Michelle and I rolled away from our previous positions, but that break gave the guys in the kitchen the chance to join in. We flipped the coffee table up on its side. It wouldn't last long under this barrage, but some cover is better than none at all.

Flipping over one of the end tables and adding it to our meager barrier, Michelle gasped, "Remind me to accessorize our next house with grenades, babe."

Then a shot came in from above—the guy on the roof was back. Michelle cried out as the bolt hit her leg. Terror surged through me as I spun to check on her. Gritting her teeth against the pain, Michelle lay with her leg limp and unmoving. The guy on the roof was still using the stun setting—probably hoping for one last chance to capture us.

Anger replaced the terror I'd felt only a split second earlier. Rolling onto my back, I found the shooter on the roof just as he took a second shot. His bolt splashed the spot I'd vacated. Rolling over, I returned fire. My second shot caught him in the hip. His leg collapsed and he fell head-first into my third shot. It caught him in the neck and blew his head from his shoulders. Two more shots tore into the body before I brought my rage under control.

Probably remembering my reaction the last time I killed a man —Paco, the Rockville Station bully boy—Michelle risked taking her eyes off of the fight and fixed them on me. Concern was plainly written on her face.

"Are you going to be okay, babe?"

In answer, I shouted to our attackers, "I killed your guy on the roof—blew his head right off. I'll do the same to anyone else who takes a shot at my wife!"

To drive home my point, I opened fire on the guys hiding behind our bed. Michelle used her good leg to spin about and open fire on the butcher block in the kitchen doorway. The men in the kitchen stayed behind the huge chunk of wood while those in the bedroom remained hunkered down behind what was left of our bed.

"Can we blow away their cover before the power cells run dry?" I asked.

"You might blow apart the bed," Michelle responded, "but there's no way I can get through that block of wood. Our best bet is to get the guys in the bedroom and hope the ones in the kitchen make a run for it."

Before I could respond to that, we heard a crash from the kitchen. The men behind the butcher block shouted in surprise. Then came the deep, powerful crack of a blaster rifle sounded. It was followed by three more in rapid succession.

A familiar—and very welcome—voice called from the kitchen, "How many more, pumpkin?"

"Two hiding behind the bed in our bedroom," Michelle responded. "There's a third, but he's been down and unmoving since the beginning."

"Are you or Matt hurt?"

"Not really. I took a stun bolt to the leg."

Jonas sprang through the kitchen doorway, firing into our bedroom as he came. The men fired a couple of wild shots in return, but Jonas ignored them. He rolled as he landed, tossed something into the other room, and called, "Duck!"

I threw myself on top of Michelle and carried us both to the floor behind what was left of the sofa. Something went 'whump' in our bedroom. Jonas charged into the room, gun held at the ready.

A couple of seconds later, he called, "Clear. You can get up now."

"Daddy, could you do me a favor?"

Jonas appeared in the doorway, coming toward us. "Anything you need, pumpkin."

Michelle squirmed behind me. "Don't come any closer, Daddy!"

A look of concern appeared on Jonas's face, but he stayed where he was. "What's the matter? I thought you said you weren't hurt badly."

"I'm *not*," Michelle snapped. "I'm naked. And so is Matt."

I barely refrained from laughing as both Michelle and Jonas blushed. Instead, I asked, "Is our closet blown to pieces or can you get us some clothes, Jonas?"

A few seconds later, pants and shirts came flying over the sofa. I helped Michelle pull short pants up over her stunned leg, made sure she could balance well enough to pull on her shirt, and then dressed myself.

Another off-duty member of our security team called Jonas on his comm and reported the on-duty team was only stunned. Glancing around the remains of our little house, Jonas growled, "They're going to *wish* they were dead when I get through with them. Get a med team up here. Michelle has a minor wound and a couple of the attackers are still alive."

Jonas signed off and, having been given the okay to approach by his now-clothed daughter, gave us both a hug. "You're sure you're both okay?"

"Yes, we're fine." As her father released her, Michelle held up her new blaster and grinned. "By the way, Daddy—best. Anniversary. Gift. *Ever*!"

Michelle and her father were deep in their discussion about the new guns when the med team arrived. Having checked his daughter's leg for himself—Jonas had intelligently selected a pair of shorts for Michelle—he waved the team into what was left of our bedroom to check on the two surviving members of the attack squad. With their arrival, Jonas stopped discussing hardware and got our after-action report.

Michelle gave it, wrapping up with a question. "Do you think it's Psi Corps, Daddy? I mean, who else would even know half-a-dozen psychic nulls, much less have a trained strike team of them?"

"That's the most reasonable answer, pumpkin," Jonas said. "Assuming that's true, it's a safe bet the only reason you're still alive is because Psi Corps still wants Matt for themselves. If the team simply wanted to kill you, they'd have succeeded."

"Yeah, I know," my wife said. "We left our home on Draconis to get away from them. We left the Federation to get away from them. Why can't they just leave us alone?"

I wrapped an arm around Michelle's shoulders. "Because they know we won't leave them alone. We're already laying the groundwork for our campaign to repeal the psychic impressment laws. A lot of people will lose a lot of power and prestige if we succeed. Some of those people are probably behind this attack."

"May I suggest you back off from that plan, sir?" Jonas always calls me 'sir' when he falls back into full bodyguard mode. "As hard as my men and I will work to protect you, we cannot stop the entire Terran Federation. If they want you, they'll get you." Jonas gave me a level stare. "And they'll get my only child at the same time."

"Dammit, Daddy, don't you *dare* try using me against Matt like that!" Michelle leaned toward her father and actually poked him in the chest for emphasis. "You trained me. You put me on Matt's detail in secret. You knew there would be risks."

Jonas didn't back down. "Risks from kidnappers, pump-"

"Don't call me 'pumpkin' when we're fighting!" Michelle snapped.

"By all means, *Mrs. Connaught*," Jonas shot back, his voice rising. "But whatever I call you, it doesn't change the situation. I cannot protect you from the full might of a government that controls a hundred and eighteen star systems!"

I tried to stem the argument with some misdirection. "A hundred and eighteen? Does that mean the Federation finally accepted the Briap System's petition for membership?"

Father and daughter rounded on me.

"Don't change the subject!" they snapped in unison.

This is where Jonas and Michelle should have laughed and turned sheepish looks on each other. Instead, it they turned their white-hot glares back on each other and both opened their mouths to speak. Then one of the med-techs appeared and knelt down next to Michelle.

"Excuse me, ma'am," she said to Michelle, "but I just need to examine your wound."

Michelle sucked in a breath as the tech gently probed the blaster burn. Nodding to herself, the tech reached into her case and pulled out a small medical device I didn't recognize.

"It's not a serious wound, ma'am, but you'll want to take it easy on the leg for a couple of days." She placed the device directly on top of the wound. Michelle winced and then her face relaxed.

"That ought to take care of the pain for a while. I'll put a Second Skin patch on it to protect it while it heals. I do recommend you get a doctor to check it out tomorrow." The med-tech glanced at Jonas and Michelle as she expertly applied the patch. "That's all I have to say. You two can go back to shouting and glaring each other to death."

Unlike my pathetic attempt to break the tension, the med-tech's words sliced right through it. Jonas and Michelle suddenly burst out laughing in response. The woman turned a knowing smile my way and winked before addressing Jonas.

"We've got the two surviving assailants stabilized, sir," she said. "One of them will make it, for sure. The other one caught the brunt of the grenade blast. I wouldn't bet any money that he'll pull through."

"Thank you, Sarah," Jonas said. "When will the ambulance be here?"

Sarah checked her wrist comp. "They're pulling up outside now, sir. There's also a note that your wife and the Connaughts are at the perimeter."

"Of course. How foolish of me to forget about them." Jonas checked his own wrist comp and then tapped the screen. "Tendack, you can let the families through, now."

"They're on their way, sir."

As he keyed off the wrist comp's comm, Jonas gave Michelle a rueful smile. "I'm just like any father—I just want to keep my little girl safe. Even if she's not a little girl anymore."

"I know, Daddy," Michelle smiled gently.

Then our families rushed into the house and distracted all of us from the argument. Michelle and I had been in tight situations before, including a few gunfights, but this was the first time our families reached our sides so quickly afterwards—including our escape from the pirate base in Pegasus Station. After the excitement of celebrating our anniversary, the gut-wrenching tension of the attack, and then the elation of survival, watching my mother, adopted sister, and mother-in-law rush toward us with red-rimmed eyes and tear-tracked cheeks brought both of us crashing back to earth in a heartbeat.

Cassie reached us first, throwing herself into our arms. "I'm sorry! I'm sorry! I should have seen this!"

Michelle and I hugged her in return and I stroked the girl's head. Michelle said, "Hey, no, Cassie. This isn't your fault!"

"It is! I used to *always* see stuff about you two—but I haven't in weeks!" Tears began flowing down Cassie's cheeks again as she pulled back and looked between us. "What if...What if...I never see you in my dreams again?" Her face screwed up and Cassie finally blurted out what was really worrying her the most. "I...I don't ever see my birth parents and I think it's because they don't love me. Do...Do you think I'm a...a freak, too?"

"What?" Michelle said. "Where did you get that idea? Of course, we still love you!"

But Cassie didn't hear us, even though Mom and Magda joined us in comforting her. Michelle pulled Cassie close, rocking like she would with a small child. Michelle looked over Cassie's head at me. "I think Cassie needs the same gift you gave me, babe. Are you up for it?"

"Sure. It's easy moving good emotions around. It's the negative ones that drain me." That wasn't really true—it's just as taxing, but I feel a lot better moving around joyful emotions.

I concentrated on everything Cassie meant to me, gathering it into a package. Then, careful to maintain my own feelings, I reached into Michelle and did the same thing. It was hard juggling two sets of emotions—much harder than I thought it would be—but too much was riding on this for me to fail. I managed to carefully move them from us to Cassie. When I released them, Cassie's crying stopped as if someone had flipped a switch. And I guess you could say I had.

"Oh!" Cassie breathed in amazement as our emotions filled her mind. When her tears began again, they were accompanied by a big smile.

As with Michelle, I did my best to keep the emotions in Cassie's mind for as long as possible. After half a minute, it was just too much for me. I slumped back against our shot-up sofa and our emotions slipped away from Cassie's mind.

Our mothers stopped fussing over Cassie and turned surprised faces my way. Mom found her tongue first. "What did you do to your sister?"

"Matt didn't do anything *to* me, Mom," Cassie breathed. "He did something *for* me."

I shrugged. "It's something new I've been working on. I... bundled up our love and put it in Cassie's mind."

"It was his anniversary gift to me," Michelle added. "And it really is the most wonderful feeling ever."

Being a guy, I had reached my tolerance for this sort of talk. Turning to Cassie, I said, "There's another reason you didn't dream anything about the attack. The team was made up of psychic nulls. I didn't know they were here until they crashed through our bedroom windows."

Magda looked puzzled. "Then why didn't they get you first thing? Surely you and Michelle headed back there as soon as we were gone."

Mom was nodding in agreement and even Cassie, not quite a teenager, had a curious expression on her face. Before I found the right words, Michelle said, "Matt gave me his gift while we were sitting on the sofa. And we had the quilt Lilla and Raal gave to us, so..."

"Oh to be young and flexible again," Mom murmured, which made me blush.

Before things could get any more embarrassing, Jonas joined us. He had the framed painting Cassie and Rob gave us—or what was left of it.

"I'm sorry," he said, handing it to me.

I felt a chill run down my spine. The painting had two holes in the canvas. One burned away Michelle's face. The other burned away mine.

DIRE DREAMS

L ooking at the remains of the painting, I felt a knot of fear forming in my gut. By logic, I should dismiss the damage as just bad luck. By logic, I shouldn't take it as a premonition. But Cassie and Rob defied that same logic. My mind swirled around the issue without ever coming down on one side or the other. Leave it to Cassie to bring me out of it.

"Rob and I spent weeks working on that painting. Now we have to do it all over again," she said. "Goddammit!"

"Language, young lady!" Mom said, tapping Cassie lightly on the head.

"I'm sorry, Mom," Cassie said, not sounding sorry at all, "but all of the other words I want to use are worse."

Mom raised one eyebrow. "And just where did you learn worse language than that?"

Cassie studiously kept her eyes on the floor, not wanting to give anyone away—such as her big brother—by looking at them. Knowing how Mom could focus on little issues when she was faced with bigger, far more difficult problems, I came to Cassie's rescue.

"Oh, come on, Mom—are you denying you knew those same words when you were Cassie's age? *I* sure knew them." Mom opened her mouth, but I got in one more line. "I love you, Mom, but I'm going to read your emotions if you claim you didn't."

My mother hesitated for just a second before saying, "Of course, I knew worse language—but I didn't use it."

"Neither did Cassie," Michelle inserted.

Magda laid a hand on Mom's arm. "You're not going to win this one, Angela. Best retreat from the field in good order and let the kids have their moment."

My mother nodded. "You're right, Magda. Though I will remember this moment when Matt and Michelle find themselves dealing with their own preteen children."

Magda gave a contented sigh. "Now that *is* something to look forward to."

Cassie stood, a determined look coming over her face. "Well, I've got to get home and get some sleep. I need to find out what this means for the future."

That started the logic-premonition swirl in my gut again. "Are you saying that having our heads burned out of the painting might be a prediction of the future?"

Cassie gave me a scornful look. "What are you talking about, Matt? How can damage to a painting predict the future?"

"Um, wasn't that what you were talking about?" I asked.

"No." Brown eyes rolled under brunette hair as Cassie headed for the door. "I meant the attack. Jeez..."

Jonas stopped her. "Just a minute, Cassie. Let me get a guard detail to go with you." He glanced our way. "Michelle, you and Matt should go, too. There's nothing you can do here and you both need sleep."

"Good idea, Daddy," my wife said. She held a hand out to me. "Matt? I could use a big, strong man to help me up."

Taking Michelle's hand, I said, "The big, strong men are all busy. Will I do in their place?"

Everyone laughed a lot more than my cheesy line deserved. Once Michelle was on her feet, she took a couple of half-hopping steps before I swept her up in my arms and carried her out to a waiting car. Minutes later, I carried her to a spare room in my parents' house after a team of guards gave the all clear.

We slept late into the morning, assured by our mothers that no one would bother us. After waking, we simply held each other and tried to figure out what we should do next. We considered dropping our anti-impressment law campaign within the Federation, but neither of us could stomach the idea of untold millions of psychics living in fear of discovery.

Michelle's leg was well on the way to recovery, letting her walk downstairs when hunger drove us out of the room. We found all four of our parents sitting around the kitchen table, serious expressions on their faces. They pasted on smiles when we came into the room.

Dad got up and brought steaming omelettes to us. "I popped these into the stasis box the second they came off the stove."

"Where's Cassie?" I asked around my first bite of breakfast.

"Still sleeping," Mom said, her eyes troubled.

We all knew Cassie only slept late when she was having precognitive dreams. At first, it was unsettling to realize a twelve-year-old girl was learning about my future—my *possible* future, as Cassie would point out—but it became a regular part of my life, and Michelle's once my sister came into our world. That meant I also knew how everyone reacted when Cassie was having precognitive dreams. Judging by our parents' unnaturally calm reaction to Cassie sleeping so late, something else beyond her dreaming was bugging our parents.

Michelle spoke just before I could. "All right, spill it. What's really bothering you?"

All four parents exchanged glances. By unspoken agreement, Jonas responded.

"One of the Ark's Landing Council members and I went to the Federation embassy this morning. We filed an official complaint with Ambassador Reynolds, concerning last night's attack." Jonas gave a flip of his hand. "She dismissed our concerns, of course. Claims it must be freelancers who found out about the reward."

A chill ran down my spine. "*What* reward?"

"The Federation has posted a large reward for your capture, Matt," Jonas said. "The reward includes all sorts of legalese requiring bounty hunters to follow all local laws, but you can tell not even Ambassador Reynolds believes the Feds really care about that."

Michelle bit her lip, trying to puzzle through this new development. "But that doesn't make sense, Daddy. The psychic laws only apply within Federation territory. Surely, they won't risk tarnishing their precious reputation by advocating the kidnapping of psychics living beyond their borders?"

"No, pumpkin, they won't. But the reward doesn't mention anything about Matt's psychic abilities." Jonas met his daughter's eyes over the table. "The Federation has charged Matt with the murder of that psychic, Sadie Johnson, during your escape from Piscain Station. On top of the Federation's posted reward, Ambassador Reynolds is officially petitioning the Ark's Landing Council to extradite Matt to Earth."

I tried to brush aside Jonas's words, to show they didn't affect me. After all, I was innocent. I mean, I *did* kill Sadie, but I only acted in Michelle's defense.

John Thomas, the odious chief of the Piscain Station Psi Corps office, claimed my wife was as good as dead unless I surrendered to him. My defense would all be so straightforward if the man had threatened her with a normal weapon. But he threatened Michelle with a deadly psychic—one who answered only to him and whose deadly psychic abilities weren't found in any of Psi Corps' official records.

In the end, my defense claim would come down to my word against that of the office chief. But the case would never come to trial. If I ever ended up in Federation custody, I'd vanish into Psi Corps and never be free again.

"The Council isn't thinking of giving in to that asinine request, are they?" Michelle demanded, her omelette forgotten.

"If they are, it will probably be the last thing any of them does in office," Dad said. "Nancy Martin came with us to file the complaint. Her response was quite...vociferous."

"And extremely graphic," Jonas added.

"She only said what the rest of us were thinking." Dad jerked a thumb at Jonas. "While Nancy went for frothing-at-the-mouth rage, your father took a different approach. Do you have any idea just how menacing he can be when he goes all quiet and intense?"

Michelle's eyes widened. "You pulled the 'bad Dad' routine on the ambassador?"

Jonas shrugged. "When you were growing up, it's how I made sure you knew I meant what I said. I wanted the ambassador to understand that, as well."

Fascinated, I tried imagining Jonas threatening the ambassador just with an expression—and had no trouble picturing it. Even after a year as his son-in-law, I found 'menacing Jonas' much easier to picture than 'family man Jonas'.

"Yes, dear heart, that worked *so* well on Michelle," Magda said.

Michelle grinned. "I'm sure it works well on people who don't call him 'Daddy'."

The moment was broken when Rob burst into the kitchen—and came to an abrupt halt as Jonas leveled a blaster at his head. I barely even saw my father-in-law move.

"Uh, friend?" Rob stammered, swallowing visibly and slowly raising his hands.

The gun vanished as quickly as it appeared. Jonas gave Rob a hard stare. "Don't do that again, Robert. Bursting in on us isn't wise at the best of times. This morning is definitely *not* the best of times."

"I understand, sir. I...wasn't thinking."

I suddenly realized Rob wasn't his usual, impeccably turned-out self. He wore mismatched pants and shirt, no shoes, and his hair was mussed as if he just woke up. Michelle was even quicker on the uptake.

"You look like you just woke up, threw on whatever clothes

were handy, and came straight here." She patted the chair next to her. "Did you see something important in your dreams?"

Rob nodded as he sat. "Yeah. Is Cassie awake? She was dreaming about you, too."

"How do you know that, Rob?" Mom asked.

"I don't really understand it all, Mrs. Connaught." Rob ran a hand through his hair, unconsciously trying to straighten it. "But I think I saw Cassie talking to Matt and Michelle in her dream."

I felt my eyes widen. "Say what?"

Michelle interjected, "What my husband meant to say is, would you please explain what you mean? We didn't think you could interact with people in your dreams."

Rob gave Michelle a curious glance. "That's what Matt said— only he didn't use as many words."

"No, it isn't," Michelle said.

"Whatever," Rob shrugged. "Anyway, about Cassie-"

"What about me?" Cassie walked into the kitchen, her hair as tousled as Rob's, rubbing sleep from her eyes.

"Rob dreamed that you were dreaming, and talking to Matt and Michelle," Mom said. "At least, I think that's what he told us."

Rob smiled. "Yes, ma'am, that's what I said."

"Oh, good," Cassie said, and then gave a big yawn. "Sorry, I was really deep in the dreams this time."

"And you dreamed you talked to us?" Michelle asked. "And then Rob dreamed about your dream?"

Cassie cocked her head and gave Rob a look. He shrugged again. "I haven't had time to explain everything yet. I just got here a couple of minutes ago."

"Oh, okay." Cassie took a seat and smiled at Michelle and me. "I didn't dream I talked to you. I talked to you in my dream."

I glanced at Michelle to see if this made any sense to her. She was glancing at me while biting her lip, a sure-fire indication she was puzzling through Cassie's words, too. We both turned back to Cassie and Michelle asked, "Isn't that the same thing?"

"No," Cassie said, rolling her eyes at us. "In my dream, I talked to the two of you. The real world, wide-awake two of you. In the future."

Rob smiled and nodded. The rest of us found ourselves at a loss for words. Finally, Dad managed to find something to say.

"How?"

Cassie tilted her head and gave it some thought. "I think it has something to do with what Matt did last night—sticking his and Michelle's feelings inside my head. I think it made it possible for me to do more than just watch."

"Okay, that makes some kind of sense. I guess," I said. "What did you tell us?"

"Not much. Really, you guys did most of the talking. I mean, you two were expecting to see me, so you knew what to say."

A look of concern crossed Mom's face. "Honey, why would Matt and Michelle expect you to talk to them from your dream?"

"Because I just told them I would," Cassie said. "Jeez, Mom!"

"Of course..." Mom gently massaged her temples. "It's all so clear, now."

"What did we tell you to tell us?" Michelle shook her head as soon as she finished asking the question. "God, I think I sprained my brain, asking that question."

"I'm supposed to tell you to go to Earth. Today."

"No, absolutely not!" Jonas said. "The Federation has filed criminal charges against Matt. You're a good girl, Cassie, but I am not letting my daughter and son-in-law head straight into danger just because of something you dreamed!"

"I dreamed it, too, sir," Rob said.

"I don't care. There's no way we can be sure this wasn't just a regular dream," Jonas replied. "Unless you can find a way to prove it-"

"I can," Cassie said.

"How?" Jonas snapped the word out. From the look on his face, he instantly regretted his tone of voice. "I'm sorry, Cassie, I didn't mean to sound so harsh."

"It's okay, I was expecting it. Future Michelle told me you'd react that way. And since she and future Matt already knew everyone would doubt me, Matt told me how to convince him I really did talk to him." Cassie turned to face me. "You remember when Michelle saved you from the gang outside the maglev station, right?"

I took Michelle's hand. "Of course. It was one of the most terrifyingly wonderful nights of my life."

"After you jumped into the car, your head ended up in Michelle's lap with her bare stomach right in front of you."

I felt goosebumps forming on my arm. "Yeah?"

"You've never told anyone—not even Michelle—but you almost buried your face in her belly and blew a raspberry."

Michelle turned an incredulous look on me. "Is that true?"

I felt my cheeks turn red. "I think it's more accurate to say I had an irrational temptation—which I resisted—to do that."

"So, what does this mean, babe?" Michelle asked.

Pulling my wife into a hug, I said, "It means we'd better start packing."

My pronouncement hung in the air for a couple of seconds, then all four parents spoke at once.

"No! There's got to be some other way!" Magda exclaimed.

"Maybe Cassie dreamed of a past where you actually did blow a raspberry and she just doesn't remember it," Dad said. "Her dream last night could be a normal dream where that memory surfaced."

"If you go—and I'm really against that idea—you're going with a full security team led by me," Jonas declared.

"Would you like some help packing?" Mom asked, strangely calm amidst all of the uproar.

That pulled the other three parents up short. Jonas looked like he wanted to ask Mom what the hell she was thinking, but couldn't quite bring himself to speak to his employer that way—even if she was part of his family, now. Magda and Dad just stared at her for a second.

My father found his voice first. "Angela, do you support this reckless action?"

"It doesn't matter what I do or don't support, Richard," she responded. "Matt and Michelle have to go to Earth."

"Unless something has changed, you're an empath, not a precog. How do you know that?" Dad asked.

I suddenly realized why Mom had so readily accepted Cassie's pronouncement. While everyone else—including me—was busy reacting to spoken words, Mom must have taken the time to read Cassie's and Rob's emotions.

"Nothing has changed, darling. Well, except I now know the training Zav has been giving me is working." Mom turned her gaze on Jonas and Magda. "I wish there was some other way, but Rob is sure there isn't. He's got a lot to tell us, but he's just too polite to tell us all to shut up and listen to him. And, Richard, you know Cassie is a precog, not a postcog—if that's even a thing. She sees the future, not the past. None of her drawings show anything from the night Michelle saved Matt from the gang on the maglev." Mom sighed, running a hand through her hair. "I can't tell you how much I hate saying this, but what I'm picking up from Rob says all of the other choices are worse. Is that true, Rob?"

"Yes, ma'am," Rob said. "I don't know why, but I think Cassie dreamed of Matt's and Michelle's best future. I dreamed about all of the worse ones. Last night, I saw my two best friends in the universe die over and over and over. I saw Michelle screaming as she held Matt's body. I watched Matt sobbing over Michelle as she died. I watched each of them throw their lives away in grief-driven attempts to kill as many of the attackers as possible before joining their one true love in death. I saw all four of you, broken by sorrow, bury Matt and Michelle in matching graves. I saw horror after horror after horror, and there was nothing I could do to end it."

Rob ground to a halt, hanging his head and drawing in ragged breaths. When he looked up, tears streamed down his face. "By all that is holy, you have *got* to let them go to Earth. And they have to go alone. The *only* time I didn't see them die was when they went by themselves." He looked at both sets of parents, his eyes filled with anguish. "No one should ever have to go through even a fraction of what I saw last night."

Michelle pulled free of my embrace and wrapped Rob in a tight hug. Without even thinking about it, I reached over and clasped Rob's hand. I didn't need the contact to feel the despair welling up inside of my friend, but the contact helped when I used my own ability to gently engulf that despair and draw the roiling emotions out of him and into my own mind. As I shoved the emotions into a corner of my mind, Rob's tears stopped and a look of surprised relief replaced his grief.

"Oh my God, Matt," he whispered. "Thank you."

By then, Cassie had come around the table and added her hug to Michelle's. Kissing Rob on the cheek, she said, "It's not easy being a precog, but I'll help you learn how to handle it."

Mom looked from Dad to Jonas to Magda. "I wish there was something else we could do, but if our two precogs haven't seen it, I don't believe it's there to be seen."

As Mom and Magda helped us pack, Dad and Jonas began planning how to smuggle Michelle and me into the heart of the Terran Federation—the planet Earth.

LEAVING HOME—AGAIN

Like most guys, I always found packing easy. Pick out a few shirts and pairs of pants, make sure you've got enough underwear, and then toss it all in a suitcase. It got a little more complicated after I married Michelle. "You're not really taking *that*, are you?" became a question I dreaded. But it wasn't my fashion sense—minimal as that was—that Michelle questioned.

"Babe, make sure you pack two or three sports coats," Michelle called from inside our closet. "Pick ones you can wear with just about everything you pack."

"Whatever you say, dear," I responded.

"And make sure you include a nice selection of long sleeve shirts."

"Of course, dear."

"And don't forget your paisley socks."

I do not and never will own anything paisley.

"Yes, dear, I really am listening to you."

Michelle leaned out of the closet. "Oh, good. Then I'm sure you can explain why I want you to pack those things."

"Earth doesn't allow open carry, so the jackets are to hide a shoulder holster. The long sleeves conceal the dagger sheaths and miniature blaster we'll strap to my forearms." I folded my arms and leaned against the dresser. "And you should have told me to select loose clothes so the weapons are less obvious to observers and easier for me to draw."

Michelle sauntered over to me and wrapped her arms around my neck. "Excuse us for a minute, Moms."

As our mothers exchanged puzzled glances, Michelle kissed me. Despite the audience, this wasn't a quick peck on the lips. It was a long and lusty kiss.

When Michelle finally broke our lip-lock, her mother said, "You know, you really ought to save something for the long trip to Earth, Michelle."

"That wasn't really about sex, Mom." Magda gave her daughter a skeptical look, so Michelle added, "Okay, it *was* about sex, but it's also the only reward I can give Matt right now."

"Reward for what?" Mom asked.

"My lovely wife—no doubt encouraged by Jonas—has been pushing me to learn more of the practical aspects of security," I said.

Michelle nodded. "And everyone knows proper rewards encourage more of that behavior. It's simple psychology."

I smiled innocently at Mom. "Michelle says I'm a very fast learner."

Magda snorted a laugh. "Just don't let your hormones get the better of you in a dangerous situation."

"Don't you worry, dear mother-in-law. That wouldn't be smart security behavior."

We managed to finish packing without any further interruptions and went in search of the others. We found Rob and Cassie talking quietly in the living room, while Dad and Jonas made plans in the kitchen. Rob looked a lot better than he had earlier, even giving us a smile as we filed toward the kitchen. To my surprise, our fathers had done a lot in the short time it took us to pack.

Jonas looked up as we entered. "Ever since the two of you got married, Richard and I have prepared for as many emergency situations as possible. That's why we had that spare spaceship waiting on Draconis, a few months ago, and it's why we have a few contingencies in place, now. The good news is, we can smuggle you to Earth. The bad news is, we don't know how to smuggle you *off* of Ark's Landing."

Dad held up his hand, as if forestalling an argument. "I know we brought the *M&M* here, but it's certain the Federation Embassy is watching it. They don't even have to try very hard since it's docked a couple of kilometers from them. We think we can get you out in a specially modified cargo container but there just aren't that many shipments leaving Ark's Landing. The next one isn't for another month, which Rob and Cassie have assured us will be far too late."

Michelle bit her lip and gave her father a thoughtful look. "Daddy, how did the team that attacked us, last night, get down here?"

"I don't know, pumpkin. My teams are digging into it, but those men aren't on any of the security vids from the spaceport. There's only been one passenger ship and a handful of private ships. The team wasn't on any of those. The last incoming cargo shipment got here about the same time you two did, so they can't have come in that way."

Planning was briefly interrupted when Nancy and Lilla came by to check on Michelle and me. After giving them both a minute to fuss over us, I told Lilla how her quilt saved us from the initial attack. That part of the story didn't draw the amused reaction I hoped it would.

"You shouldn't need any kind of saving, Matt," Lilla fumed. "The Federation keeps telling us Ark's Landing will be better off if we become a member planet, but then they pull crap like this?"

"It's not the entire Federation, Lilla," I said. "It's just Psi Corps."

"That's just semantics," Nancy countered. "Psi Corps is a major department of the Federation government. Their actions are the Federation's responsibility."

Before I could respond, Michelle asked, "Nancy, what kind of coverage does the spaceport sensor array have?"

I looked at Michelle and realized she wasn't biting her lip anymore. "What have you got, hon?"

"That depends on Nancy's answer," my wife replied.

The heroine of Ark's Landing shrugged. "It's about what you'd expect on a newly settled world. We've got satellite coverage on both wormholes and another satellite in geosynchronous orbit above the settled part of the planet."

"So a ship could enter the atmosphere undetected, if they came in on the far side of the planet?"

"It could, Michelle, but space control tracks all ships entering and exiting the wormholes for just that reason. They alert the Council, if they lose track of a ship—and that's never happened."

"Richard and I thought of that, pumpkin," Jonas said. "We already checked the records and didn't find any discrepancies."

"I know, Daddy, but what if one of the ships launched a smaller ship during its transit from one wormhole to the next?"

"The sensors would have picked that up, too," Dad said. "It's a good thought, Michelle, but-"

"*But* a Federation carrier passed through the system two days ago," Michelle interrupted. "Couldn't it have launched a ship without the sensors detecting it?"

"No. Launch signatures are easy to detect," Jonas said. "And they couldn't have just dropped a ship in space because the sensors would have picked up the engine signature when they headed toward the planet."

"Oh." Michelle's shoulders sagged a bit. "I thought-"

"Bloody hell!" Nancy exclaimed. "Which carrier was it?"

Jonas checked the list. "Um...The TFS *Javelin*. Why?"

"Of course." Nancy nodded, more to herself than us. "At least, it wasn't my old ship."

Lilla waved a hand in front of Nancy. "Ship to Nancy. Would you tell the rest of us what you've figured out?"

Nancy shook herself. "Back during the Fringer war, a few of the older carriers were modified to insert commando teams on Fringer worlds. One launch tube was changed to use a linear accelerator. It could fire a small insertion ship toward a planet. The launch signature for the accelerator is completely different than a normal launch tube. My ship, the *Phoenix*, had one. So did the *Javelin*."

Now Michelle began nodding. "They just launched the ship on a course to the far side of Ark's Landing. Once the planet blocked it from all of the sensors, the ship's crew fired up the engine and came in undetected."

Unable to resist, I pulled Michelle into a deep and lusty kiss.

"Uh, son," Dad began, "I don't think-"

"Let it go, Richard," Mom said. "He's practicing simple psychology. At least, that's how Michelle describes it."

When we finally broke apart, everyone was studiously looking everywhere but at Michelle and me. Grinning, I asked, "So, what next?"

"I'll redirect the teams to search for the insertion ship," Jonas said. "Nancy, did those ships usually have inertial dampeners?"

"Always," she responded. "The commando team couldn't count on a carrier being nearby when they finished their mission."

"Good. All we need is a distraction to make sure the Feds are looking somewhere else, and you two can slip away in the insertion ship."

"Give me the access codes to the *M&M*," Nancy growled. "I'll distract the hell out of those Fed bastards."

Jonas's search team found the ship that afternoon. Michelle and I said our goodbyes, boarded the little ship, and gave Nancy the go-ahead. Without any communication from the *M&M*, Nancy made a sudden, noisy liftoff from the spaceport.

As the comms filled with complaints and official orders for the *M&M* to return to port, I flew the insertion ship low over the horizon and began a gradual ascent into orbit. I ran under full acceleration as long as possible, shutting off the engines when we approached sensor range. Using a directional comm, Michelle fed our position to Nancy. She swung the *M&M* alongside our ship.

She was far closer than I would have preferred, but Nancy's days as a fighter pilot gave her a lot of experience with close order formations. Our two ships entered the nearest wormhole together, completely masking the insertion ship's departure.

For the third time in the last year, Michelle and I left our home behind us.

As the gray void of the wormhole closed around us, I felt a knot of tension loosen in my gut, only to be replaced by a growing knot of frustration.

"You know, I'm getting sick and damned tired of the Federation chasing me from my family. I spent seven years trying to figure out how to rescue my parents. When you and I finally do that, do we get to spend the rest of our lives in peace?" I felt the frustration giving way to anger. "Hell, no, we don't. Because of some stupid-ass laws created four hundred years ago, the Feds won't simply let us be. And when we leave the goddamned Federation, they *still* come after us!"

Michelle leaned over from her seat and hugged me. "I know, babe. I hate it just as much as you do. I know how much this makes me miss *my* parents, and they weren't held captive for seven years. I can only *imagine* what you feel." She slid over into my lap and rested her head on my shoulder. "And how are we ever going to raise a family, under these conditions?"

For a long time, we both just sat there entwined in each other and with our thoughts and feelings light years away on Ark's Landing. Finally, Michelle kissed me lightly and moved back to her seat.

"As tempting as it is to just sit here and feel sorry for ourselves, I think we should do something. Take our minds off of our sorrows and our anger." She smiled at me. "And I know just the thing."

I tried returning her smile, but my heart just wasn't in it. "I know sex during wormhole transits is sort of a thing for us, Michelle, but this just isn't the time."

"I agree, babe. Fortunately, that's not what I had in mind."

I felt my eyebrows climb in surprise. "Okay, you've got my attention. Not that you don't *always* have my attention."

"That's very sweet, Matt," she said. "And I definitely want you concentrating fully on me, but I want you to use your empathic ability."

"Hon, I use my ability on you all the time. How will this be different?"

"I want you to practice getting past my mental shields. Smash through them, find a seam you can slip through, whatever it takes."

"What if I hurt you?" I asked.

"I'll get a headache and then I'll recover." Michelle brushed golden hair away from her eyes and gazed intently into mine. "I have a feeling we're going to run into a lot of people trained to shield their minds—not to mention more than our share of psychic nulls. You need to be able to affect all of them."

I shook my head. "I can see practicing against your shield, but there's nothing I can do about psychic nulls. They're immune to psychic abilities. That's why Psi Corps likes them so much."

"You're wrong, Matt. You have already affected psychic nulls. Don't you remember when we burst into the Psi Corps office on Piscain Station and you threw that blast of fear at everyone in the office?" Michelle paused for a second, just in case I really needed time to recall that moment. "Do you remember what Thomas, the ass in charge of the office, said to you?"

"Yeah, he told me I was even more powerful than he imagined, and then sicced Sadie on you."

"Babe, he also said your psychic blast affected six psychic nulls." Michelle leaned forward in her seat. "If nulls truly were immune, you could *never* have affected them."

I collapsed back in my seat, considering the implications of what Michelle said. "Have you talked to Zav about this?"

"Yes, but he's as stuck in the Psi Corps way of thinking as everyone else. He theorized it was a physical reaction, probably induced by some of the psychics whose powers manifest in a physical manner—telekinetics and healers and the like. He claims their violent reaction to the fear you broadcast caused them to lash out at those around them, including the psychic nulls. He and the other five nulls just misinterpreted it as your power affecting them, especially after the office chief said it."

"But you think Zav is wrong, even though psychics are his life's work?"

I tried to keep my tone level, but Michelle's eyes flashed at my question. "I think Zav is wrong *because* psychics are his life's work. He knows vast amounts about psychic powers and next to nothing about psychic nulls. No one does because everyone *knows* they're simply people who are immune to psychic powers."

"I concede your point, hon. What do *you* think psychic nulls are?"

Michelle drew a deep breath. "I think they're just people who have natural mental shields—strong shields obviously, but just shields. I think, if you can learn to get past my shields, maybe it can help you get past a null's shields, too."

"And why do you think we're going to have to deal with psychic nulls on Earth?" Michelle simply stared at me in response to my question, her head cocked to one side as if asking why I was asking such a stupid question. I shrugged. "I thought it was worth asking in case Cassie or Rob said something else to you before we left."

"They didn't. But I made the reasonable assumption that Psi Corps, having already thrown six psychic nulls against us, would use as many as they had available if it meant capturing their most wanted rogue psychic."

Michelle settled back in her chair and visibly relaxed. She kept her eyes open, but they weren't focused on anything. After a minute, she said, "I've got my shield up. Come at me."

I reached out with my empathic power and tried reading Michelle. There wasn't anything to read, which was pretty impressive. Ever since I made my big breakthrough and found Michelle floating alone in space, I've never had any problems reading her. Finding myself unable to read her now was somewhat disturbing. It was as if Michelle was simply gone, even though she was sitting right in front of me.

Ignoring the animal part of my brain, which was trying to make me panic over Michelle's 'disappearance,' I took my time examining the shield. In a way, it was like the filters I used to keep from being overwhelmed by all the loose emotions surrounding me. Her shield wasn't a solid mental barrier, but rather a series of overlapping barriers. Her control was really good, though, showing the effects of Zav's training. I felt the seams, but couldn't find a way through them. I tried quickly sliding from one seam to another, hoping for some slight opening. When that didn't work, I took a different approach.

"Have you been gaining weight, hon?"

"No, but that was a good try," she replied, her voice calm and centered.

"You're the one who taught me to fight to win, even if it means fighting dirty." I paused for a few seconds, letting my eyes wander up and down her body. "I was so busy preparing to leave that I never really noticed what you were wearing. You know I always liked you in that school shirt, right?"

"That's why I wore it, babe."

"I was always surprised how all of the girls in our old school could wear the same shirt but look totally different from each other," I said. "Is that something they teach you in a secret class? Inscrutable Female one oh one, or something?"

"No, Matt," Michelle laughed. "And you're not getting through my shield with silly jokes."

"Did you ever notice how Molly wore the shirt?" My power skated around Michelle's shield as I talked. "Us guys never could figure out how she always managed to end up with the left side of her shirt untucked and the right side tucked."

"Molly worked very hard at that. And then she'd find excuses to spin to the right and make the shirt tail flare out, giving you guys a peek under her shirt."

"That was intentional?" Michelle's concentration was good. I hadn't found a way through her shield yet. "I know half-a-dozen guys who loved calling to her in the hallway for just that reason. Sneaky of her."

"Babe, you don't know the half of it. Girls learn what guys like to see and then find a way to 'accidentally' let them see it—or something close, at least."

"Huh." Without knowing it, Michelle gave me the lead-in I was looking for. "So you're saying that it wasn't a mistake when four of Jayna's buttons popped off and exposed her breasts to the guys' PE class?"

"What?" Michelle's eyes opened wide in surprise. "I never heard about-"

Her concentration broke for just a split second, but it was enough. One of the seams widened and I launched my power through it and read Michelle. She felt a strange mixture of chagrin at herself and pride for me.

"Not bad for a first time, Matt. It was downright evil of you to distract me with that story about Jayna. That didn't really happen, did it? I mean, it would have been all over the school!"

"No, it was just a fantasy concocted by some of the guys after she walked through the gym, one day."

"Thought so." Michelle leaned in and gave me a reward kiss. "As happy as I am that you found a way to make me break my own shield, next time I want you to find a way through using only your power. I doubt a psychic null is going to lose their shield from something you say—and that's assuming you even know what to say to provoke a reaction. Okay?"

I nodded. "Fair enough. But I think I'm going to have to use force and I don't want to hurt you."

"I know, Matt," Michelle said, caressing my cheek in sympathy. "But I really don't want to lose you to Psi Corps. If giving me a headache helps you learn how to defend yourself against their agents, then I'm all for it."

We settled in for another try. Neither of us spoke, this time. I wasn't gentle, but I ramped my power up slowly. Using less than half of my power, I shattered her shield and read the pain I caused her. I tried wrapping it up in my power, but it wasn't emotional pain. In the end, I simply held Michelle while she endured it. And

I wished we had another empath around who could take away the guilt overwhelming me.

I have never been so happy to have a wormhole transit end. Even after the pain I caused smashing through her mental shields, even after the time I spent cradling her as she recovered from the pain, even after my fourth time breaking her shield reduced both of us to tears—hers from her all-but-blinding headache and mine from emotional agony—even after all of that, she insisted I keep practicing. I never found a way to gently infiltrate her shield, but I found several different ways to blow through it with brute force. And every one of them hurt the woman I love more than life itself.

She winced, sitting up after my last mental attack, and wiped her eyes. "Okay, I'm recovered enough for you to try again."

I shook my head, not willing to look into her red-rimmed eyes. "No. I am not doing that to you again. Not now, not ever."

Still rubbing her temples, Michelle said, "Matt, honey, we've been over this. What if your life depends on being able to break shields?"

"I've already proven I can break your shields, Michelle. I've done it over and over and in at least half-a-dozen different ways. And watching what that does to you is tearing me up inside!" When I looked up, she was blurry because of my own tears. "If *this* is what it takes to save my life, I'd rather die."

"I know how hard this is for you, but–"

"No, Michelle, you only *think* you know how hard it is." I wiped my eyes so she could get the full intensity of my glare. "Imagine if I made you practice spin kicks on my head because I insisted your life might depend on your ability to knock out a man with one kick. Imagine kicking me repeatedly while I just stood there taking it. Imagine me getting up after every kick and telling you to do it again. After an hour and a half of knocking me around, imagine how you'd feel when I insisted you do it yet again."

I slumped forward against the pilot's console, unwilling to let my wife see the fresh tears spilling from my eyes. "That's how I feel. And that's why I can't ever do this to you again."

Any reply Michelle planned was cut off by the nav computer's announcement. "Wormhole exit in five minutes."

"Thank God." I sat up, wiping my eyes one last time, and began checking the ship's systems. "You should go get some rest, hon."

Michelle rose to her feet and kissed the top of my head. "I'm sorry, babe. I'll never ask you to do this again."

"Thank you," I breathed as she went aft to one of the less-than-comfortable berths. By the time we exited into normal space, I could hear regular breathing coming from the back of the little ship.

The proximity alarm sounded the second we broke free of the wormhole. I verified it was simply reporting the *M&M* and then switched it off.

I aimed a tight-beam comm laser at the other ship. "Nice job back there, Nancy. You sure put on quite a show with your escape."

"You did a good job staying off the sensors, Matt," she replied. "I've got a few messages for you, including final instructions from Jonas and your father. Are you set to record them?"

I tapped a quick command on the comm console. "Ready to receive, Nancy."

After sending the message, Nancy asked, "Doesn't Michelle usually handle comm duties when you two fly?"

"She's sleeping right now, Nancy."

"Damn, boy, you must have really worn her out during the transit!" Nancy laughed. "You sound a bit ragged, yourself."

"Well, our anniversary night *was* interrupted by that attack." I saw no point in correcting Nancy's impression. She'd just feel guilty and then I'd feel even worse. "The wormhole jump was our first chance to make up for lost time."

"Just make sure your hormones don't get the better of you at the wrong moment," Nancy said. "Okay, I've got to break off now and get clear of you two. I've got to say, you and Richard did a good job rebuilding the *M&M*. She's no starfighter, but she is a nimble ship."

"Thanks, Nancy. Take care of yourself and please give our love to everyone when you get back to Ark's Landing."

"Will do, Matt." She paused for a second. "You two be careful, okay? I don't want to lose two of my best friends."

"We'll try not to disappoint you," I replied. "And we both love you, too."

Nancy increased the *M&M's* throttle and the ship leapt forward, quickly leaving us in her wake. I didn't listen to any of the messages Nancy sent to us. There was only one other worm-hole out of the system, so Jonas's and Dad's final instructions could wait. The other messages were probably personal and I wanted to listen to them with Michelle. Last, I set the proximity alert to it's widest possible perimeter, giving me plenty of warning if a ship approached. Putting aside my curiosity concerning the instructions and doing my best to still the guilt I felt over the pain I caused Michelle, I settled back for a much-needed nap.

The feel of soft lips pressed against mine pulled me out of the depths of sleep. I blinked and brought Michelle's smiling face into focus.

"How's your head feel?" I asked.

"Much better, now that I've had some sleep." Her expression turned serious. "I *am* sorry for everything I put you through earlier, Matt, but I also think some good will come of it."

"I suppose so. After all, I did learn a bunch of different ways to attack mental shields." I leaned my head back, not meeting Michelle's eyes. "But it's going to take a very long time to get past the guilt I felt—and still feel."

Michelle settled into my lap and laid her head on my shoulder. "I know, babe. But, sick as it sounds right now, even your guilt might be useful. You know your empathic ability is at its strongest when you tap into strong emotions. Maybe you can tap that guilt if things get really desperate."

"Let's hope things never get that bad." I shuddered at the thought and then forced my mind away from it. "Before she left us in the stardust, Nancy beamed messages to us, including final instructions from our fathers. We should listen to them."

Michelle moved to the copilot's seat and waved an imperious hand. "Queue them up, husband."

I grinned, readily accepting Michelle's lightening of the tone. "As you command, wife."

The plan for smuggling us onto Earth was surprisingly straightforward—at least on our end. After our troubles getting clear of the Federation a few months back, ever-paranoid Jonas convinced Dad to build a bunch of special shipping containers, each one a self-contained mini-apartment, stocked with food, clothes, money, false identities, and a small arsenal of weapons. They scattered the containers throughout the GenCo shipping fleet, placing one on each of the company's container carriers. Almost entirely automated, the container carriers only have two or three man crews whose sole concern is piloting and overseeing the loading and unloading of the containers. All we had to do was intercept one of the carriers, board it, and slip into our special container.

"You're *sure* the codes included in the message will tell the carrier's sensors to ignore us?" Michelle asked.

"Dad is. And your father didn't voice a protest." I shrugged. "They've had a lot more time to think about this than we have."

"Okay, I guess..." Michelle still sounded unsure. "It just seems dangerous to have a code that makes a ship invisible to sensors. What if pirates figure it out?"

"You know how careful Jonas is. I doubt even our mothers know about the code." I opened the file containing the code. "And look at it—the thing is at least fifty characters long. There's no way anyone would just stumble across it."

"If you're satisfied, babe, I'm satisfied, too. After all, you're the team tech-head. I'm just the brawn."

"And the beauty."

"That's so sickeningly sweet, Matt. I'm just glad I don't have any lunch to lose in response."

"Fine, be that way. See if I ever call you beautiful, again."

Michelle checked the ship's chrono. "I give you a max of six hours before you do it."

"Do I really say it that often?" At Michelle's nod, I scratched my head. "Huh. I guess that either means I'm blind or I'm right. Which one do you think it is?"

"Blinded by love, babe. No doubt about it."

"Wow, Michelle, and you complained about *me* being sickening!"

"What can I say? You're a bad influence on me. Why don't we both shut up and listen to the other messages."

"Good idea, hon," I said, queuing up the next message.

We listened to personal messages from our parents, Nancy, Lilla and Raal, and Zav and three of the kids who had been living with him on Piscain Station. The last message was from Cassie and Rob.

"Hi, Michelle! Hi, Matt!" Cassie's chipper voice said. "Rob's with me. You know we both love you and miss you and all that stuff, right? Rob, they can't hear you nodding like that."

"I know, Cassie; I was just waiting for a chance to get in a word." His tone was light and bantering though it sounded forced. "Anyway, Cassie speaks for me, too."

"How about that, Michelle. I won't turn thirteen for another month and I've already got Rob properly trained to let me speak for both of us." She giggled at Rob's inarticulate sound. "That will come in *so* handy ten years from now."

"Hey!" Rob protested. "I thought that was one bit of precognition we weren't sharing with anyone."

"Oops. Sorry, Rob."

Michelle and I looked at each other in surprise. Michelle found her voice first. "Does that mean what I think it means?"

Cassie spoke before I could. "I know we should erase that from the message, but I've wanted to tell you both ever since Rob and I dreamed we would get married. Yes, we *both* dreamed it—and on the same night—so it's *got* to come true. It's not as romantic as your story, but you could say we're going to have a *dream* wedding. Get it? Because we both dreamed it?"

"They get it, Cassie. Look, guys, I know you must think this is weird right now—especially since Cassie is so much younger than me. Hell, *I* think it's weird. But...I guess it makes sense that a couple of precogs would end up together, right? And, Matt, I will not even think about asking Cassie out until she's eighteen, at the very least. You know you can trust me to do the right thing, here." I could almost hear Rob shrug in the brief silence. "What can I say? It's what we dreamed."

"But it will only happen if you two do whatever it is you're supposed to do on Earth and come back safe," Cassie said. "So don't die or get caught or anything, okay?"

"I do have one other thing to tell you," Rob said. "You've got to go to Cairo. There's something or someone you've got to find at the Cairo Catastrophe Memorial. Or maybe in Psi Corps head-quarters, since it's there, too. I wish I could tell you more, but that's all I got from my dream."

"Rob couldn't tell you that before you left. He dreamed about doing that and it ended up really bad because of the way Mom and Dad and Michelle's parents reacted. Anyway, I'll talk to you again when you're on Earth. Even though *I* already talked to you last night in my dreams." Cassie paused for a second. "Wow, that's hard to work through, even for a precog."

"You two take care of yourselves and each other," Rob said. "I wish there was more we could do to help."

"Bye," Cassie chimed in. "We love you and all that stuff. See you soon!"

The recording ended, leaving Michelle and me still staring at each other. This time, I found my voice first. "Well, that...was..."

"Unexpected." Michelle finished the sentence for me.

"So, Cassie and Rob."

"But not for another ten years."

"Right, right," I said. "Yeah. That's...okay. I mean, it makes sense. Doesn't it?"

"Sure," Michelle said, perhaps a bit too quickly. "They're both precogs and all. So...yeah."

"That's okay then," I said. "And Rob... I mean, I know we can trust him to wait until Cassie is old enough."

"Of course, he will." Michelle's voice held absolute conviction. "But it sure is..."

"Weird. Yeah." I shook the surprise out of my head. "Uh, I'd better get started plotting our course. We've got a container carrier to catch, after all."

For what it's worth, Cassie's not-so-unconscious slip was the only real surprise we had during the trip. We intercepted the container carrier late in the next day and slipped aboard in our space suits. We found our special container right where Dad said it would be and settled in for the trip. I programmed our borrowed spaceship to wait one hour and then dive straight into the system's star, erasing our tracks as effectively as possible. I coded the container for Earth, with delivery from the orbiting warehouse to Cairo. After that, we settled in for the week-long trip.

As usual, we found ways to keep ourselves entertained during the trip. All too soon, the carrier unloaded us at the warehouse. The next day, our container was flown down to Cairo. Neither of us knew what our future held—except for a conversation with dream-Cassie, that is—but we both felt the final battle in our little psychic war with Psi Corps was near.

RANEEM

As you might guess, our fathers had made sure each container had an extensive selection of makeup, hair coloring, lift shoes, and whatever else they thought would help Michelle and me change our appearance. I sat patiently while Michelle transformed me into someone my own mother wouldn't recognize. She did most of her own transforming but allowed me to help with some parts—under her careful supervision, of course. It took a few hours, which gave me plenty of time to hack into the warehouse's surveillance system and stop it from recording us when we slipped out of the building.

After spending a week inside the container, it felt good to be outside. After spending the last several months on sparsely populated Ark's Landing, Earth felt extremely crowded. It wasn't much worse than my home world of Draconis, but the change took some getting used to. Perhaps that's what made Michelle and me look like a couple of goggle-eyed tourists from a backwater planet. Whatever the reason, we drew some unexpected attention.

I noticed the woman and the girl when we exited the dockyard. The girl wasn't more than ten years old. The woman looked a few years older than Michelle and me, though Michelle's work with the makeup made us both look closer to thirty than our actual age of twenty-one.

It was second nature for me to keep an empathic scan going. I didn't really concentrate on anyone in particular—until I picked up the girl's nervous fear. Concerned, I scanned deeper hoping to discover what was scaring the girl. I didn't find any source for her emotion, which is very strange. Wondering if the woman next to her was also afraid, I shifted my scan to her and got one hell of a surprise. The woman was broadcasting low-level fear to the girl!

She bent most of her attention to the short-range broadcast, so she was either self-taught, not particularly powerful, or both. But why was she doing it? What did she gain from frightening a small girl? Then the woman caught sight of us. She said something to the girl and the fear cut off. In its place, I felt the woman working to project curiosity at Michelle and me.

"Keep a wide-eyed expression, Michelle," I murmured.

"Okay. Why?"

"See the woman and the girl, ahead?" I asked. "The woman is an empath and she's working very hard to use her ability to make us curious."

"What the hell for?" Michelle asked.

"I have no idea, but before she saw us she was broadcasting fear to the little girl."

"We *are* going to find out what's going on, right? And should I worry about her getting through my mental shield?"

"Yes, we're going to investigate. And no, she's not strong enough to even detect your shield, much less get through it." I turned a smile on Michelle and pointed toward the woman and girl —just as the woman wanted me to do. "I'll keep a read on the woman and change my attitude to match what the woman is trying to force on us. Just follow my lead."

"You got it, babe."

"Hi there," the woman called as we drew near. "Looks to me like you two aren't from around here."

Doing my best to sound like someone from the backend of

the Federation, I said, "Nope. We're from Briap. This trip to Earth is just our little way of celebrating us joining the Federation."

Michelle smiled and nodded. "We've been saving up for it for years and years."

That caught the woman's attention and triggered a nice spike of avarice in her. "I'll bet you two want to see all the sights, eat authentic Earth food, and maybe even see some of the places we Earthers don't tell the tourists about. Am I right?"

I grinned at Michelle. "That sure would be wonderful, right, honey bunny?"

"Oh, my," Michelle replied, "that would be just about the best thing, ever!"

"Well, folks, this is your lucky day!" The woman's greed eased as she tried broadcasting trust into our minds. "My little sister, Raneem, is just the person to show you around. She knows just about everything there is to know about Cairo."

"Does she?" Michelle turned a bright smile on the girl. Bending over to look the girl in the eyes, she said, "You are just about the cutest little girl I've ever seen! Would you like to show us the sights, Raneem?"

Raneem radiated resignation tinged with a fair bit of self-disgust. In a monotone voice, she said, "Yes, ma'am. I sure would like that."

I beamed at the woman. "Well, if my wife likes her then we want to hire her. You *do* want us to pay her, don't you?"

"That's so generous of you, sir!" A big smile broke out on the woman's face and her emotions turned to smug satisfaction.

I looked at Michelle. "This is a once in a lifetime trip, honey bunny. What do you think we should pay this girl?"

Michelle scratched her head. "We're going to be here for a whole week. Will Raneem be able to show us around that whole time?" At the woman's enthusiastic nod, Michelle looked my way. "Do you think two hundred credits a day is enough, dear?"

The amount surprised the woman—and pleased her no end. I

pretended to think for a few seconds, then said, "That might not be enough. How about two-fifty? Will you accept that?"

Smug satisfaction radiated from the woman for a second time, though she tried playing it cool with her response. "I think that's a fair offer, sir. Just tell me where you're staying and I'll make sure Raneem is there first thing in the morning."

"We're staying at the Masika House," I said, "but why bother sending Raneem around each day when she can just stay with us all week? We can give her a place to sleep and we'll pay for all her meals."

"That's on top of the two fifty a day?" the woman asked, sending fear to the girl again.

Watching Raneem almost fold up on herself was more than I could take. I reached out with my own ability, gently engulfed the fear inside the girl, and redirected it to my far better-protected mind. Raneem's eyes widened when the fear disappeared, but she kept her folded-up posture. Acting for the woman's benefit, no doubt. Michelle, meanwhile, assured the woman that my offer was on top of the daily payment.

"It's customary to pay half up front," the woman added.

"Of course," I said, fishing out a credit stick and checking its balance. "Let's just round it up to an even thousand, now, and the other seven hundred and fifty at the end of the week. Okay?"

"That's very fair of you, sir." The woman took the stick from me.

"We never did get your name, miss," Michelle said as the woman turned away.

"Hm? Oh, how silly of me. My name is Shafira." The woman looked at Raneem. "Bye, little sister. You behave, all right? And never fear, I'll be around if you need me."

As Shafira turned and walked away, Michelle flagged down a robo-cab. I the cab the name of our hotel and then looked at Raneem. She, in turn, was looking back and forth between the two of us. I decided to make the first move.

"How long has that woman been terrorizing you?" I asked. "I assume she's not really your sister."

Raneem cringed at my question. "I don't know what you're talking about."

Michelle wrapped an arm around the girl. "You're safe with us, honey. Whatever Shafira—if that's her real name—has done, we can protect you."

The girl's head drooped and I didn't need my ability to read her dejection. "No, you can't. No one can protect me from Shafira. That's her real name."

"Don't be so sure of that, Raneem," I said, plucking out her dejection. "Shafira doesn't scare me in the least. And she won't scare you, either, once my wife teaches you a few things. But we'll talk more about that in the hotel, okay?"

"Okay," Raneem said as the tiniest flicker of hope came to life in her mind.

I felt Raneem's little flame of hope wax and wane and flicker and waver for the rest of the drive to the hotel. When we arrived, the girl stayed with Michelle while I checked us in.

The check-in process was all automated, and completely strange to me. It was easy enough, but I was used to dealing with human clerks. Of course, you only get those in five-star hotels or on sparsely populated worlds like Wolf and Ark's Landing. I selected a small suite from the list of available rooms, maintaining our image as an average couple making the most of their once-in-a-lifetime trip. Soon, the three of us were settling into the room.

Raneem marveled at the place, no doubt finding it luxurious beyond her wildest dreams. Michelle did nothing to dispel that idea when she opened up the listing of in-room services.

"Raneem," she said, "why don't you go into your bathroom-"

"I have my *own* bathroom?" the girl blurted.

Michelle laughed gently. "Yes, honey. Why don't you use it to take a nice, hot bath? Take as long as you want. When you're finished, I'll come in and we'll get the fabricator to make you some new clothes."

Raneem's eyes went wide and a look of pure joy spread across her face. It lasted for almost three seconds before her face fell. Then the girl just crumpled to the floor, sobbing. Michelle rushed to envelop her in a hug, rocking back and forth while stroking her hair and making little shushing sounds. I didn't even need to use my empathic ability to see how much the girl trusted my wife—Michelle has the almost-magical ability to make people comfortable—so I just sat quietly and waited. Raneem's sobs slowly subsided into little hiccuping whimpers, which then faded into ragged breathing.

"Do you want to tell me what that was all about?" Michelle asked.

"Y-you're being s-so nice to me," Raneem began, her voice climbing with every word. Wailing once again, she said, "And Shafira's going to make me rob you!"

"Ah, her." Michelle looked at me. "Babe, I think this one is for you."

Surprised at Michelle's matter-of-fact tone, Raneem's wail subsided to sniffles. "What can *he* do?"

"For one thing, I can make you feel better for a few minutes," I said. "Not with drugs or anything like that. I can do it with my mind. It's a lot like how Shafira makes you scared all the time, only I'll take away the fear."

"You can do that?"

"Yes, but only if you want me to."

"Can you keep Shafira from killing me with her mind?"

"Did Shafira tell you she could do that?" Michelle asked. At the girl's nod, Michelle's eyes hardened and her lips compressed. "Well, she's lying. And even if she wasn't, Matt can protect you."

"How do you know?" Raneem asked, looking for as much assurance as she could find.

"Because the one person in the Federation who *could* kill with her mind tried to kill me." Despite herself, I felt Michelle's emotional shiver at the memory of our run-in with Sadie on

Piscain Station. Michelle jerked a thumb my way. "*He* defended me and defeated her."

"Did he kill her with his mind?" A look of morbid fascination appeared on the girl's face.

"No," I said. "I used a blaster. But I used my mind to stop her from killing Michelle."

Raneem considered this for a moment. "Then I guess it's okay if you make me feel better with your mind."

"You're already feeling better, Raneem," I said, smiling. "But I'll do what I can."

As I'd done before, I reached into the girl's mind and extracted what was left of her fear and sorrow. The transformation wasn't as impressive as it would have been when Raneem was sobbing, but at least the girl knew what to expect.

"Wow," she breathed. "What happened to the fear? Did you give it to someone else?"

"That wouldn't be a very nice thing to do." I tapped my head. "It's in here, stuck off in a corner of my mind where it can't hurt anyone. It'll fade away, after a while."

"Doesn't it scare you?"

"No. I've got it...um, surrounded is as good a word as any, by my own ability." I smiled warmly at the girl. "I can protect you from Shafira's mind. And if she tries anything else, my wife can kick her butt all around this room and then up and down the hallway outside."

"And when it's time for us to leave Earth," Michelle said, trying to get ahead of any other fears which might plague Raneem, "we'll either take you with us or make sure you're somewhere safe. Okay?"

"I've heard that from other couples. They never take me away, though." Raneem's tone was emotionless and matter-of-fact, as if she was already preparing for a similar disappointment from us.

"Did you warn any of those people about Shafira?" Michelle asked.

"No. I was too scared to."

"So, you helped Shafira rob them?"

Raneem hung her head. "Yeah."

"Since none of Shafira's victims knew you were a victim, too, they probably thought you were in on it." Michelle reached over and brushed hair away from Raneem's eyes. "You can't really blame them for not sticking to their promise, can you?"

"I guess not."

"But, you warned us and, even before you did, we knew Shafira was forcing you to help her. This is a totally different situation than those other times, and Matt and I aren't like any of those other couples." Michelle flashed her brightest smile. "So, things are going to be different, this time. Okay?"

"Okay." A shy smile broke out on the girl's face. "I guess I'm ready for that bath and then some new clothes."

"That sounds like a plan," Michelle said. "After that, we'll order room service and you can get anything on the menu that you want."

Unsurprisingly, Raneem didn't get many opportunities to bathe and she took full advantage of this opportunity. The girl sounded shy when she and Michelle went into the bedroom, but it didn't take long for Michelle to coax Raneem out of her shell. After that, the young girl chatted excitedly to Michelle about anything and everything. Michelle stayed with her, patiently listening and responding as needed.

I never doubted Michelle would make a wonderful mother. She showed it with Cassie and showed it again with Raneem. Between the long bath and clothes fabrication, the two of them stayed busy for nearly two hours. When the bedroom door finally opened, Michelle stuck her head out and grinned at me.

"Someone would like to show off her new clothes. Are you up for a fashion show, babe?"

Without even trying, I could feel the excitement radiating from the Raneem and wouldn't dream of disappointing her. "You bet!"

For the next twenty minutes, I admired everything the ten-year-old modeled for me. With each compliment, Raneem radiated joy, which made me work all the harder to find new ways to compliment her. Of course, I was also casually reading the girl's emotions. If she was particularly excited about her current outfit, I made sure I was more complimentary than normal. It was such a simple thing, but it was huge to Raneem.

After the last outfit was modeled and Raneem returned to her room to change clothes one more time, Michelle sat next to me and gave me a hug and a kiss. "You made a little girl very happy, Matt."

We ordered a big meal from room service and watched that little girl really pack in the food. Raneem ate all of her meal and finished off what Michelle and I didn't eat of ours. And she still had room for a piece of pie with ice cream on top. Between bites of food, we got as much of Raneem's story as she would share.

"There's not a lot to tell," the girl said. In a disturbingly matter-of-fact voice, she continued, "My parents are dead and I've been with Shafira ever since they died."

"Is Shafira a relative of yours?" Michelle asked. "A cousin or aunt?"

"Nah. She's just the person who got to me first when my parents died."

Michelle and I exchanged glances and I asked, "Isn't the planetary government supposed to find someone to take care of you, in that case?"

"Yeah, but they don't do a good job of it. A lot of kids just end up in orphanages or in homes where the family wants them for the extra money they get from the government." Raneem paused to shovel some more food into her mouth. "At least, that's what Shafira told us."

"Us?" I asked. "Are there more kids besides you?"

"Oh, sure. Shafira runs eight or ten of us. Sometimes the boss has her run twelve or more, but that doesn't happen much."

"Shafira isn't the one in charge?" Michelle asked.

"She's in charge of us, but she's just part of the boss's gang.

She's real scared of the boss, too. Just like we're all scared of her." Raneem paused to take a drink. "Do you think *he* can kill with his mind?"

"Probably not," I replied. "Earlier you said Shafira would make you steal from us. How does she do that?"

Raneem's eyes grew troubled. "Are you *sure* you can protect me from her?"

"Absolutely, sweetheart." Too many extremely knowledgeable people insisted I was one of the most powerful empaths since the Cairo Catastrophe for me to have any doubts. "What does Shafira make you do?"

"She'll sneak up here tonight, long after you should be asleep. I'll know she's at the door because she'll make me scared. I'm supposed to let her in so we can steal everything you've got." Raneem shrugged. "That's the plan, anyway. This is the first time I've gone to a hotel room. Usually, it's one of the older girls or boys who gets invited. Sometimes, they're crying when they come back."

I shared a very troubled look with Michelle, then she said, "Well, we're going to put a stop to all of that, honey. And it will start tonight. Do you think you can pretend we're sleeping and let Shafira in?"

"I...think so."

"Good," Michelle smiled. "Now, here's what we're going to do..."

We slept in shifts, waiting for Shafira. It was nearly three in the morning before she finally showed up. Raneem sprang up in her bed, eyes wide with fear. I quickly pulled the emotion from her mind. Michelle and I took our positions while the girl went to the door. She quietly unlocked and opened the door. Shafira shoved her way in, knocking the girl to the floor.

That was too much for Michelle to tolerate. In one smooth move, she uncoiled from behind a chair, grabbed Shafira's wrist, and flipped the woman over her shoulder. By the time I shut the suite's door and flicked on the lights, she was standing over Shafira with her brand new blaster trained on the other woman.

"Hello, Shafira. Raneem has told us *all* about you," Michelle purred. "Please do something stupid so I can have an excuse to give you the ass-kicking you deserve."

The surprise on Shafira's face flowed quickly from surprise to anger. "You just made a *big* mistake—and all three of you are going to pay for it!"

The woman summoned her full empathic power and broadcast terror at Michelle. I thought it was a good choice on Shafira's part since simple fear might just make my wife pull the trigger on her blaster. Unfortunately—for Shafira—her ability just wasn't powerful enough to get through Michelle's shields, much less affect all three of us, at once. Maybe she planned on alternating between us? Or probably she just let her mouth get ahead of her brain. It didn't matter since neither plan would work—not against *us*, anyway.

After a minute, I took pity on Shafira. Okay, not really. I just decided to end the farce. "Michelle? You're supposed to be quaking in terror, hon."

"Really?" Michelle's brow drew down in concentration. "I can't even feel her knocking on my mind. She must really suck at this."

Confusion replaced anger as Shafira looked back and forth between Michelle and me. Then her eyes lighted on Raneem and Shafira grinned. "Maybe I can't get you, but I can get her!"

Raneem shrank against me as Shafira shifted her psychic attention to the girl. I hugged her and said, "Don't worry, Raneem. She can't do anything to you."

I felt Shafira throw her power at the girl, all but yelling, "The hell I can't!"

I caught the terror before it even registered in Raneem's mind and drew it to me. "You just don't know when you're beaten, do you, Shafira?"

Michelle looked at me. "She tried to terrorize Raneem?"

I nodded and Michelle turned her attention to the girl. "Are you okay, honey? Did any of it get through?"

Raneem shook her head. "I got scared, but only because of the way Shafira looked me. Nothing happened, so I stopped being scared."

Our casual conversation and utter lack of terror enraged Shafira. She poured all of her rage into her minor power and threw it at the one target she hadn't tried yet—me.

"Now, she's turned her power on me, babe. She's certainly a determined woman, I'll give her that." I glanced at Michelle. "Should I show Shafira the error of her ways?"

"Yes. Send it all back, with interest."

I opened my mind and drew in the fear felt by those in the hotel. Much as I wish it was otherwise, fear is one emotion I can always find in abundance. So many things cause fear—or fear's close cousins, concern, doubt, and worry—that our minds are never truly free of it. That's as true of me as it is for everyone else. In other words, I had lots of fear to draw upon—including Shafira's, since the woman just kept broadcasting at me, even though it wasn't working.

I blasted Shafira hard, pouring the gathered fears of dozens of people into her mind at once. Her eyes opened wide in surprise and her mouth opened in a silent scream as I hammered her mind with fear. Then, she curled up into a ball, wrapping her arms around herself and shaking her head back and forth.

I knew the woman deserved everything I was giving her, and more. Within her mind, I felt echoes of the pleasure she took from inflicting fear on others—especially children. I knew just how rotten she was, at the core of her being. I could have kept up my onslaught for hours, but I'm not like Shafira. I kept up the assault only long enough to make my point.

The woman remained in a ball, whimpering, even after I stopped blasting her. Knowing she'd get over it, I scanned Raneem and picked up conflicting emotions. The girl wanted to enjoy Shafira's terror because she knew the woman deserved it. But, despite the horrors life dealt her during her short life, Raneem isn't emotionally broken. She very much wanted me to stop what I was doing.

"I've stopped sending fear at her, Raneem. What I sent to Shafira will fade away quickly."

Raneem looked up at me. "You don't look happy. Shafira always looks happy when she makes us afraid."

I went down on one knee to put myself on the same level as the girl. "I'm not like Shafira. I don't like making people afraid—but I'll do it to protect people like you and Michelle."

Raneem bit her lip and nodded. The gesture reminded me so much of Michelle that I smiled. "What I did to Shafira didn't make you happy, either. And that's good, Raneem. That's very good, indeed."

The girl suddenly yawned and her eyelids drooped. She blinked her eyes wide, but the lids began drooping almost immediately. I called to Michelle, "Hon, why don't you get Raneem tucked back into bed while I have a little conversation with our guest."

Michelle handed her blaster to me. She took Raneem's hand and led her into the bedroom. I settled into a chair near Shafira, who was still balled up and rolling around. I read the woman's emotions. She was filled with fear, but it was all of her own making. She suffered as badly from shock over the unexpected turn of events.

"Being on the receiving end of that isn't a lot of fun, is it?" I asked. "Honestly, you deserved what you got and then some."

I read disbelief welling up in the woman's mind. To my amazement, I even felt feelings of innocence surface. "How in God's name can you possibly believe you didn't have that coming? Are you truly that delusional?"

Apparently, she was. I felt Shafira gather her empathic ability, preparing for another blast of fear. Her cunning plan was a surprise attack while she pretended she was still overwhelmed by my blast. I sighed and formed a barrier around the woman's mind. Her blast of fear—powderpuff of fear was more like it—rebounded off my power.

Lashed by her own attack, Shafira writhed some more. And then she tried again. And again. After a while, I propped my head on one hand and just waited for her to give up. She was still at it a few minutes later, when Michelle returned.

"Raneem is fast asleep." Michelle took the chair next to mine and gave Shafira an inquisitive look. "What's going on here?"

"Shafira decided to make a surprise attack on me. I sensed her brilliant plan and walled off her mind with my own power. The attack rebounded on Shafira, so she tried it again." I waved a hand at the writhing woman. "She's been at it ever since. I think she's trying to wear me out. There's no chance of that, but I might fall asleep from sheer boredom in an hour or two."

"You want me to just shoot her?" Michelle asked.

Shafira stopped rolling around and, finally, stopped throwing her meager attacks at the shield I built around her mind. She glared at us. "You made a big mistake, standing up to me. You are going to pay for that!"

Michelle turned an incredulous look my way. I nodded. "Yep, she believes that. I don't know why, after everything that's happened to her tonight, but Shafira is positive we're going to regret this."

My wife leaned forward and met Shafira's defiant glare. "What gives? You know you can't do anything to us. You've been trying, ever since you got here, and it hasn't worked, yet. Tell us, please, why we should be worried about you?"

"It's not me you should be scared of, bitch." Shafira grinned and radiated absolute certainty when she said, "The boss can kill you with a thought!"

Michelle and I ruined this dire pronouncement by laughing. Shafira got all huffy and insisted, "He can! And he can do other stuff, too. Like, he's immune to my power and everybody else's power, too."

"*I'm* immune to your power," Michelle said, "but that doesn't mean I can think someone to death."

"But I've seen him do it!" the woman insisted. "I was waiting to make my report and turn in my money one time. And this guy who ran the pickpockets got uppity with the boss. The boss just looked at him real hard and blood started running out of his nose and then he just fell over dead." She snapped her fingers. "Just like that!"

Michelle glanced at me. "What do you think?"

"I can think of half-a-dozen ways to fake that sort of thing with some high-end technology. I mean, not even Sadie could make someone just keel over dead. But, however he did it, this boss guy scares the hell out of Shafira. It also sounds like he's the center of underground psychic activity in Cairo."

"Damn straight he scares me," she said. "And if you don't let me take the girl and all your money, he's going to scare you, too. But it'll be too late because he'll already be killing you."

Michelle raised an eyebrow at me and I nodded. She turned back to Shafira and said, "We want to meet with him. Go arrange it."

"You want to meet the boss?" Shafira asked, her voice turning silky smooth. "Yeah, I can make that happen."

Her emotions overflowed with duplicity and something I could only call evil glee. I could readily imagine her cackling and rubbing her hands in anticipation of the horrors she would have the boss inflict upon us. As it happened, it didn't take an empath to see this.

Michelle squatted down in front of Shafira. "Any idiot can see you're planning a nice little double-cross—it's written plainly on your face."

"No," Shafira insisted, shaking her head and trying to mask her emotions. "I wouldn't do that!"

"Listen to me very carefully, woman." Michelle's voice dropped to a whisper colder than a winter wind on a pitch-black night. "If you try a double-cross, I will personally hunt you down and end you —but not until after my husband has inflicted so much terror on you that you beg for the sweet release of death. Are we clear on that?"

Eyes wide and mouth slack, Shafira just nodded dumbly.

Michelle smiled brightly and stood up. "Good! Now, be on your way."

Shafira looked toward the door and her already-wide eyes grew wider, still. Babbling incoherently, she scuttled backward in a terrified crab walk.

Michelle turned a questioning gaze toward me and gave a startled jump of her own. I looked to my left and, prepared for an unexpected sight, managed to keep from mirroring Michelle's reaction.

A ghostly image stood in the room, looking around in wonder. In a wispy voice, Cassie said, "Hi guys!"

Shafira moaned in terror and curled up into a ball. "Don't let the ghost take me! I'll be good and I'll do what I said and I won't double-cross you or nothing! Just don't let the ghost get me!"

Michelle whispered to Cassie, "Play along with us, here. We need to make sure this woman does what we want. She is *not* a nice person, so don't feel guilty."

"Why aren't you surprised to see me?" Cassie asked. "I didn't even know I could do this."

"You'll tell us about it at breakfast," I said. "But let's discuss that once Shafira is out of here."

Cassie shrugged. "Okay. Should I make 'wooooo' noises or anything?"

"Whatever you feel like, honey," Michelle grinned. "Just make it good. Oh, and use her name every time you speak to her."

"Got it." Cassie returned my wife's grin. She raised her hands over her head in a stereotypical 'haunting ghost' pose and sang out, "Shafiiiiira—I've come for you."

A terrified moan rose from the curled up woman. Her emotions, once filled with artless guile, were overrun by gibbering-in-the-corner terror.

"No, Cassie, you can't have her," Michelle said, walking over to Shafira. "At least, not yet."

Cassie followed Michelle. Sticking to the sing-song voice, she said, "But I'm sooooooo hungry!"

I almost burst out laughing but then Shafira's whimpering stirred compassion inside me. Not much compassion, but enough to want to hurry this along. I caught Michelle's attention and made a hurry-up gesture.

Michelle nodded, dropped to one knee, and prodded the woman. "Hey, are you listening Shafira?"

The woman moaned in response.

Michelle poked her again. "Pay attention or I *will* let the ghost take you!"

Shafira's head rose and her wide eyes flicked back and forth between Michelle and Cassie. "I- I- I'm listening."

"Good. You're going to arrange this meeting with the boss. You're not going to double-cross us. You're going to set it up some-place public. And then you're going to come back and report to us. Got it?" Shafira's head bobbed rapidly. Michelle smiled. "See, that wasn't hard. You can go now."

The woman climbed to her feet, never once taking her eyes off Cassie. The girl reached toward the woman and said, "I'll be watching you, Shafira. Everywhere you go, I'll be watching and waiting. Waiting for you to go back on your word. Then you'll be *mine*!"

Shafira shrieked one more time and bolted for the door. She ran right through dream-Cassie, removing any lingering doubts Shafira might have harbored about Cassie's 'true nature.'

When the door slammed behind her, Cassie doubled over laughing. "Wow, that was cool! I can't wait to tell you about that in the morning."

I shook my head. "You can't do that, Cassie. We're about a week into your future right now, so you can't tell week-ago-us much at all. You can only tell us to go to Earth."

"And you're going to need to convince our parents," Michelle said. "Daddy is going to snap at you when you tell us we need to come to Earth, so don't be upset. He'll apologize right after that."

"Okay. Is there anything else I should know?" Cassie asked.

"Yeah," I said. "You're going to need something to tell everyone so they know you talked to us. So... Um, you remember the story about Michelle rescuing me from the gang outside of the maglev station?"

"Sure. That's when your stories joined. It sure was a lot easier dreaming about you two once you were together."

"And you remember how my head ended up in Michelle's lap?"

"Of course. You both told me all about it."

"I know, but you only have one chance to convince everyone," I said.

"Well, you're here aren't you? That means I didn't screw it up." Cassie's ghostly eyes rolled. "Can we get to whatever it is I'm supposed to say while I'm not screwing it up?"

"I felt an irrational desire to bury my face against Michelle's stomach and blow a raspberry."

"Whoa—really?" Cassie's eyes danced. "I wonder if you two would have gotten married if you did that?"

"Absolutely not," Michelle said.

"I think she would have forgiven me." At Michelle's skeptical glance, I added, "Eventually. I did say it was an *irrational* desire and I did *not* give in to it."

"As a result, you've been happily married to me for just over a year," Michelle smiled at me.

Cassie looked back and forth between the two of us. "I know what *that* look means. You two can go get all lovey-dovy. I'll deliver your messages in the morning."

"Uh, mentioning getting lovey-dovy..." I said.

Cassie gave me a look of exasperation. "Did Rob tell you about us?"

"No, you did," I said. "Or, you will."

"Oh. What about Rob and me?"

"Isn't he a little…old for you?" I asked. "He's a great friend, but does he really see you as a love interest?"

"No, I'm more like a little sister to him. It really weirded him out when he dreamed about our wedding. But he'll change his mind when I'm older." Dream-Cassie came over to me and put her arms around me—and through me in a couple of places. "This is supposed to be a hug. Don't worry, big brother, Rob hasn't changed and neither have I. He won't even kiss me on the lips until my eighteenth birthday."

"It's still a strange idea, but I can't think of any guy I trust more." I returned Cassie's supposed-to-be-a-hug. "And I'm sure you'll make a beautiful bride—but not for another nine or ten years."

"Rob says I'll be as beautiful as Michelle, but I think he's just being nice."

"I think he's telling the truth," Michelle said. "Now, get out of here so Matt and I can get busy."

Cassie nodded and faded away.

"In a week full of strange stuff, that has got to be the strangest of them all," I said. "And I even knew it was going to happen."

"I know what you mean," Michelle said as she led me toward our bedroom. "Meanwhile, let's get well and truly screwed tonight so we don't get well and truly screwed when we meet Shafira's boss."

"That has worked out well for us ever since you had the idea back on Piscain Station." I shut the door and started unbuttoning Michelle's shirt.

"I know," she replied, reaching for my belt, "and I plan on being *very* thorough tonight."

I pulled Michelle close and kissed her. "I had that very same idea."

THE MEMORIAL

After our 'Sex for Success' ritual, Michelle and I did something we didn't normally do after a round of love-making. We put on pajamas before going to sleep. Properly attired for bed, we left the door to our suite's sitting room open. If Raneem woke before us, we didn't want any kind of barrier between her and us.

I woke up as someone climbed carefully over my legs. Raneem wormed her way up to my back and curled up there.

"You can get under the covers," I whispered.

"I didn't mean to wake you up," Raneem whispered back. "I'm sorry."

"It's okay."

"You can both stop whispering," Michelle growled. "I'm awake, too."

"Sorry," Raneem and I said at the same time.

Michelle checked the time and sat up. "I need to get up anyway."

Raneem propped her head on my side. We both watched Michelle get up, stretch, and head to the bathroom. The young girl didn't say anything after Michelle shut the door, but she radiated curiosity.

"Go ahead and ask whatever is on your mind, Raneem."

"How do you-? Oh, yeah, you're a psychic." The girl was quiet for a few seconds, probably trying to figure out the best way to ask her question. "How did you and Michelle meet?"

I was ready for a momentous question about her and the future and how we could protect her, so this question took me by surprise. "We met in school—sixth grade. I fell madly in love with her the first day and loved her even more as I got to know her better."

Raneem sighed. "That's sweet. Did she love you from the beginning, too?"

"I think she was actually pretty mad at me," I said. "Her father moved from Earth to Draconis—that's where my family lived—to take a job with my father. Michelle had to leave all of her friends and the only home she ever knew. But she got over that and eventually fell in love with me."

"And then you got married?"

"Um, sort of." I squirmed onto my back, ending up with Raneem's head on my stomach. Stroking her head the same way I remembered Mom stroking mine, I asked, "Do you want to hear the whole story?"

At Raneem's nod, I launched into an abbreviated version of Michelle saving me from the gang at the maglev station and our search for my parents. A part of me protested against telling this waif everything she needed to destroy our lives. The rest of me—including the well-trained, powerful empath part—knew Raneem was trustworthy.

The girl listened with rapt attention and, when I wrapped up with our second wedding, breathed, "That is *so* romantic!"

Exiting the bathroom, Michelle asked, "What is so romantic?"

"Our story," I said.

Michelle paused and looked at me. "Our real story?"

"Yes." I tapped my head, hoping Michelle understood I wasn't just blindly trusting the girl.

Smiling in response, she said, "While you're getting a shower, I'll tell her the rest of the real story."

"What do you mean? I told Raneem everything."

"And all of it from your point of view, babe. You probably made it sound like you were incredibly lucky to end up with a girl like me and a bunch of other crap like that."

I slid out from under Raneem's head and climbed out of bed. Kissing Michelle lightly on the lips, I said, "I *am* incredibly lucky to have you."

As the bathroom door slid shut, I heard Michelle say, "Let me tell you the story about how I became the luckiest girl in the galaxy and married the guy of my dreams."

By the time I came out of the bathroom, Raneem and Michelle were giggling over something. Maintaining an air of manly indifference, I gave my wife a kiss on the top of her head and then did the same with the girl.

Raneem fell into a pretend swoon and, through her giggles, said, "Read me now!"

When I cocked an eyebrow at Michelle, she grinned and said, "I can't believe you just glossed over our first kiss. Don't tell me you've already forgotten it?"

I sat down on the bed and pulled Michelle close. With a significant glance at the still-giggling girl, I gave Michelle as deep and romantic a kiss as I could in front of the ten-year-old Raneem. "Does that answer your question?"

Michelle pulled back just enough to look into my eyes. "Magnificently."

"Wow," Raneem sighed. "I wonder if I'll ever meet a 'Matt' of my own?"

"Stick with us, kiddo, and it's almost guaranteed," I said. "But right now, I'm hungry and we've got some preparations to make before Shafira comes back."

Just mentioning the woman's name stopped Raneem's giggles. "What are we going to do if she tries to take me back while you two are gone?"

"You don't want to come with us to the meeting?" I asked. "Not that we were going to take you, but I expected an argument."

"Michelle explained that to me while you were in the shower. I understand why I can't go, but I'm still worried about staying here, alone."

"You can stop worrying," I said. "We're going to take you someplace really safe. Someplace that can get you to our family even if something happens to Michelle and me."

Michelle smacked herself on the forehead. "The container! Why didn't I think of that?"

I shrugged. "That's why we're a team—so one person doesn't have to think of everything."

"Uh, are you talking about putting me in a box or something?" Raneem asked.

"Not the kind you're thinking of," Michelle assured the girl. "Don't worry, Matt and I came to Earth in it. We'll show you right after breakfast."

I left a note on the door in case Shafira showed up while we were gone and then we went in search of a restaurant.

"You don't want to get room service again?" Raneem asked. "I liked it last night."

"I looked over their breakfast menu and they don't have waffles," I said. "Never trust a breakfast place that doesn't have waffles."

"What are waffles?" the girl asked.

I gasped in pretend horror. "You don't know what waffles are? Child, they are God's gift to breakfast."

"Along with bacon," Michelle added.

"I know what bacon is," Raneem said. "I've seen Shafira eat it a few times."

"But you've never tasted it?" Michelle asked. When the girl shook her head, Michelle took her by the hand and led her out of the hotel. "Then it's past time you did."

It didn't take long to find a proper breakfast restaurant. I don't know where she put it, but Raneem ate two waffles and three plates of bacon. Then we flagged down a cab and returned to the spaceport.

We spent an hour in the container with Raneem. First, we coded it to obey her instructions. Then we showed her everything we could about the container, including how to call up books and watch vids. We made sure she knew how to have meals prepared for her. Most importantly, we taught her how to contact us and, in case of an emergency, how to have the container shipped back to Ark's Landing.

When we were ready to go, Michelle hugged the girl and asked, "Do you understand everything?"

"I think so. And if I forget, it's real easy to just ask the container how to do stuff."

"Will you be okay staying here alone?" I asked, also giving her a hug.

"Yeah. I *never* get to be alone, so this is kind of a treat." She turned big eyes on the pair of us. "But please be careful. You've been so good to me and I don't want anything to happen to you. Shafira's boss can be real mean, so don't trust him."

"We won't, honey," Michelle said. "We're pretty good at this stuff, you know."

With one last hug, we left to await our meeting with Shafira's boss.

We took a taxi away from the spaceport, stopping a few blocks from our hotel. From there, we played tourist while waiting for Shafira to get my note and contact us. By the time she called, Michelle and I were in an out-of-the-way diner eating something I didn't recognize and whose name I couldn't pronounce, much less remember. It was good, though. My mouth was full, when my comm buzzed.

"Hello," I said around my food.

"Where are you?"

I finished chewing and took a quick drink. "It's nice to hear from you, too, Shafira."

"Why didn't you wait at the hotel like you said you would?" Shafira sounded flustered.

"Hang on a minute, Shafira." I ignored her squawk and muted my comm. I looked at Michelle and said, "She sounds pretty agitated for someone who was just supposed to set up a meeting."

Michelle shrugged. "She's a pawn stuck between two powerful players. That's scary enough, but I'll bet her boss is forcing her to do exactly what we warned her not to do. Her boss hurts or kills her if she doesn't bait us into a trap. She believes we'll give her to a ghost if she does. The trap bit was always going to come down to who scared her the most."

"It looks like it's not us. What do you want to do, hon?"

"You've been pretty deep into Shafira's mind—is there any chance you can read her from this far away?"

"Sure. Back at Pegasus station, I found you from a lot farther away. But filtering Shafira out of the mass of people around her and us is another thing. I just don't know her well enough to pick the right filters."

"That's about what I thought." Michelle bit her lip, meaning she was puzzling through the problem. After a few seconds, she smiled. "We both know she's up to something, just not what. Can you bluff her?"

I grinned back at my wife. "I think I know just the thing."

A string of profanity sounded from the comm when I put it back to my ear. I unmuted it and said, "Watch your language, Shafira!"

"Then don't cut me off when I'm trying to tell you about the meeting *you* wanted!"

"I muted you so I could pay attention to our friend's report without you overhearing everything she said."

Shafira was quiet for a few seconds. When she spoke again, her voice was low and much less confrontational. "Um, what friend is that?"

"Come on, Shafira, you know exactly which friend. The one from last night. She appeared after Raneem was asleep. I was quite disappointed in her report. She, however, was pretty excited about it."

"W-why?"

"Why do you think, Shafira?" I used the same gentle voice I would use comforting Raneem, doing my best to convey pity for Shafira. "The ghost is very hungry and she thinks we're going to let her have you."

"Y-you won't do that, right?"

I heaved a sigh. "I don't want to, but I may have to. If you double-crossed us and we don't give you to her, it would break our binding on the ghost and then she'd be free to come after us. When the choice comes down to you or us, well, I'm sure you can understand why we'll choose ourselves."

"The boss picked the Cairo Catastrophe Memorial for the meeting," Shafira said in a rush. "He's going to have a lot of his people in there with him. There's only one way in or out, so they're going to grab you when you leave. If he can't grab you, he'll turn you over to Psi Corps."

"He does realize Psi Corps will take everyone in the memorial —including him and you—and test them?

"He says he's not worried."

Shafira sounded worried—and for good reason. If she helped us, Psi Corps would grab her. If she helped the boss, we'd turn the ghost loose on her. Too bad the woman didn't know the 'ghost' threat had no teeth. Then again, knowing our parents and our friends—Jonas in particular—Shafira probably wasn't worried enough.

"Where are you right now?" I asked.

"Right outside your hotel."

"Wait for us there, but keep this comm connection open. I'm going to mute on my end, but I'll be listening. And the ghost will be watching and listening."

I muted the comm without waiting for a response. We paid for our lunch and left the diner.

Michelle looped an arm through mine. "Have you got a plan,

babe?"

"Not exactly," I said. "I'm pretty sure I can handle any psychics the boss throws at us, but any kind of psychic battle in the memorial will almost certainly alert Psi Corps. They've got to have some high-powered psychics at their main office. Have you got any ideas?"

"Two—go in heavily armed and find another way out of the memorial."

"How are you going to go heavily armed? Earth doesn't allow open carry."

"I've got a wonderful, one-of-a-kind backpack that your father gave to me just before we left. It's got lots of places to hide weapons and is designed to fool scanners."

I whistled appreciatively. "I know GenCo has technology that can do that, but it's not cheap. How much did the backpack cost?"

"Eight point six million credits—and worth every centicred if it helps us get out of this."

"I won't argue with that. What about finding another way out?"

"That'll be a team effort. I'll smile and ask memorial employees —males, of course—if there's another way out. You'll read them and see what you can find out."

"Our brilliant plan is very short on details," I said.

"That's why we know it's going to work," Michelle said.

"That's...counterintuitive."

"Oooh, that's a nice turn of phrase, Matt. It's much better than saying, 'That doesn't make any sense.' We've always done our best work when we were making it up as we go. I don't see any reason why this time will be different."

"We had surprise on our side, in the pirate base and when we were escaping from Piscain Station. Shafira's boss knows we're coming."

"Her boss knows some psychic and his wife are coming. If he knew it was the infamous Connaughts, he'd wet his pants."

"Let's hope you're right."

On the way to the hotel, we stopped in a family restroom and checked our makeup. Michelle used a pocket pad to verify our retinal overlays were working properly. When we reached the hotel, Shafira was right where she said she'd be. I stayed outside with her while Michelle ran upstairs to prepare her fancy backpack.

As Michelle disappeared into the hotel, I looked at a spot right next to Shafira. "No, Cassie, you can't have Shafira. She's cooperating with us."

Shafira jumped to the left, staring at the same spot. "The ghost is here?"

"I told you the ghost was watching you, Shafira."

"How come I can't see her?"

"Yes, Cassie, it is a silly question." I looked at Shafira. "She's a *ghost*. You can't see her unless she wants you to."

"How come you can see her?"

"I bound her." I sighed and shook my head. "Don't you know *anything* about ghosts?"

"My mama told me all about 'em when I was little. One took my dad and mama saw it all. He used to beat her and mama warned him the ghost was angry. He just laughed at her—until the ghost threw him across the room and out the window. It was a long way down."

I read absolute certainty from the woman, though the explanation was probably a lot more psychic than paranormal. Her mother sounded like a strong telekinetic who didn't even know she had powers. With psychic powers of her own, why hadn't Shafira figured this out? Since we needed Shafira, I wasn't about to point this out to her, but it puzzled me.

"Did the ghost ever threaten you?" I asked.

"Some. It picked me up and pinned me against the wall one time when I was talking back to mama. I couldn't breathe and was sure I was going to die. Mama was screaming and begging for the ghost to let me go when I passed out. When I woke up, mama said the ghost didn't like me. For my own safety, mama put me out on the street."

"How old were you?" I asked.

"Eight. Mama was right, though, 'cause the ghost got her less than a month later. Threw her out the window, just like my dad."

Obviously, Shafira's mother was a telekinetic, and a powerful one if she threw a grown man out of a window. That didn't explain how her mother went through the window, though, since telekinetics can't use their own power on themselves. I guessed Psi Corps was involved in that, though I doubted we'd ever learn the details.

"Is that when you started working for the boss?"

"Yeah. He took me in, put me on a team. He made me learn how to use my powers. The boss can be mean and scary, but I'd be dead if it wasn't for him." Shafira looked at me. "So remember that when you ask me to betray him."

It was a sobering story, one that could have had a completely different outcome if only Psi Corps didn't essentially enslave psychics. Without the fear Psi Corps engendered, Shafira's mother could have received training and made something of herself. Shafira wouldn't have ended up on the streets and also could have been trained.

How many similar stories could I find all across the Terran Federation?

How much suffering had Psi Corps caused?

It was long past time for this to end.

It was long past time to bring Psi Corps down.

And where better to do that than the heart of the entire operation?

I don't know what I expected from the memorial site, but it definitely wasn't what I got. Maybe I thought such an important place would be more...noticeable? It definitely wasn't ostentatious, but it wasn't soberly grand, either. The entrance ran between two buildings—it was probably just an alley four hundred years ago—and was unmarked except for a simple metal plaque with 'Cairo Catastrophe Memorial - Entrance' engraved upon it. The entrance to Psi Corps headquarters, fifty meters to the right of the alley and marked with large block letters over the entrance, was garish in comparison.

Michelle spoke my thoughts aloud. "This is it? The entrance is awfully subtle for one of the most famous memorials in the Federation."

"What did you expect? Clowns and games and rides?" Shafira sneered.

"No, Shafira, I expected something similar to other memorials around the Federation," Michelle said, keeping her tone even. "Signs big enough to read from a distance, a somber reminder of the event, and maybe a prayer for the souls of the dead."

"They've got stuff like that inside." Shafira made a sweeping gesture with her arm. "So let's not keep the boss waiting and get on in there."

Michelle and I led the way into the alley-cum-entrance. Signs on both walls listed items prohibited inside the park and warned we would be scanned before we were allowed to enter. I found myself praying Michelle's incredibly expensive backpack was up to the task of masking our weapons.

At the end of the alley, an armed guard directed us to different scanners. To my relief, all three of us passed through the scanners without incident. Then a guard stopped Michelle.

"What's in the backpack, ma'am?"

"Bottled water and snacks." Michelle pulled the pack off, undid the fastenings, and opened it for the guard to look inside. "Is it okay to bring those into the park? The signs didn't mention food or water."

My pulse rate doubled as the guard stuck his arm into the pack and rummaged through the contents. "Food and water is fine, ma'am. We just check the contents of the bags as a precaution. Thank you for your cooperation and enjoy your visit."

"Say, is there another way out of the park besides that alley back there? It's on the complete opposite side of the memorial from our hotel."

"I'm sorry, ma'am," the guard said. "This is the only public entrance and exit."

Michelle gave me a significant glance, making sure I heard the qualifier. There were other exits if we could find them.

Slinging the pack over one shoulder, Michelle joined us and we wandered away from the scanners. When Shafira's attention was elsewhere, I caught my wife's eye, darted a look at the backpack, and raised my eyebrows. She gave me a quick thumbs up.

Michelle wrapped an arm around me, pulled me into a hug, and whispered, "The stuff in the pack gives the guard something to concentrate on other than the pack, itself. And I didn't let him hold it because the pack weighs too much for what's inside. Since the scan was negative, he was just going through the motions, anyway."

"You'd better put your shields up. I don't know where the boss's people are, yet, but-" I felt a familiar tingle, followed by three more. "Okay, I just picked up an empath and three telepaths. They aren't trying anything yet, but they're scanning, too."

Shafira pointed off to the left. "We go that way."

Checking the signs in that direction, I asked, "We're going to the hologram replay site? Why there?"

Shafira actually shivered. "Because it's creepy and hardly anybody ever goes there—especially us locals."

I nodded in understanding. "Your boss wants us distracted by the holograms. Are they really that bad?"

"They're great if you don't mind watching people go crazy and kill each other or kids beating their heads on the sidewalk until they smash their skulls open."

"That's disgusting," Michelle said. "Why would Psi Corps desecrate the memorial with something like that?"

"Because it's what happened,"Shafira said. "They used vids of the catastrophe to make sure they got everything right."

"And it serves as a horrible reminder of the terrible psychic forces Psi Corps holds in check," I said. "That's the intent, at least. Make sure everyone leaves here certain the only thing standing between normal citizens and total chaos is Psi Corps."

"It works, too," Shafira said. "Anybody sees this, they leave all pale and scared and ready to back Psi Corps completely. Idiots."

"Yeah, thank God you and your cheap-ass psychic buddies are doing something worthwhile to counter the message Psi Corps is sending." Michelle paused briefly as if having a revelation. "Oh, that's right, you're *not* doing something worthwhile. And when Psi Corps catches you, they'll parade the lot of you in front of the cams and make you the face of rogue psychics everywhere. Who's the idiot, Shafira?"

"Don't you go preaching to me, bitch," Shafira shot back. "You don't have any idea what it's like living on the streets."

We entered a large square ringed with warning signs about disturbing images and telling parents to remove young children from the area before the next show—an incongruous word for the display—began. An older man watched us from the center of the square. Six other men and women, ranging in age from late teens to late middle-age, lined up about ten meters behind him.

A quick scan told me all six were psychics of some kind, though I didn't take the time to check more thoroughly. I broadened my scan and picked up nine more psychics scattered around the square but out of our sight.

I felt a psychic signal pass between one of the six and someone else. Without looking away from the man, I said, "Be ready—something is about to happen."

Before Michelle could respond, the square suddenly filled with people calmly going about their day. Their clothing was four hundred years out-of-date, but everything else about them was recognizable. Here was a businessman impatiently fighting the crowd, obviously late for an appointment. There were parents out with their children. In between them walked a gaggle of schoolgirls about Cassie's age, laughing and chatting and scoping out the boys around them. The boys, in return, cast less-than-furtive glances at the girls. Only the lack of sound—something I found odd in such a detailed hologram—exposed the scene as a recreation.

Then horror swept over the crowd like a tidal wave. People

clutched their heads or dropped to the ground or ran screaming from unseen terrors. Some curled up on the ground, shivering, while most stampeded away from the source of the terror. The young and those curled up on the ground were trampled by the mob. And, yes, here and there children—they were all children—fell to their knees and began banging their heads on the pavement.

Terrible as the sight was, my empathic scan picked up the same emotions as it did before the hologram began. This knowledge steadied me and let me view the catastrophe somewhat dispassion-ately. Then I felt Michelle's shield drop as the horrible sight over-whelmed her. Realizing she was vulnerable to the boss's psychics, I reached into her mind and blocked the effects of the hologram.

"Th-thanks, babe," she stuttered.

"Close your eyes, hon. That should help you clear your mind," I said. "And then get your shield up again. I can feel the boss's people preparing something."

"I'm working on it."

I felt one of the empaths broadcast fear at Michelle. Her shield would have stopped the attack, if it was up. Since it wasn't, I inter-cepted the little blast. I gathered it in with the horror Michelle felt at the hologram and threw it back at the empath with every-thing I had. Behind the boss, a woman close to my own age suddenly screamed and pitched backward. The woman's compan-ions turned their attention on me and threw all of their psychic might against me.

I caught the empathic attacks, letting the telepathic whispers pass. As I hoped, the incompatibility between telepaths and empaths, between pure thought and pure emotion, meant those attacks mostly slid off me. I caught a few fragments in passing—words of doubt meant to sap my will to fight—but ignored them.

Even as I prepared a return attack, I sensed a dozen more psychics hurrying our way. Despite my huge advantage in raw power and Zav's formal training, I had no idea if I could handle attacks from so many sources at once. Too much was at risk to stay here and psychically slug it out with the boss's team.

"Michelle, can you concentrate enough to shoot any of them?"

"Probably not, babe. It's taking all of my concentration to hold my shield up. I doubt I can aim worth a damn right now."

"Then I'm going to suck up every negative emotion near us and blast every one of the boss's psychics."

"This close to Psi Corps headquarters? Won't that alert them?"

"Probably, so finding that other way out of here is going to be really important, in a minute."

I cast my mind wide. In a memorial to a catastrophe, I had no trouble finding an abundance of negative emotions. Sorrow, muted horror, fear—they were all around me in abundance and I drew them all into my mind. And, back in the Psi Corps offices, I picked up a new emotion—alarm that such a powerful psychic was operating in their backyard. What the hell; I grabbed the alarm and added it to my arsenal of emotional hell.

Stepping in front of Michelle and Shafira—who was rooted in place—I blasted everything in my mind at the boss and his gang of psychics. I felt all of the psychics reel under my assault, though the empaths got the worst of it by far. Even the boss stumbled back a few steps—the smug expression wiped from his face—and then fell on his ass.

And just like that, the battle was over. All around us, holograms ran and screamed in grotesque silence while the boss and his gang groaned and held their heads. My head drooped from the exertion of containing my blast to just the boss and his gang of psychics. I desperately wanted to sit down and rest for a while. But I could already sense Psi Corps mobilizing to find me and, at all costs, capture me.

"Time to get out of here, babe," Michelle said, handing me my brand new blaster. "Don't worry, it's set to stun."

"Any idea which way we should go?" I asked.

She pointed to our left. "How about that way?"

"No," a familiar voice called. "Follow me."

And then Raneem appeared out of the hologram crowd, grabbed Michelle's hand, and dragged us in the opposite direction.

THE SNARE

"Raneem, what are you doing here?" Michelle asked as we pelted after the girl.

"I'll tell you, when we're safe," Raneem said over her shoulder. "It's not far."

I stumbled as the fatigue from exercising such exacting control over my last psychic blast caught up with me. Michelle grabbed my arm and steadied me.

"Are you okay, babe?"

I nodded. "Just tired."

She jerked her head toward the little girl leading us out of the square. In a low voice, she asked, "Too tired to check?"

"Already did." I kept my voice low, as well. "There's nothing in Raneem's mind but an earnest desire to help us."

Michelle's deeply concerned expression eased a bit, but the easing stopped at seriously concerned. Trapped inside Psi Corps' own little park and with Psi Corps headquarters alerted to our presence, who could blame her? And I had to add to her worries.

"If I get captured, promise me you'll take Raneem and escape."

"Not a chance, Matt," Michelle snapped.

"You *have* to," I said as we ran into an alley, finally leaving the wide-open square behind us. "If Psi Corps holds you, they hold absolute power over me. You know I'll do anything they want if they threaten you."

"I'm not leaving you, babe, so just drop it."

We exited the alley and followed Raneem to the left. She stopped and tried a door, flashing a fierce grin when it opened. "Come on, there's a tunnel under this building."

We slowed to a walk, making it easier for me to talk with Michelle. "What if Psi Corps tortures you? I won't just see it, I'll feel it through my connection to you. It won't matter how tough you act or how hard you fight against screaming, I'll know how bad it is for you. Jonas taught both of us that everyone breaks eventually. I'm pretty damned sure empaths break faster than most people—and the most powerful empath in four hundred years will break fastest."

"Matt, I-" My wife's voice faltered.

"Michelle, if you love me too much to leave me, then show me you love me enough to kill me."

Raneem opened an unmarked door. "Be careful on the stairs. This building is real old and the lights don't work."

We followed the girl down the stairs. I shut the door behind us, cutting off the trickle of light from the outside. We groped for a few seconds before I heard Michelle fumbling with something. A weak light appeared in her hand as she turned her pocket pad on. It wasn't much light, but it was a vast improvement over absolute darkness.

At the bottom of the stairs, Raneem paused, looking up and down the walls around us. "Let's see, it should be here somewhere."

"What should be here, honey?" Michelle asked.

"A yellow and black symbol painted on the wall. He said it would be hard to see."

Michelle and I exchanged alarmed glances. I asked, "Who said?"

"The guy who commed me in that container you left me in," Raneem replied, never taking her eyes from the wall. "Jonas."

"My *father* commed you in the container?" Michelle asked, her voice incredulous. "Raneem, he was on a planet outside of the Federation a week ago."

"So were you," the girl said. "He said that answer ought to satisfy you."

"But we were supposed to come to Earth alone," Michelle objected.

Knowing how my father-in-law thought, I said, "We did come alone."

Raneem suddenly pointed at a mark high up on the wall. I recognized it from my Earth history classes. It was a radiation symbol with an arrow pointing down the hallway to the left.

Michelle remembered her history lessons, too. "It's showing the way to a fallout shelter."

"Yeah, that's what Jonas called it," Raneem said. "And he said the precognitive told him it was okay to come to Earth."

"*The* precognitive?" I asked as suspicion blossomed in my mind.

The girl nodded. "Cassandra."

Michelle's eyes widened. "No one calls her Cassandra."

My eyes met Michelle's and we both said, "It's a trap."

I felt fear rise up in Raneem. "No, no. He's your father. He has to be."

"Well, he's not." Michelle switched on the infrared sight on her blaster and I followed suit.

Tears welled up in Raneem's eyes and her lip trembled. Swinging my gun in an arch overhead, I said, "It's not your fault, Raneem. You didn't know."

"Crap," Michelle muttered as her infrared sight picked up heat signatures from the floor above us. "How did Psi Corps know about the container, much less Raneem?"

"They've got precogs of their own, hon," I said, watching red splotches appear on my own sight.

"How very perceptive of you, Mr. Connaught," an amplified voice boomed from above. "We do, indeed, have precognitives of our own.".

"Th-that's the voice I heard over the comm in the container!" Raneem said.

"Quite right, young lady," the man said, his tone quite jovial. "You have been an enormous help to us. I might even let you go free—provided Mrs. Connaught has the good sense to surrender along with her husband."

"No," Michelle shouted. "Hell no."

"I have over a dozen psychic nulls blocking the only way out of the building. My equipment lets me hear everything you say and see everywhere you go. My psychics know your every thought and emotion. Psi Corps spent the last two months preparing for this operation. We set a snare, baited it for your precognitive, and then waited until you ran into it." The man's tone shifted from triumphant to demanding. "There is no escape, Mr. Connaught. There are no options available to you. You can watch your wife and your little friend die or you can end this without bloodshed. Make the smart decision. Surrender to Psi Corps."

Despair welled up inside me as the man from Psi Corps proclaimed victory. I had no snappy comeback. Hell, I had no comeback at all. Trapped, with our only escape route blocked by Psi Corps, what choice did we have besides surrender? I grasped at the only one available to me.

"What if I just shoot myself, rather than surrender to you?" I called.

"You never struck me as the self-destructive type, Mr. Connaught," the man replied, "but, should you make that choice, I'm afraid that Psi Corps will simply tell the galaxy they cornered a dangerous rogue psychic who was killed in the subsequent battle. Tragically, the rogue psychic's wife, and an innocent child they took hostage, also died in the struggle."

My blood ran cold at the man's matter-of-fact tone. "You would kill an innocent woman and child out of spite, because you couldn't get me?"

"If Psi Corps can't use them as pawns to ensure your good behavior, they are of no use to us."

And that was the end. I couldn't let Psi Corps kill Michelle and Raneem, not when I could save them by surrendering. My head dropped and my shoulders drooped. I sighed deeply and tried to find the right words to explain this to Michelle.

Then Michelle placed Raneem's hand in mine and took my other hand, herself. "I've figured out which of those bastards is the one doing all of the talking."

Irritation overwhelmed despair for just a moment. "So? What can I do about it?"

Anger flashed in Michelle's eyes. "You can stop feeling sorry for yourself. You can stop feeling guilty for us. You can stop planning your noble surrender to save us. You can draw emotions from Raneem, from me, from the psychics above us, and from the panicked crowds in and around the memorial park. And you can find out if I'm right about psychic nulls."

"Does that mean Matt is going to kick that son of a bitch's ass?" Raneem asked.

"Damned right it does, honey," Michelle said.

I looked at Raneem. Hope and excitement shown in her eyes. But those emotions were nothing compared to the absolute confidence she radiated—confidence in me.

I looked at Michelle. Her eyes blazed with an intensity I'd never seen in her, before. Anger, fear, and hope shone from her, but they were all drowned out by her love for me.

"We *never* give up, babe—and that means *you* never give up, either." Michelle squeezed my hand. "I want to meet my children, Matt, and I'm going to need you to make that happen. Now, do like Raneem said and kick that son of a bitch's ass."

As if on cue, the man said, "My patience is wearing thin, Mr. Connaught. Your chances of avoiding bloodshed run out when my patience vanishes."

"Which one is he?" I asked.

Michelle held her blaster in front of me. "The guy the sight is centered on."

I closed my eyes and stretched out with my feelings. Bright

minds flashed all around me, blinding me to the subtle feel of a shielded mind. With an assurance I wouldn't have believed a year ago, I filtered out those bright minds. Almost like a man moving in utter darkness, I extended my empathic power and felt for anything blocking me.

Slowly, an image formed as my mind flowed through the floor above us. The differences were subtle, but my mind flowed around certain points—almost like a stream flowing around rocks. Once I knew what to look for, I found the talking man's mind in a few seconds. And that is what gave me hope that Michelle was right. If psychic nulls truly were blank to psychics, I could never have found the man or any of his companions. But I *did* find them—all of them.

Gently, I drew power from Raneem and Michelle. I did the same from the panicked people in the park. Their panic eased and then vanished as I summoned all of their fear and terror, packing it into my mind. Last, I ripped every shred of emotion I could from the psychics above us. I heard the empaths cry out in pain. I heard the telepaths—usually immune to empathic abilities—gasp as they felt me take what emotion I could from them.

"What's going on?" the man asked, concern evident in his voice.

That's when I attacked. I threw everything I had at the man's mind. I struck from all directions. I struck with every emotion available to me. Terror pounded his forehead. Shame bashed his temples. Hatred hit him behind the ears. Greed clobbered the top of his head. Lust smashed the back of his head. Concern, doubt, guilt, grief, horror, worry, fear, dislike, distaste, disgust—they all battered the man. Like an eggshell crushed between two hands, the man's defenses shattered.

Disbelief coursed through the man's mind for a split second. I grabbed that emotion and turned it against him, too. Though he had worked with psychics his entire life, the man had never felt our power. He had never even worried about our power. The man was as unprepared for my onslaught as a person could be. He quivered in terror. Withered in shame. Burned in hatred. Writhed in guilt. Our brains are designed to deal with one or two strongly felt emotions at a time. I hit the man with dozens, forcing his mind into contortions it simply couldn't handle.

His mind protected itself in the only way it could—it shut down.

One second, the man was screaming and crying and beating his fists against his head, the next he fell silent and folded into a heap on the ground.

Watching it all on the infrared sight on her blaster, Michelle breathed, "Damn, babe."

Raneem leaned over and looked at the blotchy image. "Is he dead?"

I leaned against Michelle as fatigue washed over me. "No, Raneem, he's not dead."

"Will he recover?" Michelle asked.

"I don't know." Ignoring my fatigue as best I could, I called, "Does anyone else want to threaten my wife and Raneem?"

Silence stretched for almost thirty seconds before we heard a woman's quavering voice. "What did you do to Mr. Toma?"

"I used him to prove psychic nulls are just normal people with a natural mental shield. I broke his shield and hit him with every emotion I could find."

"What are you?" the woman whispered, her voice laced with fear.

"I'm just a man. A man with a wife and plans for a family. I'm a man who has *never* used his powers for anything other than defense. I'm a man who is sick and damned tired of Psi Corps' attacks and lies." Righteous rage overcame my fatigue and I found myself shouting, "I'm simply a man who wants to be left alone— but you bastards at Psi Corps won't do that. Now I'm a man who is out to bring this whole damned organization crashing down around you!"

Michelle brushed a hand down my cheek, concern reflected in her eyes. I stopped speaking, took a deep breath, and squashed the anger boiling in me. "I simply want to be left to live in peace with my family. Back off, let us leave, and I'll return to my home outside of Federation Space."

"I- I can't do that. I don't have the authority." In a terrified whisper, she added, "Please don't kill me."

"Toma isn't dead. And since you haven't threatened my wife and Raneem, I see no point in attacking you." I didn't have the energy for another attack, but she didn't need to know that. "Who am I speaking with?"

"C-Coleman. Kathleen Coleman."

"I won't claim I'm pleased to meet you, Kathleen, but at least you had the courage to speak to me. As a reward, you're the only person I'm going to speak to."

"Lucky me." Her voice held fear, but she sounded determined to hide it.

"Since you don't have the authority to deal with me, I'm willing to wait while you go get someone who has the authority."

"I can't do that—I'm just a low-level handler. The only reason I'm here is because Mr. Toma used my telepath squad. Nobody important is going to speak to me."

"If they won't talk to you, I'm just going to randomly attack psychic nulls until they do. You've got two hours."

"But-" Kathleen began.

I hardened my voice. "Two hours, Coleman, and the clock is running."

Then I sat down against the wall and fell asleep.

I slept. I dreamt. I wandered through a land of walls. Towering walls. Squat walls. Flat walls. Round walls. They surrounded me. They hemmed me in. They kept me from Michelle, from my parents, from Cassie and Rob, from Raneem. I heard my family and friends shouting, their voices echoing off the walls and losing all sense of direction. They needed me but the walls blocked me. And the walls mocked me, their hysterical laughter further confusing me. In frustration, I banged my fists on the walls and the walls laughed all the more.

"Foolish boy," they laughed, "you cannot hurt us!"

I stopped banging on the walls and started punching them. My fists hammered away, pounding the walls with ever-increasing strength and speed. And still the walls laughed and taunted.

The cries of friends and family grew more frantic. The walls cackled in maniacal mirth. I screamed in frustration, pounding faster and harder. And then my fists changed.

No longer were they flesh. No longer did blood course through them. When next my fist struck, I heard the sound of metal on stone. My hands were gone, replaced by mallets of the hardest metals known to man. When they struck, walls screamed. Where they struck, walls shattered. Wall after wall fell before my onslaught. But before the dust settled from one wall, another took its place.

Walls screamed and fell. I screamed and flailed. I forgot my family and friends. I thought of nothing but destroying the next wall. And the one after that. Wall after wall broken by the force of my blows, the force of my will. It was my destiny and it was glorious!

And so I crushed the lovely golden wall that reached out for me. It's dying scream pierced my mind like a lance. My fists stopped. My hands returned. I wrapped them around Michelle, broken and battered, as she died. With her final breath, I heard her whisper, "I love you, Matt."

I willed my fists back into hammers so I could break myself as I broke my wife. My hands remained flesh. Feeling the trickle of warm blood over that flesh, I screamed.

Something shook me. "Matt? Babe? Wake up!"

My eyes flew open. A pair of bright blue eyes gazed into mine. Framed by soft, golden hair, the eyes were filled with concern.

"Are you okay?" A tentative smile spread across my wife's face. "You looked like you were having one hell of a nightmare."

"I was." Wrapping my arms around Michelle, I pulled her close. "It was horrible."

"It's over now, Matt. And it was just a dream."

"I don't think so. I think it was my subconscious sending me a warning."

Michelle sat back, biting her lip and just looking at me. After a few seconds, she said, "A warning about your ability and breaking that Toma guy's mental shield?"

I nodded. "I don't think I should do that again. Maybe if there's no other choice. Maybe."

"You're afraid you'll start enjoying it." It wasn't a question.

"Exactly. I'm afraid I'll turn into the monster Psi Corps is afraid I already am."

Michelle offered a tentative smile. "Then it's a good thing I was never going to ask you to do that again."

"You weren't?"

She shook her head. "I only asked you the first time because I wanted Psi Corps to back off for a while. Everyone is outside of my blaster's infrared range, so we're likely outside of their infrared range, too."

That didn't strike me as a particularly safe bet. "What makes you so sure of that? What if their IR scanners are closer to the cutting edge than ours?"

Michelle gave a disbelieving look. "Yeah. Right."

"What makes you so sure our new blasters' IR sights are a match for Psi Corps equipment?"

"Daddy picked out our new guns, personally." Michelle stated flatly, as if it settled the matter.

And it did. When it came to protecting Michelle and me, Jonas never settled for anything less than the absolute best. If he chose these guns, they were from the bloodiest part of the bleeding edge.

"I concede your point, hon."

I looked around, realizing Raneem was missing. Alarm must have been written all over my face because Michelle cupped my chin in her hand and turned my head toward her. "Relax, she's just gone to the bathroom."

As if on queue, the girl came out through a nearby door. "Is he okay? He scared me when he started screaming." At Michelle's nod, a smile replaced Raneem's look of concern. "Have you told him your plan?"

"We have a plan?" I asked.

"Now that I've had a chance to explore a bit, without Psi Corps looking over my shoulder, we do," Michelle said. "We're going to make a daring escape by blowing a hole in the wall between this building and the one next to it."

"Uh, how is that going to help us? Won't Psi Corps shift and cover that building too quickly for us to get out of it? Even if they don't, we'll still be trapped in the memorial park."

My wife grinned. "Yes and yes—except we aren't really going to leave this building."

"Is this some new form of escaping that doesn't involve actually, you know, escaping?"

"You could say that, babe. Do you still remember how to broadcast disinterest, like you did back on Piscain Station?"

"You, of all people, know I can't hide you and Raneem that way. Besides, they have infrared scanners. I can't make the scanner techs ignore the big red blob that will represent us."

"You won't need to, Matt," Michelle said. "You only have to keep people from spending any time searching the radiation shelter below us."

I shook my head in confusion. "I'm completely lost. Maybe I should just shut up and let you explain the whole plan."

"It's pretty simple—if you know all of the stuff Daddy packed into the extremely expensive backpack besides our new blasters."

"You mean like explosives?" I asked. Michelle cocked one eyebrow at me. "Sorry. Shutting up and listening."

"Don't tell me you're surprised Daddy packed explosives?" Before I could respond, Michelle held up a hand. "Don't answer that or we'll get bogged down again. He included some concealable blasters, vibroblades, stuff like that. *And* he packed a big piece of thermal dampening material. All we have to do is set the explosives, retreat to the shelter below us, and cover ourselves with the thermal dampener. As soon as Psi Corps comes back, I blow a hole into the next building and Psi Corps assumes we're making a run for it."

"But they'll search this building, too, which is where I come in."

"Exactly. As long as the search team stays away from the shelter, we're fine. But if anyone comes our way, you make them lose interest and leave."

"What about Psi Corps' own psychics? Won't they pick up my broadcast?"

"I hope they'll be part of the pursuit team. If not, I really hope they'll be just as susceptible to disinterest as us normal folk are."

"Won't it help if someone really is running away?" Raneem asked. "I could—"

"No!" Michelle and I exclaimed simultaneously.

"But-"

"We said no, Raneem, and we mean it." Michelle spoke in a firm tone, brooking no argument. "You'll be safer with us. Is that clear, young lady?"

"Yes, ma'am," the girl mumbled.

I leaned over and kissed Michelle. "You are going to be one fantastic mom."

"Thank you, dear," she said. "But first, I'm going to be one kick-ass explosives expert."

Forty minutes later, a section of the basement wall was rigged with explosives and the three of us were huddled under the thermal dampening material. It was a tight fit under there, with Raneem tucked in between Michelle and me. Finally, an hour and fifty-three minutes after I gave Kathleen Coleman her deadline, we picked up movement on the IR sights of our blasters.

Michelle grinned. "Showtime!"

She tapped a button on her pocket pad and an explosion rocked the building.

SLIPPING THE SNARE

The explosion still echoed through the halls of our building when the red splotches on Michelle's infrared sight scattered. Apparently satisfied with what she saw, my wife pulled her hand holding the blaster under the thermal dampener and turned the weapon off.

"That ought to keep them busy for a while," she whispered.

"I didn't want to distract you from the delicate task of placing and arming explosives," I said, my voice equally low, "but is there more to your plan than blowing stuff up and slipping away during the resulting chaos?"

"Yes, though not a lot more." Michelle turned her head, pointing her right ear toward the shelter's door. "It's muffled, but there's a lot of shouting going on outside the building. I think the plan is working."

"Great. While we wait for everyone to clear out, would you care to share the rest of your plan with us, hon?"

"Sure. Once the way is clear, we're going to slip out of this building and go hide in another one—one closer to the main entrance would be best. We're going to have to spend the night in here, but tomorrow we can just mingle with the normal park crowd and quietly leave through the main entrance."

"Is the park even going to be open tomorrow?" I asked. "Won't Psi Corps lock the place down after a battle between rogue psychics?"

Before Michelle could reply, we heard doors bang open and shouts erupt from inside the building. Feet pounded down the stairs and into the basement above the shelter. More doors banged open and slammed shut. And the voices were close enough for us to understand them.

"The heat signature from the explosion came from the far end of this hallway," a man said.

Footsteps hurried down the hall, then the same voice spoke again. "It looks like the precognitives missed this possibility."

"Or they chose not to tell us about it," a woman said.

"Have you ever been assigned to precog duty?" the man asked. The woman must have shaken her head, because the man continued, "The department has spent centuries learning how to condition psychics, but it's especially easy with precogs. Offer just the right threats, in just the right way, and the precog's dreams do the rest."

"The precogs never call the bluff?" the woman asked.

"Every now and then. The last time was five years ago. A teenage boy started giving false information and we lost a whole family of rogue psychics. That night, the news reported the boy's little sister was killed in a hit-and-run accident." the man replied. His voice shook a bit when he added, "Psi Corps doesn't bluff."

"Damn, that's rough," the woman said. "Still, I guess it's one life against millions."

"That's what I tell myself, every night," the man said. "Go tell the director what we found. There aren't any heat signatures in the building besides us. I'm sending the rest of the team through this hole. Maybe we'll get lucky and catch them between two search groups."

"Right. Are you going with the team?"

"Not yet. I'm going to poke around down here, a bit. Maybe I'll find some clue to tell us where they've gone."

Michelle vented a quiet, inarticulate sound of frustration. "No, dammit, go with the search team, like a good little Psi Corps worker."

After that whispered outburst, we remained silent and listened to the man moving around on the floor above us. Doors opened and his footsteps wandered into and out of rooms. The man whistled softly—and atonally—to himself, as he searched. Every now and then, he stood still for a few seconds. Maybe he thought he found a clue or something because I had no other theory for his random pauses.

After what felt like an eternity but was probably only five minutes, the man stopped whistling. His ambling stride turned purposeful—and came straight to the door at the top of the stairs down to the radiation shelter. I felt Michelle change position and then her infrared sight came on. The red blob representing the man came right to the door and gently pulled it open.

I carefully probed the man with my power, and it confirmed my worst fear. He was a psychic null—not surprising, in someone who works directly with psychics—so broadcasting disinterest at him wouldn't work. I gently tapped Michelle's arm twice, our prearranged signal for a null. Her blaster shifted as she double-checked the gun's setting.

"I'm coming downstairs now. Mr. Connaught, please do not break my shield as you did to Toma," the man called in a soft voice. A stair creaked as the man put weight on it. "I'd also appreciate it if Mrs. Connaught didn't shoot me on sight."

In a barely audible voice, Michelle said, "What the hell?"

I shrugged and realized Michelle couldn't see that in the darkness. Keeping my voice as low as hers, I said, "He said he worked with precogs."

"I haven't told anyone you're hiding down here," the man said. "To be exact, you're under a thermal dampener in the right corner opposite the stairs."

That was exactly where we were. Throwing caution to the winds, I said, "You know an awful lot for a psychic null."

"Ah, she was right," the man said to himself. His next words were directed at us. "My name is Harry Foster. Is it safe for me to come down there, so we can talk face-to-face?"

"Sure," Michelle said, "but I'm going to keep my blaster trained on you. Don't worry, it's set to stun. Also, who was right?"

"My daughter," Foster said, picking up his pace down the stairs. "Not by blood, but most definitely by choice. My wife and I want to adopt her and my daughter by birth wants her as a sister, but that's not the sort of thing Psi Corps will approve of."

A man a few years younger than my parents entered the room, bringing a handheld light with him. He carefully shielded its glare with his hand. "Tell me when your eyes adjust and I'll move my hand."

Michelle slithered out from under the cloth, keeping her blaster trained on Foster at all times. "Put the light down and place your hands against the wall. I want you so far off balance that the bricks are the only thing keeping you from falling."

Foster did as Michelle ordered and she patted him down quickly and expertly. "No hidden weapons. Stand up and carefully unbuckle your stun gun holster. Drop it on the floor and then kick it to me."

Once again, Foster followed my wife's instructions to the letter. When Michelle was satisfied, she said, "I've done my part. I leave the rest in your capable hands, babe."

"Thanks, ever so much, hon." Despite the situation, my dry tone sparked a bright grin from Michelle.

"Would it make things easier, if I told you my story?" Foster asked. "The short version, anyway."

It was a place to start, so I said, "Sure."

"Evie—she's my precog—came to Psi Corps from an orphanage when she was six. My own daughter was about the same age, and the director thought that would help Evie connect with me. He even encouraged me to bring my own daughter to work and let the girls play together. The girls hit it off, and it wasn't long before we thought of Evie as more of a family member than one of Psi Corps' slaves." I raised my eyebrows when Foster used that word. He barked a laugh at my expression. "Any Psi Corps employee who doesn't think the psychics are government slaves is either lying to himself, or deluded.

"Did you hear the story I told about how Psi Corps keeps psychics in line?" At our nods, he continued, "When I saw what happened to that boy's little sister, I realized why the director picked me, and why he let my family grow so close to Evie."

"Your daughter is the first person the director will threaten, if Evie ever misbehaves," Michelle said. She shook her head in disgust. "Every time I think Psi Corps has sunk as low as it's possible to go, they find new ways to disappoint me."

"What are the chances someone in Psi Corps will figure out that Evie has been lying to them?" I asked.

"About even," Foster shrugged.

"You're taking a really big risk, just talking to me," I said. "Why do it?"

"My daughters are sixteen, now, Mr. Connaught. I want them to finish growing up without the fear of Psi Corps hanging over their heads."

Something told me he was telling the truth, but I didn't know if I could trust that something. After all, I wanted to believe him in the worst way. I looked at Michelle. "I don't know. What do you think?"

"He *sounds* convincing, but-"

"He's telling the truth," Raneem said.

"How can you tell, honey?" Michelle asked.

"If you live like I do, you've got to be able to figure out—fast— who you can trust and who you can't." Raneem walked right up to Foster. He met her gaze and smiled. She smiled back and said, "I think we can trust him."

"That's what I feel, too, but I didn't know if I could trust that feeling," I said. "I assume you've got a way to get us out of here?"

"I do, but you've got to promise me one thing."

"Name it."

"You've got to find a way to break Evie out of here and take all of us with you back to Ark's Landing."

"Just to make sure we understand exactly what you want, when you say 'break Evie out of here' you mean Psi Corps' main office." Michelle waved her hand in the general direction of the main entrance to the memorial park. "The one just down the street?"

"Yes," Foster replied.

"The most heavily guarded Psi Corps office in the Federation," Michelle continued.

"Yes."

"The place with more psychic nulls per square meter than any other place in the galaxy?"

"Yes," Foster growled, irritation showing in his eyes. "The place with more psychics than anywhere. On the most heavily protected human-settled world. And probably dozens of other reasons you can come up with to just shoot me and try slipping out of here on your own."

"We won't shoot you, Mr. Foster, and we won't simply leave you and your family behind," I said. "Michelle just wants you to recognize and understand how difficult this might be."

"I know it won't be easy—I've spent years trying to figure out how to do it and Evie is still a Psi Corps slave." Foster gave me an imploring look. "I'm risking the lives of everyone I love and hold dear, just by talking to you."

Michelle took my hand. "And we're risking our lives and our futures just by listening to you. But we *are* listening."

Foster nodded, his expression softening. "How are we going to do this?"

I squeezed Michelle's hand. "This is your area, hon."

"We don't have time to plan anything, right now. Mr. Foster has to rejoin his team." Michelle bit her lip and I sensed her mind spinning fast. "I don't have nearly enough information to make any plans. Can you remember a message drop address and password?"

Foster nodded. "Shoot."

"Box address E-R-B-r-a-c-k-e-t-t, password s-t-a-r-k-w-o-o-l-a,"

Michelle recited. "It's all from a couple of ancient Terran authors my father discovered in a college lit class."

"If you say so," Foster muttered before repeating the address and the password. "Are you sure the address is still active?"

"I checked it, myself, after we landed. Check it, tonight, for the first set of questions from me," Michelle said. "Now, how are you going to get us out of here?"

Foster's plan was remarkably similar to Michelle's, except we'd stay in this building overnight. There was one wrinkle we didn't know about. "Everyone entering the park tomorrow will be given a pass with their name and a retina scan printed on it. The guards collect the passes, and do a retina scan comparison, when guests leave."

Michelle nodded. "Simple and effective. If we're still stuck in here, we won't have passes or, if we steal some, the scans won't match. The guards will know exactly who to grab."

Foster pulled out a small retinal scanner. "Exactly. Except I'm going to get passes for the three of you. I can't risk coming back in here, so tell me where you want me to hide them."

Foster and Michelle fell into a discussion about the surrounding area while Foster got our scans and the names associated with them. When the two of them were satisfied, Foster collected our retina prints, shook hands with us, and slipped away.

We settled in to wait and Michelle pulled out the snacks and water she brought with us. It didn't make for a gourmet meal, but the snacks did settle the growling in our stomachs. Shortly after that, Raneem curled up and fell asleep.

"You should get some sleep, too, babe," Michelle said to me. "You wore yourself out with those two psychic blasts earlier today."

I didn't argue with her about it. She's remarkably stubborn most of the time, and more so when she's right. At her urging, I laid my head in her lap, wrapped my arms around her waist, and was fast asleep in minutes.

I awoke feeling stiff but otherwise well-rested. Michelle

absently stroked my head as she kept watch. Unable to resist, I blew a quiet raspberry against her stomach. Michelle's shirt kept me from matching the night she rescued me from the gang outside the maglev station, but she gave a startled 'eep' and swatted my head playfully.

I laughed silently and Michelle, her tone one of mock disapproval, asked, "Have you got that out of your system for good, Matt?"

"Maybe. I guess you'll just have to wait and see."

"Great. Can I assume you're going to teach our daughters to do this sort of thing to their poor, suffering mother?"

"Don't forget our son—though it's more likely he'll learn it from his big sisters."

Michelle heaved a dramatic sigh. "I'm not even pregnant, yet, and you're already corrupting our children."

"Isn't that a father's job? Well, along with embarrassing the children, once they hit puberty?" An idea occurred to me. "Hey, wouldn't it be cool if we were *both* cleaning blasters the first time we meet a boy interested in dating Nancy? Or, are we naming our first daughter Nora? Did we ever decide?"

"Our first daughter will be Nora," Michelle said. "We got married because of her, after all."

"We got married a year ago because of her, you mean," I said. "I'd have proposed after we rescued my parents."

"But finding them would have been harder without the private apartment we had after our wedding. You'd have been hard-pressed finding a place to set up your pad and leave it running."

"You make an excellent case, wife. Our first daughter will be Nora. Besides, Lilla already named her daughter after Nancy." I stopped and thought for a moment. "What were we talking about before we got off on this tangent?"

"Your plan to terrorize the first boy to take an interest in Nora," Michelle said. "Something we most certainly are *not* doing."

"Can I at least speculate about it until Nora complains to you?"

"We'll see," Michelle laughed. "Now let's switch places, otherwise my eyes will be too tired to open for the retinal scanner when we leave."

As Michelle and Raneem slept. I kept watch with my blaster's IR sight and a subtle empathic scan of the area. By a stroke of good fortune, or because of Foster's misdirection, no one came near the building the rest of the night.

As the sun cleared the tops of the buildings and the workday began, the three of us made a breakfast of the remaining snacks and water. We cleaned up and straightened our clothing as best we could. Then we waited patiently for lunchtime. When it neared, we took one last IR scan around the building and slipped out into the bright and hot late morning. The three passes were right where Michelle and Foster agreed he'd hide them.

We wandered into the square with the horrific hologram while it was running. Once in and among that chaos, it was easy enough for us to trail along after other families hurrying away from the overwhelming images and join those queuing up to leave the park. We finally reached the front of the line and presented our passes.

As the guards verified my retinal scan, Michelle asked, "Can we use the same passes when we come back after lunch?"

"I'm afraid not," the bored guard intoned. "We have to issue new ones each time you enter the park."

Groans sounded from those behind us in the line and one woman complained, "It took forever to get in this morning."

Michelle turned a weary look on the woman. "Yeah, I know what you mean. I guess we'll find something else to do this afternoon."

The guards scanned Raneem and Michelle and compared their prints to their passes. After a few seconds, that seemed like years, they waved us on. We were out of the park and free of Psi Corps —for now.

GOING UNDERGROUND

We caught the first available taxi and headed toward the tourist center of the city. No one said much, both because of possible recordings and because we were simply too tired to do anything beyond collapse in the seat. When we climbed out of the taxi twenty minutes later, Michelle consulted her portable pad and led us off with a purposeful, if slower than normal, stride.

"I hope you're taking us someplace where we can get real food, hon." This was my subtle way of asking where we were going. It also told her I was hungry, just in case she hadn't figured that out yet.

"Not yet," she said. "We need to change our look, from clothes to makeup. You can bet our...friends...have vid recordings from the park and will have our images out on the net soon."

"They're hushing up our confrontation with the boss and his people, so how do you think they're going to explain their interest in us?"

Michelle put an arm around Raneem's shoulders. "In their place, I'd claim we kidnapped Raneem. No one in their right mind will ever think you and I are her parents. Your hair is almost as dark as hers, but my blue eyes and your gray ones don't combine to make brown any more than our pale complexions could combine into Raneem's darker one."

"Does that mean you'll be safe if I go away?" Raneem asked, her voice small.

Michelle pulled the girl close. "Of course not, honey. It just means Matt and I have to make sure we blend in better. We'll dye my hair and use makeup to darken our skin. I've got some lenses in the backpack to change our eye color and retinal prints, too."

"I'm afraid you're stuck with us," I smiled down at Raneem. "And we're going to have to buy even more new clothes since we can't risk going back to the hotel for the stuff we fabricated last night."

Raneem turned a troubled look on me. "New clothes are expensive, Matt. Maybe-"

I glanced at Michelle. "I thought you told her our story while I was in the shower?"

"I kind of glossed over the money part," Michelle said. "It's nice and all, but it's not romantic in the least."

Raneem looked back and forth between the two of us at this exchange. "What are you talking about?"

I met the girl's gaze. "Have you ever heard of GenCo?"

"Of course." In case her dismissive tone wasn't enough, Raneem rolled her eyes for good measure.

"My family owns it."

Raneem's eyes went wide and then narrowed in suspicion. "You're making that up!"

"Not a bit," I said. "But the important thing is you need to stop thinking of yourself as a burden. You're not. You're a little girl we care about, very much, and will do everything in our power to help."

Raneem blinked rapidly for a few seconds, and then wrapped her arms around both of us. We didn't say anything else until Michelle found the shop she'd been looking for. Raneem and I waited on the street while my wife bought everything she needed.

Our next stop was a run-down, fully automated virt theater. In the theater's single comfort station, Michelle performed her magic on us. When we left, thirty minutes later, our skin tones closely matched Raneem's, as did our hair and eyes. We spent another half hour at a low-end clothing fabricator. Raneem and Michelle assured me the fashions were years out-of-date, which is why they were so cheap. I nodded sagely as if I had any idea what they were talking about. Once Michelle was satisfied with our appearance, we finally got some lunch.

One advantage to eating so late was that we missed the lunch rush. That far from the tourist centers, though, it was possible the place didn't have much of a lunch rush, anyway. Still, we had the diner to ourselves, making it much easier to discuss our plans. As usual, Michelle took the lead.

"We need a place away from the bright parts of the city, preferably with several exits. It's also got to be somewhere we won't raise any eyebrows. The clothes help some, but they're too new for us to vanish into the worst parts of the city."

"I'd rather avoid those areas anyway, hon." I pulled out my pad. "If there's another one of Dad's special containers on Earth, maybe we can have it moved to Cairo and use it as a base."

"Psi Corps already knows about one of the containers. We've got to assume they know about the rest," Michelle said. "We need to go somewhere Psi Corps won't ever think to look."

"Like where?" I asked. "If they've got precogs trained to dream about us, how do we know we won't find them camped out wherever we decide to go?"

"We've got to go somewhere. Besides, if their precogs were that well trained and that accurate, our friend wouldn't have dared approach us last night. And if they know our every move, why hasn't Psi Corps already picked us up?" Michelle shrugged. "I'll bet they got lucky with some of their precogs but mostly have no idea what we're going to do."

"Good point, hon. And even Cassie dreamed a whole range of possibilities for us."

"I know where you can hide," Raneem said around a mouthful of food.

"Don't talk with your mouth full," Michelle said. She immediately clapped a hand over her mouth, her eyes going wide. "Oh my God, why did my mother's voice come out of my mouth?"

Raneem giggled as I shook my head sadly. "I hear that happens to people as they get older—and you *are* older than me."

"By thirty-three days," Michelle growled.

"A yawning gulf between our ages. No doubt, it was during those thirty-three days that you learned those feminine wiles which led poor, innocent, *young* me astray and into your clutches."

"Says the guy who's been in love with me since the sixth grade."

"Indeed. A long-ago time when those same thirty-three days were an even greater barrier between us."

"You two are weird," Raneem said, her mouth now empty of food.

"So true, my young friend. It's why we work so well together," I said.

"Now, what was this about a place to go?" Michelle asked.

"I can take you to Shafira's place. She's real careful to keep us out of sight of the police—at least around her place. Her boss helps keep people away, too. None of the other kids will turn you in, either."

The last we'd seen of Shafira, she was standing still, watching the boss and his pet psychics reel under my empathic attack. I glanced at Michelle and said, "What if Psi Corps caught her? I can't see Shafira holding out for long under psychic interrogation."

Before Michelle could respond, Raneem said, "Uh-uh. Shafira's real good at getting away from trouble. Besides, if she is caught, we need to help the other kids. Some of them are my friends."

Michelle bit her lip, thinking through the problem. "You can always scan the place before we go in, babe. We won't be in any rush, so you can take your time and not blow a lot of energy doing it."

"Or," Raneem said, "I can just go inside and see what's going on. You can read me the whole way and take off running if Psi Corps grabs me."

"Not a chance, Raneem," Michelle said. "We stick together. Period."

"Michelle is right," I said to the girl. "But I think your idea is better than anything else we have."

"Me, too," my wife said. "As soon as we're done eating, we'll go visit Shafira."

Forty minutes later, we set off walking. The place wasn't very close, but we were leaving the areas taxies frequent and entering areas they avoided. After we'd been walking for an hour, Michelle took the precaution of pulling a couple of concealable blasters out of her amazing backpack. I know I felt better having one of those in my pocket, especially when we began attracting stares from the locals.

Michelle and I were waiting for someone to start something, and hoping we could end the confrontation fast enough to get away. Then Raneem took care of the problem.

"Hey, Abasi," she suddenly called to a man lounging against a building, "I'm getting tired of everyone eying the people I'm taking to see the boss. Get the word out so they don't do something stupid."

"I'm not your messenger, girl," the man snapped.

Raneem shrugged. "Something happens to these folks, I tell the boss it's your fault."

With a grunt, the man levered himself from the wall and stalked off ahead of us, muttering the whole way. I don't know what he said but, after that, people went out of their way to avoid us.

Finally, Raneem stopped at a corner. "Not far now. I can go ahead and-"

"We've been over this, Raneem," Michelle interrupted. "We all go or no one goes."

The girl looked at Michelle and then at me. Nodding, she led us around the corner and down a very narrow, unlighted street. After a few meters, she turned into an even narrower and darker alley. She stopped after the alley turned to the right. In the darkness, I barely saw her reach out to the wall on her right. A section of it popped out, leaving a pitch black opening framing her. Without a second thought, Raneem led us through the opening.

Following Raneem and Michelle into absolute darkness, I put my left hand out to brush against the wall. Since I had no idea what was around me or where we were going, touching the wall gave me more psychological benefit than anything else. Even recognizing that fact, I didn't bring my hand down.

"Matt, can you shut the door?" Raneem asked.

"Sure," I said, hoping I could find it in the Stygian darkness.

When I turned around, light seeped in from the alley and dimly illuminated the entrance. I caught the edge of the door and pushed it closed. Dim lights came on, illuminating a short corridor ending in a second door.

Raneem opened the far door and led us into a small storage room. Haphazard stacks of boxes and crates were scattered around the floor and stacked against the walls. The girl walked toward a stack of crates against the right wall. She grabbed the corner of one of the crates and pulled. It swung out, revealing a meter-high door leading to a narrow staircase heading down. Raneem ducked inside easily while Michelle and I bent double to get through the door. Relieved to find a full-height ceiling beyond the door, we unfolded and followed the little girl down the stairs.

"Is this the way into the boss's...lair? Hideout?" Michelle asked.

"We just call it home," Raneem replied, "but I like 'lair'. That sounds exciting, like something out of a vid. The boss doesn't live with us, but we can get to him from our area."

The stairs went down at least ten meters before ending in a door. Our guide opened the door and stepped through, calling out, "It's me. Got friends."

Following Raneem, Michelle and I found ourselves in a long, pipe-lined service tunnel. We looked around, expecting a guard or something, but didn't see a thing.

"Who were you talking to, honey?" Michelle asked. "Is there a hidden camera and comm or something?"

"Nobody down here is rich like you and Matt—not even the boss." Raneem waved her hand toward a jumble of pipes. "It's Anwar's turn on watch."

"Do you see anyone over there, hon?" I asked.

Michelle shook her head. "No. If this Anwar is in there, he's very good at hiding."

"Hey, Anwar, can you wave to my friends?" Raneem called.

"Hi, Raneem's friends," a shadow said before resolving into a waving boy. "Hey, girl, you be careful. Shafira be back and she be mad at you."

"Thanks for the warning, Anwar," Raneem said. "Is she waiting for me to come back?"

"Nah. She say you dead or caught by Psi Corps."

"She wishes! Thanks for the warning," the girl said.

We walked in silence, for a minute or two, then Raneem said, "Anwar is okay. Can we take him with us if we get out of this?"

"Yes, along with any other friends of yours who want to come with us," Michelle replied. "How much farther have we got to go?"

"Not much. We'll be there in five minutes."

Michelle looked over her shoulder at me. "Are you scanning yet, Matt?"

I nodded. "I was just about to kick my normal, low-level scan up a notch or two. If you want to stop for a minute, I can give the scan all of my attention."

"Yeah, do that, babe," Michelle said as she and Raneem stopped walking.

I closed my eyes to block out distractions and broadened my scan. I slowly added filters to block out most of the emotions that weren't coming from ahead of us. Within seconds, I picked up our old friend Shafira along with six others. Like Anwar said, Shafira was not in a good mood. I picked up a bunch of little emotional spikes as she used her minimal empathic power to punish the six others around her. Those six mentally cringed away from the woman, not that it helped them any.

"Dammit, Shafira is lashing out at six other kids with her power," I said as my temper flared.

My anger was nothing compared to Michelle's fury. Her eyes sparked dangerously as she said, "Get me to that woman fast, Raneem, so I can kick her ass again."

Raneem took off running, with Michelle and me pounding after her.

"I can block her power from here, you know," I said.

"And warn Shafira we're coming?" Michelle said. "No way."

"Okay, but I can't just let those kids suffer, Michelle. I'm going to redirect Shafira's attacks."

"Just don't tire yourself out too much, babe. We might need you at full power later."

Recognizing the truth in my wife's warning, I settled for siphoning off some of her power. About half of it still hit the kids, but I could tell it helped ease their fears a little bit.

A minute later, Raneem turned off the main tunnel and led us through a short, disorienting series of twists and turns that ended in a door.

"Shafira's on the other side of the door," I said.

"Open the door and then stand aside, Raneem," Michelle said.

The girl nodded. When she reached the door, she turned the very old-fashioned knob, pushed the door open, and then flattened against the wall. Michelle never broke stride. Charging through the door, she launched herself at an extremely surprised Shafira. My wife punched the other woman in the stomach and followed with an uppercut as Shafira bent over. When the other empath didn't collapse, Michelle gave her a spin kick to the head. Shafira dropped to the floor and Michelle immediately went to her knees straddling the other woman.

Shoving her concealable blaster under Shafira's chin, Michelle said, "Hi Shafira. Did you miss us?"

Shafira's eyes took a couple of seconds to properly focus on Michelle. Still dazed from her beat down, the woman's face screwed up in obvious confusion. "Who-?"

"Our disguises must be better than I thought if they confuse a genius like *you*, Shafira," Michelle said. She bent down close to the other woman's ear and, in a stage whisper, said, "Here's a hint—I'm Michelle."

Shafira's eyes widened and then quickly narrowed in obvious anger. "Get off me, you bitch!"

"She's throwing all her power at you, hon," I said. "I guess she didn't pay enough attention to the lessons we taught her, back in the hotel room."

"Tsk tsk," Michelle shook a finger at Shafira, "you're being very naughty, Shafira. You don't want us to turn our ghost loose, do you?"

"You don't have a ghost," the other woman said. "If you did, it would have taken me after everything that happened at the memorial yesterday."

"Maybe we kept a tight rein on the ghost because we thought you might still be useful to us," I said.

"I don't know how you made me see that ghost before—maybe you got some kind of power I don't—but I wouldn't be here anymore if you had a *real* ghost."

While the three of us held this discussion, Raneem gathered the other children together and talked quietly with them. With Shafira still directing her power against Michelle's shielded mind, the kids were recovering from the emotional lashing Shafira had given to them.

"Are those kids okay, Raneem?" I asked.

A bunch of heads nodded as Raneem said, "Yep. They like the way Michelle kicked the crap out of Shafira, too."

"*You!*" Shafira snarled. "I'll teach you a lesson, you little brat!"

Two days before, Raneem would have recoiled in fear at the

threat. Now, she just smiled at Shafira and said, "Give your best shot. I bet Matt stops it before I even feel it."

Shafira redirected her power from Michelle to Raneem. As I'd done in the hotel room, I blocked it all. Raneem's smile never wavered.

"I was about to give you credit for figuring out about the ghost, Shafira," I said, "but you totally blew it with this stupid attempt to use power while I'm around to stop you. Why don't you just give up so we can all get on with our lives?"

"I must concur," a voice said from the door. "Shafira, stop this foolish display so Mr. Connaught and I can get on with our business."

A man I recognized from the encounter at the Cairo Memorial stood in the doorway. He must have snuck up on us while I was concentrating on Shafira. Mentally kicking myself for letting my guard down like that, I immediately scanned him. All I got for my trouble was static.

"Telepath?" I asked.

"Yes."

"And the boss's right-hand man?" At the man's nod, I said, "You obviously know our names. What's yours?"

"You may call me Thoth."

Michelle gave a sharp laugh. "The Egyptian god of the mind. Cute."

"I thought so," Thoth said. "Now, if you would be so kind as to come with me, Amun awaits."

"Is that your name for the boss or is his ego really that big?" Michelle asked.

"The others simply call him 'boss', but I felt it appropriate to give my leader a name higher in the pantheon than my own."

Michelle got up off Shafira. "You can't get any higher than the top. You do realize I won't use either of those names for him?"

"What you call Amun is between you and him," Thoth said. "Shall we go?"

"Sure," I said. "But the kids stay here and Shafira comes with us."

"Agreed."

Without another word, Thoth turned and strode from the room. Glaring white-hot death at us, Shafira followed.

"Take care of the kids, Raneem," Michelle said. "If we're not back in two hours, get out of here and take all of the other children with you. Go to the Cairo office for GenCo and tell them to contact my father, Jonas Young. Give them the code word 'pumpkin'. Tell him everything that's happened."

At Raneem's nod, Michelle and I turned and followed Thoth out of the room.

Michelle and I hurried to catch up with Thoth, who hadn't waited for us, and Shafira, who was getting as far away from us as possible. She kept looking over her shoulder at us, her expression a mixture of fear and fury.

"I do believe someone doesn't want to spend any time with us," Michelle said. "Have I told you how much that hurts my feelings?"

"I can't begin to imagine, hon," I said. "I just don't know what she thinks she's gaining from this. It's not like she can ever truly get away from me."

"Either she doesn't understand your range—entirely possible when you consider she still hasn't figured out she can't get through my shield—or it's something else." Michelle's eyes went wide in mock horror. "Oh dear, could it be that she doesn't like me?"

I took Michelle's hand and patted it solicitously. "There, there, darling. Don't let mean, old Shafira upset you. I'm pretty sure she doesn't like anybody."

Michelle wiped her free hand across her brow. "Phew. That certainly is a relief."

"You know that I can hear you?" Shafira said, glaring at us over her shoulder.

"Well, isn't this just *so* embarrassing?" Michelle asked. "I've ruined any chance at making Shafira my bestest girlfriend."

I kissed Michelle's hand. "Don't worry, hon, I still love you."

"In that case, who cares what Shafira thinks?"

Shafira's glare intensified and her stride stiffened.

I shook my head and sighed, "She never learns."

"What's she doing this time?" Michelle asked.

"You're supposed to be quivering in fear right now. Shafira is, once again, using her power against you."

"That will be enough, Shafira," Thoth said without turning around. "While Amun did not select you for your intellectual prowess, he does expect you to learn from your experiences. By your own admission, you have never affected either of those two with your power. What made you think it would work now?"

"I thought maybe she wasn't paying attention," Shafira muttered. "Maybe she wouldn't have her shield up."

"The woman is walking toward a meeting with the leader of a band of rogue psychics," Thoth replied. "An intelligent person, which she most assuredly is, would not do that without taking every precaution available to them. Now, kindly rein in your meager ability and be silent until Amun gives you leave to speak."

After that, our journey continued in silence. It was a tense one, on Shafira's part. Michelle and I weren't exactly relaxed, either. I didn't have to use my power to read Michelle's emotions. She was nervous.

"Relax, hon, everything is going to work out fine," I whispered.

"Have you suddenly developed precognitive powers, babe?" Michelle shot back, her voice equally low.

"Obviously not, but–"

"Then you don't know everything is going to work out fine. Also, in a situation like this, a relaxed bodyguard is an idiot."

"I do wish you'd stop with the bodyguard bit. We've been married for over a year."

"I was your bodyguard for eight years, babe. Old habits die hard. Besides, *someone* has to take care of the real world while you're off playing in your psychic realm."

"I can take care of myself, Michelle," I said. "After all, your father trained me, too."

"Sure, but not as hard, and not for nearly as many years, as he trained me. So, if this meeting goes the wrong way-"

"I'll do what you tell me to do."

"You're such a smart boy. Are we getting close to this mysterious boss?"

"I think so. There are a lot of people scattered around down here in these tunnels and that throws things off a bit, but it feels like there's a concentration of people a couple of hundred meters ahead."

"Then I think it's past time we were properly armed." Michelle dug into the extraordinarily expensive backpack and pulled out our anniversary presents from her father. Buckling the gun belt around her waist, she said, "I feel much better, now."

Thoth heard Michelle and looked over his shoulder. Spotting our guns, he stopped walking and said, "You will not be permitted in Amun's presence while armed."

Catching my arm, Michelle stopped walking. "We'll be armed or we'll turn around right now."

"Good. Run away, little girl," Shafira snarled. "We don't need you."

"There you go, Thoth," Michelle said, waving her hand in Shafira's direction. "If she says you don't need us, that seems ample proof that you *do* need us."

Thoth stood still, considering the situation. His unwavering stare was disconcerting until I figured out what he was doing.

"I'm pretty sure he's checking in with the boss—well, another telepath who can talk to the boss, anyway," I said, keeping my voice low. "Your bluff might have worked."

"It's not a bluff, babe," Michelle said. "In case they decide to force us into helping them with their problem, do you think you can find Raneem and get her to head to the nearest GenCo office?"

"I can try," I said. "But remember that emotions aren't precise like telepathy."

"I know, Matt, but we don't have any other way to contact her."

Redirecting my scan, I hunted through the many minds scattered behind us. Fortunately, a child's emotions shine much brighter than an adult's do. Children haven't yet learned to bury their feelings and experience almost everything in a much more emotional way than their elders. I ignored the many minds with muted emotions and, in a surprisingly short time, found a group of minds shining bright with emotions. It only took a few more seconds to find Raneem.

"Very well," Thoth said, "Amun grants you permission to bring your weapons. Note that Amun's guards will have their own weapons at the ready. They will fire without warning should you draw your blaster."

"That's fair," Michelle said. "Of course, I'll kill them if they fire without cause."

She took my arm, guiding me while I completed my sending to Raneem.

I began by simply sending warm feelings of love and laughter to the girl. I felt her start at the sudden emotions. She quickly returned them, showing she knew it was me. With extreme care, I gently shifted the emotions toward caution and concern. Fear flared in the girl's mind, which I quickly whisked away. I increased my broadcast of caution while trying to mix in the feeling you get when you go outside on a lovely day.

What can I say? Emotions aren't exact and that's the best I could come up with to suggest she actually go outside. I don't know if Raneem got that or not, but I finished by shifting from concern to feelings of safety and security.

When I stopped broadcasting, I picked up decisiveness from the girl. I just prayed that meant she decided to go to GenCo and not to come after us. Releasing my power, I returned to myself. Ahead of us, Thoth was keying in the code for a door.

"Are you back, Matt?" Michelle whispered.

"Yes."

"Did you find Raneem?"

"Yeah, but it's anyone's guess whether my message was clear or not."

"It'll have to do, babe."

The door ahead of us opened. Thoth turned and gestured for us to enter ahead of him.

"Are you ready to meet Amun?" he asked.

"Sure," I said.

"Then step forward. He awaits within."

Hands clasped, Michelle and I stepped through the door.

THE BOSS

A large open area, at least thirty meters across and wide, lay beyond the door. The space seemed odd after the almost-claustrophobic tunnels we'd walked through. I can't guess the original use for the big room but it was the boss's— damned if I'm going to call him 'Amun'—meeting hall now. Or maybe it was the seat of his court and the people scattered around the room were his courtiers.

I recognized the boss from our attempted meeting at the Cairo Memorial. He was on the far side of the room and seated in a lounge chair. As thrones went, what it lacked in pomp it more than made up for in comfort. I recognized some of the men and women gathered around him from the same almost-meeting, though I didn't spot the woman who made the original empathic attack on Michelle.

Thoth directed us to stop midway across the room. "We will wait here until Amun finishes hearing petitions from his people."

Looking about the room, Michelle said, "This isn't quite what I was expecting."

"What did you expect, Mrs. Connaught?" Thoth asked. "Ruffians and flatterers competing for Amun's attention with the bodies of the losers rotting in the corners?"

"Nothing quite so dramatic," Michelle replied. "But I didn't expect something quite so clean and comfortable in Cairo's abandoned tunnels."

"Amun could not attract as many followers as he has if he did not take care of them. He is a stern master, but he understands that all leaders rule at the sufferance of the ruled. As such, he avoids needless cruelty and keeps his word."

"Really?" I asked. "Then what do you call the unprovoked attack on my wife at our previous meeting?"

"An unfortunate misunderstanding," Thoth said, "one which Amun will address, when he summons you."

"What is your story, Thoth?" I asked. "You appear highly educated and out of place among these people."

"There are several among Amun's followers who come from more socially acceptable walks of life. I was a history professor at Cairo University. The man to the right of Amun was once a senior accountant for the Nextra Corporation," Thoth said, pointing toward an older man sitting next to the boss. "Each of us had our psychic powers discovered after we were well into adulthood. Each of us ran rather than bow to Psi Corps. Amun found us, took us in, and kept us and our families safe."

"You're too smart to believe he did that simply out of the goodness of his heart," I said. "The man obviously expected something from you in return."

"Of course, he did. Tell me, Mr. Connaught, is GenCo in the habit of paying people who cannot do something for the company in return for that salary? Or does your company simply give away money and the security it brings to any deserving soul who walks through its doors?"

I opened my mouth to fire off a quick retort and then swallowed it. "You have an interesting way of explaining things, Thoth. I think I'd have enjoyed taking one of your history classes."

Thoth smiled, "And I believe I'd have enjoyed teaching you and your wife. Alas, Psi Corps makes that impossible for all of us."

We waited a few more minutes while the boss dealt with one remaining issue. When the petitioners left, he motioned to Thoth.

"Amun is ready for us," Thoth said and led us forward. He bowed before the boss and said, "Amun, I present Matthew Connaught and his wife, Michelle Connaught."

"So, you're the pair who has given Shafira such problems," the boss said, looking us over.

"Shafira was an easy target," Michelle said, "and we don't have any interest in talking about her."

"Hey!" Shafira cried. "I'm going to-"

The boss silenced Shafira with a glance. "I concede your point. What do you want to talk about?"

"I'd like to know why one of your empaths attacked Michelle when we met at the Cairo Memorial," I said.

"That was done without orders from me. I am still responsible, though, so please accept my apologies for it. Rest assured, I have severely punished Sabah."

"We only have your word on that," Michelle said. "Can you prove any of that? It's not like Matt can just read you."

"True. That's one disadvantage to being a psychic null," the boss said. "Down here, my word is more than enough to prove anything."

"Yeah, that's part of the problem." Michelle waved vaguely at the people around the boss. "Your...subjects...take your word as law. We don't. Can you bring that empath—I think you said her name was Sabah? Bring her here and let Matt read her. That will convince us."

"I told you that Sabah has been punished. She is no longer available to answer any questions."

"You killed her?" I asked.

"She disobeyed my orders, made a mockery of my word, and endangered all of my psychics," the boss said, his voice stern and cold. "I had her executed."

"That's barbaric!" Michelle said.

"If we were free to fly off to worlds outside of the Federation, perhaps I would agree with you," the boss said. "But we do not have the same freedom you enjoy. We must live in the shadow of Psi Corps and the Federation. Our way of life is precarious, young woman. Those who endanger it deserve punishment both swift and severe."

I looked at Thoth. "What do you think of Sabah's execution?"

"She put my life at risk to attack Mrs. Connaught. As Amun says, our life affords us precious little room for error. Sabah agreed to Amun's rules when she joined us."

"Okay..." Turning back to the boss, I said "That puts us at an impasse. I can't read Sabah because she's dead and I can't read you, either."

"What you say is true, but there is another option," the boss said. "Before her execution, Sabah claimed Amir, one of my officers, gave her orders to attack when the hologram started."

"Claimed?" Michelle asked. "Why didn't someone read Sabah and verify it?"

"My empaths were still recovering from the effects of your husband's counterattack," the boss said. "The telepaths, of course, couldn't read Sabah because she was an empath."

"And you executed her before the empaths recovered," Michelle said. "That's not exactly a brilliant move on your part."

The boss's eyes hardened. "What part of *swift* punishment did you not understand, girl?"

Michelle shook her head in disbelief. "Whatever. It's your circus. Did you execute Amir, too?"

"Not yet. Perhaps, not at all. That depends on your husband."

"Why me?" I asked. "You've got enough empaths and telepaths down here. Couldn't one of them read the guy?"

"No. Like me, Amir is a psychic null."

I threw up my hands and asked, "Then what the hell do you want *me* to do?"

"Do to him what you did to that Psi Corps official, Mr. Toma," the boss said. "Break Amir's shield so my people can read him."

"Let me get this straight," I said. "You want me to crush the shield of another psychic null because you *think* he might be guilty of ordering the attack on Michelle?"

"No," the boss replied, "I want you to crush his shield because I think he disobeyed my orders. There was nothing to gain from attacking your wife at the memorial, and much to lose. After all, we were right there, where Psi Corps is at its strongest. My people were in just as much danger as you were."

"Really?" Michelle scoffed. "How many of Psi Corps' agents chased after your psychics?"

"The numbers don't matter. The situation, itself, was dangerous."

"Do you need a translation of the boss's answer, Matt?" Michelle asked.

"Not at all," I said. "No one chased him and his psychics. They were all after me."

"By your own admission, you are the most powerful empath since the Cairo Catastrophe," the boss said. "Are you truly surprised Psi Corps dedicated all of their resources to capturing you and not us? All of my psychics combined can't match you—something you proved during that short, very one-sided fight in the memorial courtyard."

"Everyone chased us. No one chased you. And somehow that means your psychics were in just as much danger as us?" Michelle said.

"Fine. We were in just as much *initial* danger," the boss said, irritation creeping into his voice.

"Besides, we used tunnels that go in and out of the memorial to get away," Shafira said, her tone smug. "Psi Corps couldn't catch us if they wanted to."

Shafira's sudden entry into the conversation surprised the boss. Judging by the look on his face, it angered him, as well.

"Who gave you permission to speak, Shafira?" the boss demanded.

"I- Um, I, uh, just-," Shafira ground to a stop. Then she turned eyes blazing with hatred on Michelle and said, "She's such a smug bitch, and I wanted to show her that she doesn't know as much as she thinks she knows!"

Michelle smiled sweetly at the other woman. "Thank you, Shafira, now I can add those secret entrances into the memorial to all those other things I know. I guess you showed me."

Shafira screamed in rage and frustration. She looked ready to attack Michelle, even though her fights with my wife never worked out well for the woman. Michelle settled into her fighting stance and waited for Shafira's charge.

"That is *enough!*" the boss's voice thundered. "Thoth, put Shafira in with Amir. I'll deal with her later."

The blood drained from Shafira's face. She dropped to her knees and groveled. "Please don't kill me!"

"You could still be useful to me, Shafira, but I am tired of your impetuous stupidity." The boss turned to Michelle, "It's obvious you don't like Shafira. I think I'll let you choose her punishment."

"She's unnecessarily cruel and not particularly smart," Michelle said. "But she's pretty enough and can act like she cares long enough to fool her marks. I suppose she's *some* use to you."

"Considering that, what kind of punishment do you recommend?" the boss asked.

Michelle's eyes widened. "Whoa, you were serious about that?"

"I *never* joke about punishment."

"Never let her near those children again. Assign her to some other job."

"Do you mean the children young Raneem led away from here not thirty minutes ago?" the boss asked. "Can I assume that was your doing?"

"Did you stop them from leaving?" Michelle asked.

"No, and I'm not going to send people after them, either. I'm afraid you and your husband have ruined Raneem and she is in the process of ruining the rest of them." The boss waved a hand in dismissal, "Besides, there are *always* more street urchins."

"Nice," Michelle growled.

The boss shrugged. "I prefer to think of it as practical. But does your response mean you want me to execute Shafira or not?"

"Not! Good God, what else could I mean?" Michelle said.

"I don't know. That's why I asked," the boss said. "Do you wish to beat her?"

"No!"

"Very well." The boss motioned to Thoth. "Put her in with Amir so she can think about her actions over the last few days. I'll let her out when she can tell me what she did wrong and explain why it all backfired."

"Thank you, boss! I mean, Amun," Shafira babbled as Thoth led her away. "Thank you! I'll think about what you said. I really will!"

"Now," the boss turned back to me, "about Amir..."

"Yeah, Amir," I said. "Before we discuss this any further, tell me why I should get involved in this. In other words, what's in it for me?"

"Ah, at last we are on familiar territory," the boss said. "Should you help me, I will be deeply in your debt."

"Even if Amir's mind is completely scrambled and unreadable, after I break his shield?"

"Why would you expect that?" the boss asked.

"I don't expect anything," I said. "I simply have no idea. For all I know, that Toma guy from Psi Corps is a complete vegetable now."

"He is not. In fact, he is recovering rapidly."

"That's a relief," I said.

Michelle crossed her arms and stared hard at the boss. "Just how do you know the condition of a high-level Psi Corps official?"

The boss turned an impassive expression to Michelle. "I have my ways."

"That's not an answer," Michelle said.

"No one can survive for long in my position without well-placed sources of information," the boss said. "And that is all the answer you're going to receive."

Thoth returned, reminding me of a different question I had. "Why didn't Thoth come to our meeting at the memorial? He strikes me as your most disciplined and best-trained follower. I'd think you'd want someone like that with you when you met someone like me."

"Empires, even one such as mine, do not run themselves," the boss replied. "When I go out, Thoth stays behind and runs things."

"Okay, that makes sense," I said. And the answer did make sense, but I couldn't shake the feeling that there was more to it than that. "But you took your other seventeen psychics with you—eighteen, if you count the late Sabah?"

"Yes."

"And they're all in this room with us?"

"Most assuredly, though I think you already knew that. It is my hope that the combination of psychics and armed guards will make you think carefully before attempting a retaliatory attack."

"You do realize that most people don't think like that?" I asked.

The boss shrugged. "I'd rather be unnecessarily paranoid than insufficiently paranoid."

I looked around the room, letting my gaze rest for a second on each of the psychics present. "I count six empaths, twelve telepaths, and the woman in that corner. I can only tell she's a psychic of some kind because of her emotional state."

"Ursula is a pyrotechnic," the boss replied.

"Great," Michelle muttered. "I hope she's more mentally balanced than the other pyros we've met."

Ursula's face contorted in anger and flames raced up her arms. "Whatta you mean by that?"

"Douse yourself, Ursula," the boss snapped. The flames vanished, though the pyro's glare was almost as hot. Looking back at me, the boss asked, "What difference does all of this make?"

"If we end up having to fight our way out of here, I wanted Michelle to know what we're dealing with," I said.

Michelle smiled at me and ran her fingernails up my spine. "Thanks, babe. I'll show you how much I appreciate your thoughtfulness next time we have some real privacy."

"Enough of this prattle," the boss snapped. "Are you going to help me with Amir or will your wife have to make immediate use of the information you just gave her?"

"If I do smash Amir's shield, you know that's going to be like sending up a signal flare to Psi Corps?" I asked. "I use way too much power to keep it secret."

"I have ways of keeping the...leakage...to a minimum," the boss said.

"Tell us," Michelle demanded.

"Does the great and powerful Matthew Connaught realize I am not the only psychic null down here?"

I did, having spent more time identifying the four other nulls than I did identifying the nineteen psychics. Deciding the boss didn't need to know what I'd figured out, I just shook my head. Michelle cocked an eyebrow at me and I shrugged in response. While the boss laughed, thinking I'd disappointed Michelle, my wife gave a microscopic nod.

Still chuckling, the boss said, "There are four more nulls among my people. If you agree to aid me, I will simply surround you and Amir with the nulls. They should block most of your power usage."

"They'll also block me from drawing the emotions I need to break Amir's shield."

"Can't you just gather your power before they surround you?" the boss asked.

"Yes, but that can alert Psi Corps, too," I replied. "Although if I gather the power slowly over many hours, it will probably be okay."

"Does that mean you will do it?"

"You'll owe me a big favor if I do, right?"

"I will."

"And you won't change your mind once I've done this?"

"I am a man of my word."

Michelle took my hand and whispered, "Babe, I don't think this is such a good idea."

"These people can show us how to get into and out of Psi Corps through their tunnels," I said. "Now we know how we can sneak Foster and his precog out of there."

"I don't know, Matt…"

"Trust me, Michelle," I said. "I know what I'm doing."

"What is your answer, Mr. Connaught?" the boss demanded.

Sighing, I said, "I'll do it."

The boss smiled broadly at my response. "Excellent! Make yourselves comfortable and begin gathering your power."

I looked around the spartan room. The only comfortable chairs had the boss and his top aides parked in them. I doubted they'd move for Michelle and me. Besides, I wanted some privacy.

"Michelle and I need the most comfortable and *private* quarters down here."

The boss's brows drew down in irritation. "Very well, I'll have two chairs brought in for you."

"No. This is going to take hours and a lot of concentration. I cannot gather power surrounded by all these distractions. What part of *private* wasn't clear?"

"You didn't have any trouble getting enough power to attack my psychics back at the memorial," the boss said. "And you did it while that extremely distracting hologram played."

"Please tell me you can see the difference between these two situations?"

"Instead," the boss replied, "why don't you explain it to me?"

"Nothing about the situation at the memorial was subtle. I grabbed all of the emotions I could as quickly as possible—something Psi Corps easily detected—and immediately threw it at you and your people," I said. "Now, I must gather the emotions gradually and store them longer than I've ever stored emotions before. That's going to take a lot more concentration on my part."

"None of my other psychics have ever needed peace and quiet to do their jobs."

"Two things. First, I'm not one of your psychics. Second, if your other psychics are so great, let them pop Amir's shield."

"You know quite well they cannot do that." The boss heaved a sigh, "Very well, if you must have peace and quiet to do this, then you will have it."

"Thank you," I said.

The boss motioned at Thoth. "Take the Connaughts to my room. Have one of the nulls guard the door."

Thoth, accompanied by a woman I'd identified as one of the boss's four remaining psychic nulls, led us through a few twists and turns, stopping at a door after only a few minutes. He opened the door and motioned us inside.

"Knock on the door when Mr. Connaught is ready," Thoth said. "Safa will summon me to escort you back to Amun."

"What about some food for us?" Michelle asked. "Hunger is one of those distractions Matt should avoid."

Thoth gave a single nod. "I shall have dinner brought to you."

"Include some snacks for later," Michelle said. "We don't know how much energy Matt will burn doing this."

"That is a good idea," Thoth said. "I'll see to it personally."

When the door clicked shut, we finally took the time to examine the room. Nothing in it was particularly fancy nor did any of the furniture match, but it all looked comfortable. The chairs were firm and readily conformed to my body contours when I sat in them. The large bed did the same thing when I stretched out on it.

While I tried the furniture, Michelle checked behind the two doors in the room. One opened into a large closet filled with clothes. The other opened into a well-appointed bathroom.

"Not bad," she said. "Our parents would be appalled at the

decor—well, maybe not Daddy, but Mom and your parents would be—but it's peaceful and the furniture looks comfortable."

"It is," I said. Patting the bed, I added, "Why don't you come over here?"

Michelle assumed what I've dubbed the irritated-woman pose —arms crossed, hips canted to the left, and the right foot tapping —and glared. "Matthew Connaught, if you think I'm having sex with you in that bed-"

I rose and held my hands out in a placating manner. "That wasn't my intention, hon! I just... Michelle, holding you settles my mind and I'm going to really need a settled mind to do this."

Michelle swung her hips to the right, started tapping her left foot, and kept her glare going. "Are you saying you don't want to have sex with me right now?"

"What? I...um...that is...uh-"

Michelle's laughter interrupted my brilliant response. "God, Matt, men's minds are *so* easy to play with!"

"In defense of all men, that's because we truly love you women but have no idea how your minds work."

Michelle kissed me lightly and began kneading my shoulders. "You looked like you were brooding, or about to start brooding, so I thought I'd jar you out of that mood. Lay down and let me work on your shoulders and back until they bring us dinner."

"Okay," I said, pulling Michelle into a hug. When her ear was close, I whispered, "After we eat, we need to discuss exactly what I'm going to do later."

"So, you're not going to just do whatever the boss wants you to do?" she whispered back.

"Hell no. I don't know exactly what's going on, but something isn't right in all of this."

"I'm glad you picked up on it, too, babe." Michelle climbed onto the bed and we fell into a reclined embrace. Burying her face against my neck, she said, "A bunch of the people in that room were on edge. At first, I thought it was because of the woman the boss killed, but then I realized no one reacted when the boss told us he killed...what was her name?"

"Sabah."

"Right, her. Everyone else already knew about the execution, but it's just not human to hear something like that and not have *some* kind of reaction," Michelle said. "Even if no one liked Sabah, someone should have frowned or smiled or looked down in sadness or whatever."

"I didn't detect any spikes of joy or sorrow or anger, either," I said. "It was just...weird."

"What emotions did you detect, babe?"

"Wariness. Worry. The same stuff I picked up when we first walked into the room. It's like Sabah's death wasn't even worth worrying about compared to...whatever was on their minds."

A knock sounded at the door. Michelle hopped up and answered the knock. Thoth was there, accompanied by a man we didn't know. The other man wheeled a cart full of food and snacks into the room. From the aroma, the boss ate well.

"I trust all is well, now?" Thoth asked.

"Almost," Michelle replied. "I want to watch you eat a bite from each dish. Bites *I* will select and give to you."

"You're not a very trusting young woman," Thoth said.

"Would you be, if our positions were reversed?"

"No." Thoth motioned to the woman posted outside the door. "Tomkins, please eat each bite Mrs. Connaught gives to you."

Michelle shook her head. "I said you, not her."

Both of Thoth's eyebrows rose in surprise but all he said was, "Very well."

For the next several minutes, Michelle selected bits from each dish and Thoth ate them all. He never hesitated when Michelle handed the fork to him. After ten minutes, even my overly-protective wife was satisfied.

"Okay, you can go," she said.

"Thank you." Pointing at one of the main courses, Thoth added, "The beef is excellent, by the way."

Michelle and I busied ourselves eating for a while. Thoth was right about the beef, too. Meanwhile, I began slowly absorbing emotions. Considering how long I had to hold the emotions, I avoided the sharper emotions like anger and envy. I remembered all too well the way anger overwhelmed me in that bar on Wolf a few months back. When we finished eating, we returned to the bed and cuddled like before.

With her mouth close to my ear again, Michelle whispered, "I thought about our situation while we were eating. I think everyone is on edge because they're about to do something really dangerous."

"More dangerous than sneaking into the Cairo Memorial?" I asked.

"Way more dangerous," she said. "Babe, I think they want to tire you out so Psi Corps can swoop in and capture you."

Michelle's suggestion surprised me. "I just thought this was part of a power struggle or something. If all the boss wants to do is turn me over to Psi Corps, why doesn't he just let them come get me while I'm preparing to break Amir's shield?"

"Remember what I said about tiring you out? After what you did to Toma last night, I doubt anyone from Psi Corps wants to get anywhere near you when you're at full strength." Michelle's arms tightened around me. "With you unable to put up a big fight, Psi Corps can safely overwhelm the two of us with sheer numbers. By the time you recover your strength, the bastards will have a gun at my head—probably quite literally—and use me to force you to behave and do their bidding."

"It would work, too," I said.

"It would for a while, but the longer Psi Corps used me against you..." Michelle sniffed and I felt warm tears splash onto my neck. "You'll do so many things you won't want to do and all just to keep Psi Corps from hurting me. It will take years, Matt, but you'll end up hating me just as much as you hate Psi Corps—maybe more since I'll be the embodiment of your suffering."

"Hey, no, Michelle," I whispered, "I could never hate you."

Michelle's tears fell faster and her words came in gasps, "You will...You'll hate me for the family you never had...You'll hate me for keeping you from your parents...You'll hate me for everything Psi Corps makes you do...You'll hate just seeing me because Psi Corps will only bring me around when they want something from you...You'll hate-"

"That is *not* happening, Michelle! I won't let it happen and neither will you." I held her at arm's length and gazed into her red-rimmed blue eyes. "Where did that come from, hon?"

"It's been hanging around ever since we got to Earth, Matt." Michelle wiped at her eyes with her sleeve. "I think I can handle a lot of things that might happen to us—even something as painful as you dying—but I don't think I could ever deal with you hating me."

I nodded, thinking through Michelle's fear. "The thing is, you'd probably end up hating me, too, because I'll be the reason you're kept locked up. That thought is..."

"Terrifying," Michelle said.

"Yeah...So, we won't let that happen, right?"

"Damned straight, babe!"

"Then I guess it's past time we got out of here." Looking around the room, I said, "Does the boss strike you as the type who would let himself get trapped in his own bedroom?"

"No, he doesn't." Michelle began looking around the room, also. "Where do you think he'd hide an escape tunnel?"

"I don't know, but we won't find it if we don't get off our butts and start looking," I said.

"Oh my God," Michelle said, "why did my father's voice just come out of your mouth?"

"Probably because—and it hurts me to admit this—a lot of the stuff our parents told us actually makes sense." I walked to the only wall without a door and began running my hands over it. "According to Mom, it gets even worse when you have children."

"You mean I'll have more episodes like the one I had with

Raneem, at lunch?" Michelle asked. "That's a hell of a reward for doing my part to keep the species going."

We searched in silence for the next thirty minutes, finding nothing. We were both checking the closet walls when Michelle spoke again.

"Do you think Thoth is part of whatever it is the boss has planned?"

"He's supposed to be second-in-command down here, so I can't believe he isn't in on it," I said. "I agree that he seemed like a good guy during our brief time together, but that doesn't mean much. After all, look at what my aunt and uncle were hiding for so many years."

"Good point, babe, though your uncle was okay when we worked with him on Piscain Station." Michelle glanced my way. "Do you ever wonder where he and your aunt went after he got her out of prison?"

"Yes. Dad and Mom claim they don't care as long as the two of them stay far away from us, but I can tell they're worried about both of them. They're also mad as hell at Gunther and Tess for kidnapping them and keeping them prisoner for so long."

"Family can be complicated," Michelle said, stepping back from the closet wall and putting her hands on her hips. "I don't think we're going to find a secret door hidden in one of these walls, Matt."

"What makes you say that?"

"So far, all of the walls have been solid plasticrete. That stuff is almost impossible to cut. Besides, there are so many pipes running along the walls down here, I'd bet the other sides of these walls are lined with pipes."

I followed Michelle back into the bedroom. "Does that mean you don't think the boss has a getaway tunnel?"

"No, I'm still sure he does. I just don't think it's in the walls." Pointing toward the wall without a door, she said, "Help me move that sofa."

We each took an end of the extremely solid-looking piece of

furniture. Michelle counted down from three and we both lifted. Expecting something very heavy, we almost threw the surprisingly light sofa into the air. We juggled it a bit—the sofa was still big and unwieldy—before getting it under control. Michelle and I shuffled a meter from the wall and put our burden down. A locked trap door was barely visible in the direct light.

Michelle spent a couple of minutes checking out the door. Finally satisfied it had neither traps nor alarms, she pulled out a set of picks and went to work on the old-fashioned mechanical lock. After five extremely long minutes, the mechanism finally turned and Michelle opened the trap door. A ladder descended into the dark.

"Well, there's our way out of here," she said.

"It seems kind of odd, doesn't it?" I asked.

"What's odd?"

"We came down here looking to hide and even voluntarily went with Thoth to visit the boss," I said. "Now we're sneaking away from the same people we hoped might help us—or at least not turn us in."

"I'm sure there's more to the story than we know," Michelle replied, "but everyone can't be like Zav, Nora, or Greg."

"We'll have to invite Nora and Greg out to Ark's Landing once we get back," I said. "Too bad we can't just go visit them on Pegasus Station, but I think this trip will be my last time tempting Psi Corps."

"Let's get back home, first, then we can worry about having guests visit," Michelle said. "Can I assume you're scanning down there?"

I gave Michelle my best offended-husband look. "Of course."

"Good!" Michelle nodded. "I'll go first. You pull the sofa back against the wall—no sense advertising what we're doing—and then stay close to me."

"You still can't let go of your bodyguard training, can you, hon?"

I'd given a half-smile when I spoke, hoping for light moment before we descended into the unknown. Michelle answered with a glare, reminding me just how deeply ingrained her father's training was.

Lifting my hands in surrender, I quickly added, "I mean, yes, ma'am. Whatever you say, ma'am."

That got a smile from Michelle. It was a bit on the smug and self-satisfied side, but at least it was a smile. "That's better, babe. Now, let's get out of here!"

Then we descended into the unknown.

INTO THE TUNNELS

Michelle and I descended into the darkened tunnel. As the light from the room above faded, Michelle dug into the backpack and pulled out a flashlight. The light showed another trapdoor a few meters below us. Michelle climbed the rest of the way down to the door, waited for me to join her, and flicked off the light.

"You need to keep quiet while I check out what's on the other side of the door," Michelle said.

"I kind of figured that out for myself, hon," I said.

"Yes, you're very smart." Michelle's voice came out of the darkness from below me. "Now, shut up."

"Need help with the door?" I asked.

"Seriously, babe," Michelle replied as I heard the trapdoor swing up, "be quiet so I can listen."

"Yes, ma'am," I whispered.

We both strained our ears, probing the darkness for any sound out of the ordinary. After a few seconds of listening to water dripping, Michelle turned her light on again. The bright light stung my eyes for a few seconds, but they quickly adjusted.

Michelle, silhouetted against the light shining into the tunnel, stuck her head through the trapdoor and looked in all directions. "It's clear. The floor is about three meters below the door."

Without waiting for any response from me, Michelle dropped down into the tunnel below. She landed softly and moved to one side.

"Come on down, babe," she called quietly.

A couple of seconds later I was crouching next to her in the tunnel. Make that tunnels. We were at the intersection of six of them. Michelle shined the light down each one, looking for some indication of which way we should go.

"I have no idea which one we should take," she said. "Can you figure something out using your ability, Matt?"

"I'll try."

Cautiously, I reached out with my empathic ability. To my right, I readily detected Psi Corps. It wasn't very close, but it had a huge emotional footprint. To my left, and a lot closer, I picked up the boss's little gang. Most of them were not familiar, but Shafira was easy to pick out.

I waved one hand in an arc encompassing three of the tunnels on the right, "Psi Corps is somewhere over there. The boss and his people are in the opposite direction. Shafira is close by. I'm pretty sure I could find her—especially since she's doing something with her power—anything else is a total crapshoot."

Michelle bit her lip, something I hadn't seen her do much lately, as she considered what I had said. After a few seconds, she pointed back toward the boss's territory and said, "I think we're going to need a native guide. Let's go get Shafira."

"Do you think that's such a good idea, hon?"

"No, I think it's a really bad idea. But unless you think you can quickly navigate through these tunnels to Psi Corps, I don't think we have any choice." Michelle motioned for me to lead the way, and said, "You can keep her power in check, can't you?"

I gave Michelle an incredulous look as I walked past her, "Please tell me you're kidding."

"Just being cautious, babe, Just like Daddy taught me," my wife said.

I raised one wrist dramatically to my forehead and said, "Still, your doubt has cut me to the quick. I don't know how I can go on, now."

"I suppose I'm going to have to find some way to make this up to you," Michelle sighed, matching my dramatic tone.

"Oh, good! I've got something in mind already."

"Let me guess," Michelle said, "does it involve a bed?"

"I was thinking of something more like a blanket, a jug of wine-"

"A loaf of bread, and thou," Michelle interrupted. "What, no Book of Verses? No singing in the wilderness?"

"You've heard me sing, hon, do you think I'd really subject you to that?" I asked. "Talk about ruining the mood..."

"In the poem, I'm pretty sure it's the woman doing the singing."

"In that case," I said, "we'll have some singing, too. You sing like an angel."

"That's very sweet of you to say, babe," Michelle said. "Now, can we get back to the task at hand? Shafira won't find herself."

"Oh, I've been keeping track of Shafira. She's not very far away." We came to another intersection and I immediately took the tunnel to the right. "In fact, she's right down here."

Michelle shined the flashlight down the tunnel, illuminating several doors on both sides of it. We were both relieved no guards posted at any of the doors.

"Nice of the boss to leave her unguarded," Michelle said.

"If the door locks from the outside, I can't see why he would need anybody guarding it," I said. "I mean, we are talking about Shafira, here. She's not exactly a master criminal."

"Yeah, but wasn't she supposed to be in with Amir? From what Thoth and the boss had to say, I got the idea he was not an idiot."

"Probably not, but he is a psychic null. It's not like I can easily pick him up," I said.

"I wasn't asking if you detected him with your ability, Matt. I know he's a null, but I thought he might be worthy of a guard."

"Maybe Amir is sort of like a middle manager criminal?" I asked. "Not an idiot, but not someone you put in charge of anything really important, either."

I stopped next to the third door on the left. "She's in here."

Michelle examined the door, and said, "There's just a simple external locking mechanism. It's impossible to open from the inside, but as easy as flipping a switch on the outside. Are you ready to contain Shafira?"

"Yep, just give the word."

"Do it, babe," Michelle said as she reached for the locking mechanism.

I blocked Shafira's empathic power just as Michelle slid the door open. Beyond the door, was a small room with no furniture, and two people sitting on the floor. One of them was our old friend Shafira, while the other was a man we had never seen before. He was short, very pale, and maybe thirty years old. I had to admit, he looked exactly like I thought a middle manager should look.

A nasty grin split Shafira's face when Michelle stepped through the door. She turned the grin on Amir. "You know who that is don't you? Are you ready to get your brain turned to mush!"

Amir turned a resigned gaze on me. "I suppose it's time?"

Shafira glanced my way and said, "I've been using my power to tenderize his mind for you."

Michelle gave Shafira an incredulous look. "You do know Amir is a psychic null, right? Your power has no effect on him."

"Just take a look at him," Shafira crowed. "Have you seen anybody look more depressed than him? He got that way because I was broadcasting depression at him. I must be more powerful than people think."

Michelle looked at me and said, "Good God, I think she actually believes that."

A wry smile crossed Amir's lips. "Never underestimate the power of Shafira's stupidity."

"Hey! Just for that, I'm going to hit you with my full power," Shafira snarled.

Whatever else you could say about the woman, Shafira was very determined to prove just how stupid she really was. Her pathetic attempts to broadcast depression and fear at Amir hit my power and were immediately routed into my brain. I stored them along with what little I'd absorbed while we were in the boss's room.

Amir climbed to his feet and said, "Let's get this over with."

"We're not here to do anything to you, Amir," Michelle said. "We came to get Shafira, so she could guide us through the tunnels to Psi Corps. Of course, looking at her right now, I'm having second thoughts about the wisdom of that plan."

"You should listen to those second thoughts," Amir said. "Shafira will betray you at the first opportunity."

"I knew that," Michelle said. "But she's the only one I know who can get us through these tunnels to Psi Corps, who isn't also upstairs with the boss."

"I can get you through the tunnels," Amir said. "I'm the one who taught her which way to go."

Michelle looked at me and said, "Is there any way you can figure out whether he's telling the truth or not?"

"Not without turning his brain to mush, alerting Psi Corps where we are, and bringing everybody that works for the boss down on us," I said. "On the other hand, why don't you just ask Shafira?"

A look of comprehension crossed Michelle's face and she turned toward Shafira. "So, is it true? Did Amir teach you the way through the tunnels to Psi Corps?"

"No, he didn't!" Shafira said. "I figured it out all by myself."

Shafira is a very good liar, as long as she's not lying to another psychic. Deception shone out of her mind as bright as the sun.

"She's lying," I said.

Michelle nodded and looked at Amir. "Are you willing to help us?"

"It beats waiting around to get my brain turned to mush," Amir said.

"You realize that's what is going to happen to you if you try to turn us over to Psi Corps?" Michelle said.

"Yes, I figured that out all by myself," the criminal middle manager said. "But you know Shafira is going to sound the alarm as soon as we leave, and even your husband can't block her power forever."

Michelle reached into her backpack and pulled out one of the new blasters her father gave us for our anniversary. Holding it so Shafira could see it, Michelle flipped the setting to stun, and pointed it at Shafira.

"I'm way ahead of you, Amir," Michelle said and pulled the trigger.

Even on stun setting, the blaster report echoed loudly in the small room. Shafira slumped to the floor and Michelle motioned us out the door. Eyes wide in surprise, Amir fell in behind me.

"Don't do anything unexpected, Amir," Michelle said, bringing up the rear. "I'll shoot you without a second thought."

I looked over my shoulder at the man, "Believe her. At least you know it's on stun."

"If he's stunned, will it be easier for you to break through his shield?" Michelle asked me.

Amir held his hands up in mock surrender. "You've made your point, Mrs. Connaught. Only a suicidal moron would risk your wrath. I am neither suicidal nor a moron."

"Good," Michelle said. "I'm glad we understand each other. Now, which way to Psi Corps?"

With the exception of Amir's softly called directions, we walked in silence for the next twenty minutes. At a four-way intersection, Amir broke the silence.

"From here, which way we go depends on why you want to get into Psi Corps."

I looked past the man to Michelle. "How much do you think we can trust him?"

"I'm just the brawn, babe. I leave all that thinking and trust stuff to you and your psychic ability."

I raised an eyebrow. "Who are you and what have you done with Michelle?"

Michelle's lips turned down in a slight frown. "I'm not entirely kidding, Matt. I'm pretty sure you're better at reading body language than I am. You're observant and an empath, so my best guess is that you've built up a pretty extensive physical vocabulary by both watching and reading people. That's why you believed our...friend...the other night. Your doubt is why you waited for Raneem's confirmation before saying anything."

I scratched the back of my head, working through Michelle's meaning. "I think I can follow that logic. Let's say you're right, what makes you think I can read body language without using my ability as a lens?"

"I don't know, Matt," Michelle said, shrugging. "Maybe because you have to?"

"Might I make a suggestion?" Amir asked. "It is, after all, my brain poised above the mush maker."

"Sure," I said.

"I could tell you more about myself so you'll have more to go on when judging my trustworthiness."

"That's a great idea," Michelle said, "except how will we know if you're telling the truth?"

It was Amir's turn to shrug. "If I wanted to lie to gain your trust, would I start out by admitting I work for Psi Corps?"

Michelle raised her blaster so fast I almost missed it. My own hand twitched toward my own holster, but I stopped short of drawing the gun. Amir never moved, never even flinched, at my wife's reaction.

"Thank you for not shooting me, Mrs. Connaught," Amir said. "I trust I have your attention and belief?"

"Attention, yes," Michelle said. "I'm still not sure I believe you."

"I do," I said.

Without taking her eyes off of Amir, Michelle asked, "Why do you believe him, babe?"

"I don't know. His tone of voice, maybe? His overall nonchalance? I can't really point to any one thing, but *do* believe he works for Psi Corps. Maybe you were right about me and body language," I said. Then uncertainty caught up with me as I realized how little I understood my reaction to Amir. "Or maybe I just want to believe him. If that's the case-"

"Stop doubting yourself so much, Matt. You've lived your whole life afraid Psi Corps would find out about your empathic ability. Your brain is programmed to distrust anything those people say to you but your gut is telling you something else about Amir." Michelle's eyes caught mine for a second. "I'm sure you remember what Daddy taught you about instincts."

"They're our subconscious sending us a message after processing data we aren't even aware we know."

"Exactly. So don't let your brain get in the way of your instincts." Michelle's eyes returned to Amir and she lowered her blaster. "Okay, you've got our attention and our tentative belief. Please explain why I shouldn't shoot you right now."

"Put yourself in my position," Amir said. "My superiors at Psi Corps are obviously willing to leave me to the boss's not-so-tender mercies if it means capturing your husband. Would you willingly sacrifice yourself for your employer?"

"Uh, yeah," Michelle replied. "That's pretty much the definition of a bodyguard."

"You're his bodyguard?" Amir asked, his eyes widening in surprise. "My apologies. When Mr. Connaught showed up with a woman his own age, I just assumed you were his wife."

"Michelle *is* my wife," I said. "She used to be my bodyguard and her training is never far from the surface."

"Let me try another analogy," Amir said. "If you worked in a

GenCo manufacturing facility, would you sacrifice yourself so the company could get their hands on a new product design?"

"Do you hear that, Matt? Psi Corps wants you to be their new product."

"You know what I meant, Mrs. Connaught."

"Yes, I do. But Psi Corps goes to great lengths to convince the galaxy that they exist only to serve and protect the Federation." Michelle cocked her head to one side. "If that's true, wouldn't you do anything—even sacrifice yourself—to get a powerful psychic like Matt off the streets and under Psi Corps' control?"

"Yes, if that was true. Tell me, Mrs. Connaught, have you spent much time dealing with government agencies?" When Michelle and I both nodded, Amir continued, "Then you have some vague idea what Psi Corps is really like. Surely, you've spoken of its inner workings with your friend Zavier Gordon and the psychics you took from Piscain Station, as well? Do you truly harbor any illusions that Psi Corps is anything but a large government agency dedicated to increasing its power within the Federation government?"

"No, we don't. That's one reason we're working to bring Psi Corps down," I said. "I'm still surprised you're admitting as much to us."

"You may remember I was being held as a sacrificial lamb so you would drain your strength, Mr. Connaught. I happen to like my brain just the way it is and will do much to avoid the same fate as your previous victim, Mr. Toma."

"What do you mean by that?" I asked. "I was told Toma is recovering."

"Who told you that?"

"The boss," I muttered, reddening in chagrin. "Obviously, I shouldn't have believed him."

"*We* shouldn't have believed him," Michelle said.

"You two can't be blamed for accepting his word when he told you what you wanted to hear."

"I assume you know the truth?" I asked. At Amir's nod, I said, "Tell me."

"Toma has not regained consciousness since you attacked him. I'm told telepaths have detected brain activity, but there's no evidence he's dreaming or even thinking." Amir looked directly into my eyes. "There are two healers assigned to Earth and neither of them can do anything for him. They aren't even sure what's wrong with Toma."

Numbly, I asked, "Do they think he's going to die?"

"I don't know, but I'll bet the director is hoping he will. All the better to scare the public and squeeze more funding and a broader mandate from parliament. You know, whip them into a panic over Matt Connaught by claiming you can kill them with your mind."

"Hell, if Toma dies the director won't even be exaggerating," I said.

"You do remember that Toma wanted to capture the two of us and use me to force you to do Psi Corps' bidding?" Michelle asked. "Would you feel this guilty if you'd shot the man in a gun battle and that was the reason we got away?"

"I...don't think so," I said.

"Psi Corps set a trap for you, Mr. Connaught," Amir said. "They sent me to negotiate the whole thing with the boss. He was in on the whole plan, as were the rest of his psychics. Except for Shafira, that is. No one trusted her to keep the secret."

"Even Sabah, the woman he executed?" Michelle asked.

"Yes, though that part of his story was true. I did arrange for her to attack you before the others were ready. I was observing from a nearby building and when I saw the little girl running toward you, I gave Sabah the order to attack. The timing had to be just right or you might have left before the girl could lure you deeper into the trap." Amir met my eyes again. "You aren't the only one who has blood on his hands, Mr. Connaught."

"And *this* is the story that's supposed to make us trust you?" Michelle asked.

Amir's eyes bored into mine as he said, "Yes, because I am being completely honest with you."

"Because you think that's the best way to lure Matt into Psi Corps' trap," Michelle whispered.

Amir was so focused on me, I'm not sure he even consciously heard what Michelle said. His subconscious did, though, and it made him give a fractional nod in response. His eyes widened as he realized what just transpired, but it was way too late. Without hesitation, Michelle shot him.

"Don't worry, babe, my blaster is still set to stun," she said. "Now, help me stash our friend down a side tunnel."

I was still catching up with the sudden turn of events, but knelt down and hoisted Amir up over my shoulder. "You keep a watch out for Psi Corps people. I'll take care of our former friend."

Standing at a four-way intersection, I discounted the tunnel that brought us here. I dismissed the two tunnels Amir claimed led to Psi Corps, too. That made my choice very simple.

"How far do you think the sound of the blaster shot carried?" I asked.

Michelle, backing down the tunnel behind me, said, "With all the hard surfaces down here to reflect sound, probably a very long way. For the same reason, it'll be hard to figure out which direction the shot came from, but I expect Psi Corps can bring lots of people down here to search for us."

I ignored the first three side tunnels we passed, and almost ignored the fourth. If Amir's limp bulk hadn't made me look down slightly, I would have missed it entirely.

"Shine a light over here, hon," I said.

A few meters down the tunnel, behind a row of pipes, a metal grating covered what looked like an air vent. Dropping Amir, I got down onto my stomach and scooted under the lowest pipe. The grating was hinged, but also locked.

"Hurry up, Matt. I think I hear voices in the distance," Michelle said.

"Are those little concealable blasters quiet enough that I can use one to blast a lock?"

"Probably?" Despite her uncertainty, Michelle put one of the small weapons into my outstretched hand. "Try using half-power."

I turned the power dial with my thumb and then pressed the blaster against the lock. The shot sounded deafening to me, but I was both right next to it and desperate to keep noise to a minimum.

"I definitely hear voices, now, babe," Michelle said. "Did that work?"

The grating creaked open when I pushed on it, its hinges stiff with rust and disuse. "Yeah. Shove Amir to me and get down here, yourself. The vent looks wide enough for us to fit in next to each other."

After a few minutes of wriggling and pushing Amir, we'd gotten several meters down the vent. Michelle even remembered to push the grating shut with her feet—something that slipped my mind entirely. As soon as we stopped, Michelle pulled a roll of heavy-duty tape out of the extremely expensive backpack she hadn't let out of her possession since we left our hotel the previous morning. It only took her a couple of minutes to bind and gag Amir with the tape.

"He should be out for a good while, yet, but Daddy says never take unnecessary chances." Michelle kissed me lightly on the nose. "Why don't you get some sleep. I'll keep watch and try to figure out what we should do next."

"Promise me you'll wake me if anyone comes close. If it's not a psychic null, I can probably broadcast indifference at them and keep them from noticing this vent."

"Unless they have the plans for this place, I don't think anyone will notice it even without your help," Michelle said.

"Maybe, but I have it on very good authority that my father-in-law says we should never take unnecessary chances."

"Very good, babe! You passed my 'do you listen to your wife' test."

"Aren't I supposed to get a better reward than a verbal pat on the head?"

Michelle leaned in and kissed me very thoroughly. "Anything else is going to have to wait until we're safe."

I folded my arms and laid my head on them. "It's always good to have something to look forward to."

I closed my eyes and, unexpectedly, fell asleep quickly.

Some time later, Michelle gently shook me awake. She had one hand gently covering my mouth so I assumed she wanted me to keep quiet. I raised both eyebrows in question. Michelle cupped one hand around her ear and use two fingers from her other hand to mimic someone walking. I nodded my understanding and turned my attention toward the tunnel at the end of our vent.

After a few seconds, I heard the sound of feet scuffing over a hard surface. Someone—probably several someones—was coming our way.

Suddenly remembering our 'guest,' I looked over my shoulder to make sure Amir was not making any sounds. I remembered Michelle taping his hands behind his back, his feet together, and his mouth shut but he still had enough freedom of movement to kick at the wall in an attempt to alert whoever was approaching. I needn't have worried. While I was sleeping, Michelle had hogtaped—it's exactly like hogtying except you use tape—the man's hands and feet together behind his back.

I smiled into Amir's glare before turning my attention back to the tunnel. By now the sound of approaching footsteps was clearly audible. I could also hear snatches of quiet conversation among the people approaching. Michelle and I both strained to make out the words, hoping to learn something useful from their passing conversation.

In an adventure vid, the band of minions would have been discussing important details of their search, the layout of their hideout, or something else useful to us. We had no such luck. The men were primarily griping about the local football team and its poor performance this season. In a way, though, their conversation did tell us something useful. The searchers obviously felt no sense of urgency, otherwise they wouldn't waste time on casual conversation. I was left with the impression the men were performing one last sweep of the area before moving on. The voices and footsteps faded away, but Michelle and I remained silent until a full minute passed.

"How long was I asleep?" I asked.

"Almost four hours."

"And those guys were the first ones to search down this tunnel?"

Michelle shook her head. "Three other groups came in the last few hours. They were all a lot quieter. I didn't hear them until they were nearly at the entrance to the vent. You were sleeping quietly, so I decided not to risk startling you by waking you up."

"I don't understand why you didn't wake me after the first group went by."

"If you have to use your power, a few hours of sleep might mean the difference between freedom and capture. And, like I said, you were sleeping quietly. It wasn't like we were going to get out of here while the search was going on, anyway."

"Okay, hon," I said. "What now?"

"By hiding in here, I think we've convinced Psi Corps and the boss that we've left the tunnels and returned to the city above."

"Why do you say that?" I asked. "I mean, Shafira heard our full plan and someone in the boss's group must have found her by now. She'll have told them everything she overheard. So they know we wanted to sneak into Psi Corps. That means they've got to be waiting for us."

"I'm sure they were waiting for us, but that group that just wandered by tells me they think we either never were going to Psi Corps or have given up. Between the boss's people and Psi Corps' people, they probably think they know everything about these tunnels. After spending four hours searching for us and not finding us, it's reasonable for them to assume we're not down here."

"Yeah...What do you think your father would say to that line of reasoning?"

"Daddy would probably call it wishful thinking. But he also says to trust your gut—and my gut says we've got a mostly clear path to Psi Corps." She looked over her shoulder at Amir and added, "That's assuming Amir gives us the directions we need."

Amir shook his head violently. That's about the only movement he could make but his meaning was very clear. He wasn't going to help us.

"Are you comfy, Amir?" Michelle asked. Amir's glare intensified and my wife said, "I didn't think so. Here's the deal, you tell us how to safely sneak into Psi Corps headquarters and we'll make sure someone finds you after we get back out. If we get caught, I don't think we're going to be quite so charitable. Imagine spending the last days of your life taped up like that while you die of thirst or hunger."

"Um, Michelle? I don't know about this."

"I don't like it either, babe, but I like the idea of spending the rest of our lives as slaves to Psi Corps even less." Michelle matched Amir's glare and said, "So, what's it going to be, Amir? Will you give us directions that get us around all of the guards and bypass any traps and sensors?"

Amir and Michelle held a staring contest for another half a minute before Amir's head drooped and he nodded. Turning around, Michelle pulled out what was left of the tape she'd used to bind Amir and cut off a strip large enough to cover his mouth. She peeled back one corner of the strip over his mouth but paused before removing it.

Michelle dug into the expensive backpack and pulled out a wicked-looking knife. Drawing it from its sheath, she laid it on the floor right in front of our captive's face. Then, Michelle got down on Amir's level and looked him in the eye.

"Before I pull off that piece of tape, I want to tell you something, Amir. A couple of very talented precogs have told Matt and me that we're going to have at least three children. They even gave us a painting of them. I want those children so badly, I can almost taste it. I want to feel them growing inside of me. I want to feel them moving and kicking. Hell, I even want morning sickness and labor pains. Are you with me so far, Amir?"

Eyes wide, Amir nodded.

"Good. Now, this next bit is the part you *really* need to pay attention to." Michelle picked up the knife and moved it back and forth in front of Amir's eyes. "I will interpret anything other than your absolute cooperation as an attack on my babies. Everyone knows the fiercest thing in the universe is a momma protecting her babies. I'll be that momma if you do anything stupid. If you shout, I'll slit your throat. If you send us into a trap, I'll kill everyone trying to trap us, and then come back here and slit your throat. If we get captured... Well, I already told you what will happen, then. So, before I remove that strip of tape, take a minute and imagine your blood spurting all over this tunnel. Or, imagine spending days trapped down here, as you slowly die of thirst over several days. Are you imaging those things, Amir?"

Amir's head bobbed up and down so fast that he bashed his jaw on the floor several times before he could stop.

"Good," Michelle purred. "I'm glad we understand each other."

She ripped the tape off of Amir's mouth. He grimaced in pain but didn't cry out or make any other noise Michelle might interpret as a call for help. Over the next several minutes, he gave detailed directions which my wife recorded in her pocket pad. After he finished answering all of her questions, his eyes widened in panic as she prepared to tape his mouth shut.

"Please, can't you just stun me? That way I won't be able to call for help until long after you have gotten to Psi Corps."

"Sorry, Amir, you were only out for about forty minutes the last time we stunned you," Michelle responded. "That's just not long enough for us to do what we need to do. Besides, I'm not willing to risk someone overhearing the blaster shot."

"Please? There has to be something I can do to change your mind."

"Well, there is one thing,"Michelle said.

"What? I'll do anything."

"Maybe, if you tell us the truth about Toma..."

"Yeah, I can do that! He's recovering fine, but he isn't a null any more. Or maybe he just hasn't recovered. No one knows what to expect."

Michelle's voice hardened, "Why did you lie to us?"

"Because if Mr. Connaught was feeling guilty, Psi Corps hoped he'd get careless and be easier to capture."

"Thank you, Amir."

She reached slapped the tape over Amir's mouth. His eyes widened in shock and he tried to protest through the gag.

"You aren't the only one who can tell lies, Amir," she said. "For the record, I don't take kindly to people who want to take Matt or my future babies away from me."

Hope faded from Amir's eyes as Michelle slapped a second piece of tape over his mouth. I pushed down the rising sympathy I felt for the man, reminding myself he had been leading us into a trap.

"How long do we wait before we get moving?" I asked.

"Let's give them another half an hour. Have you got any idea what you want to do when we get to Psi Corps?"

"Only in very vague terms—scope out the situation, find our friends, and get back out of there as fast as we can."

"I don't like going in there knowing as little as we do, babe. We have no idea how many guards there are, what the layout is, or even if our friend is there right now."

"We could ask Amir," I suggested.

Michelle shook her head. "The questions we'd have to ask would give Amir too much information about our friend. If we get caught and someone still finds him, that information could lead Psi Corps to them."

"I hadn't thought of that...Can your portable pad get a signal down here? We could send a message to them if it does."

Michelle checked her pad and shook her head. "What about

you? Have you got some cutting-edge, super-slicer pad GenCo hasn't made available to the public, yet? Something that can get a signal down here?"

"Mine is just like yours, hon. I don't need anything better on Ark's Landing and I didn't have time to arrange for something better before we left." I took Michelle's pad, opened the messaging app's settings, and made a few quick changes. Handing it back to my wife, I said, "Now, an alert will display on the screen as soon as the pad gets a signal. It's the best I can do."

"We'll just have to hope our friend regularly checks the message drop I told him about."

The thirty minutes crawled by but eventually Michelle said, "All right, babe, time to go."

I looked over my shoulder at Amir. "As soon as we have a signal, I'll set up a time delayed message to Psi Corps telling them where you are. Even if we get caught, you won't die down here. Michelle would've done the same thing, she just wouldn't have told you about it."

Michelle punched me lightly in the arm. "You're going to ruin my reputation as a hard ass, babe."

"I always thought of your ass as soft and shapely," I countered.

Michelle rolled her eyes. "You must be nervous if you're already making corny sexual jokes."

"Only an idiot wouldn't be nervous sneaking into his enemy's lair. And I'd like to think you didn't marry an idiot."

I scooted under the pipes and stood up in the tunnel. Reaching down, I helped Michelle to her feet.

"Which way, hon?"

Michelle pointed back the way we came, and we set off to infiltrate Psi Corps headquarters.

PLANNING

Michelle kept track of where we were going while I kept track of where we had been. We might need my map if we had to make a run for it. Also, I would include it in the time-delayed message I sent to Psi Corps. Michelle had no trouble following Amir's directions and, twenty minutes after we left him, we entered a dimly lit section of the tunnels.

"I don't know if anyone is still down here," Michelle said, "but we're not going to take any chances. Keep your blaster's targeting set to infrared and keep checking behind us."

"Roger that," I said while surreptitiously switching my blaster to infrared targeting.

"You never changed your targeting system did you, babe?"

"What makes you say that, hon?"

"You never say 'roger that' or any other semi-military responses unless you're covering something up. Usually, it means you didn't do something you should have done." Michelle grinned over her shoulder at me. "Daddy taught me that about you when I was thirteen."

"And you're just getting around to telling me this after we've been married for a year?"

"This is the first time it's come up, babe. You're usually very good at doing what I tell you to do."

"What can I say? Your father taught me well." An odd thought suddenly struck me. "Hey, since your father knew how I felt about you for all those years, you don't think he was training me to be proper husband material for his little girl, do you?"

"Oh, probably. Daddy always had my back."

"Just so we're clear, I didn't ignore your instructions. I was concentrating on setting up the mapping application on my pad."

"So noted. Now that you have infrared targeting turned on, I want you to scan behind us and down passages we don't take. You know, like I asked you to do twenty minutes ago."

"Hey, I *did* look in all those directions. I just didn't use infrared.

Every few meters, I spun around and scanned the tunnel behind us. Honestly, I felt like that unnamed guy in every adventure vid whose job it is to get shot instead of the hero. You know, the dorky rookie whose death hardens the hero's resolve. Fortunately, the similarities ended there. I didn't see anything on the infrared system and no one shot me in the back.

Michelle stopped at the first door we came to. "If there are stairs up to the surface on the other side of this door, we'll go up far enough that we can get a signal with our pads. We can send a message to Foster, and use the GPS to figure out exactly where we are. You can also set up that time-delayed message with Amir's location."

"Don't you think you ought to leave a message for your father, too? I assume the codeword you gave to Raneem will bring Jonas here as fast as possible."

"I've been debating that with myself," Michelle said. "Daddy can't get here in time to do anything to help us, and we already know he'll help Raneem and her friends."

"But he might also be able to help Foster and his family. And he'll know what happened to us. He could probably guess, anyway, but the more he knows about our plans the better the chance he can figure out a way to rescue us."

"You're right, babe. I'll leave a message for Daddy, too."

The door was locked, of course, but Michelle had an amazing assortment of lock picking tools in the very expensive backpack. I kept watch while she unlocked the door. In well under a minute, it softly slid aside and revealed stairs going up. We went up at least twenty meters before we got a signal.

While I set up my delayed message to Psi Corps, Michelle keyed messages to both her father and Foster. I finished well before she did, so I used a locator application to overlay our position on a map of Cairo. As expected, we were under the Cairo Catastrophe Memorial, but were still half a kilometer from the main Psi Corps building. I showed the map to Michelle when she finished leaving her messages.

"Is there any chance you can break into the city archives and maybe find a map of the tunnels?" Michelle asked.

"With this thing?" I asked, holding up my pad. "Not likely and, even if I could, it would take a while. You want me to try?"

"No, that's what I expected, but wanted to make sure."

We returned to the tunnels and, once again, Michelle led the way using Amir's directions. I, on the other hand, went back to acting like the dorky rookie in an adventure vid.

"Are you sure we aren't walking into some kind of elaborate trap. I mean, shouldn't there be *somebody* else down here besides us, hon?"

"I hope most of their people are searching the tunnels behind us. With any luck, we won't run into guards until we leave the tunnels. If we're really lucky, we can avoid all of the guards—including the ones above ground."

"Here's hoping..."

Our progress slowed, considerably, the closer we got to Psi Corps. We communicated entirely with hand signals, thoroughly checked every intersection before crossing it, and generally acted as paranoid as Jonas would have wanted us to.

We checked every door we came to and ascended every set of stairs to get a signal and open the message drops. Either Foster wasn't checking for messages obsessively or he wasn't in a position to check them discreetly. Michelle dutifully looked for a response from her father, too, despite having no expectation he could possibly send one. So you can imagine her surprise—and her suspicions—when she got a response from Jonas.

"Someone responded to the message I left for Daddy," she said.

"What do you mean by 'someone'? Who else could possibly know those drops that the two of you set up? Hell, you won't even tell them to me and I'm your husband."

"You've got your own message drops with Daddy, so stop whining."

"I wasn't whining, Michelle, I was simply using logic to show that no one but the two of you could possibly know about that message drop."

"Says the techie who has broken into more systems than I can count."

"Okay, hon, I'll concede that point. And it's not like Psi Corps won't have access to extremely pretty talented slicers if they really want them. So what are you going to do?"

Michelle bit her lip while considering my question. Finally, she said, "I'm going to ask him a question only he will know the answer to."

Michelle busied herself keying a response and then headed for the stairs. "Okay, let's go."

Hurrying after her, I said, "What question did you ask?"

"I'm not going to tell you. There's always the chance these stairs are bugged and I'm not giving the answer to whoever is listening."

I let the matter drop. It's impossible to reason with Michelle when she's in bodyguard mode. We slipped back into the tunnels and continued towards Psi Corps headquarters. Ten minutes later, we ascended another set of stairs and Michelle checked her messages again. As before, Foster had not responded. Her father—or whoever was pretending to be her father—had.

"Well?" I asked as soon as Michelle read the response.

"He knew the answer! It's *got* to be Daddy. He's here. In Cairo! And he brought the whole team!" Michelle looked up from her pad and met my eyes. "He wants us to come to the local GenCo offices so he can get us out of here."

"We can't just leave Foster hanging," I said.

"No, we can't."

"Even if we didn't owe him for getting us out of the memorial, he knows several of Psi Corps' deep and very dark secrets. We need to get him and his family to safety so he can tell the galaxy his story. We're never going to get a better chance than this. And Foster will never trust us again if we abandon him."

"I know, babe," Michelle said. "I'll tell Daddy to prepare to take Foster's wife and daughter to safety. Then we go get Foster and the precog he'd like to adopt."

I didn't have to ask Michelle if she was sure she wanted to do it that way. She never once bit her lip during the discussion.

Michelle's simple statement made it sound so easy. She would just explain the situation to Jonas, pass along her instructions for him, and we'd be on our way. Of course, it didn't work that way. Fathers—even ones who trained their only daughter as a body-guard—tend to be protective when it comes to their little girls.

Jonas must have been sitting on the message drop as his replies to Michelle's messages flew fast and furious. They showed up before Michelle could close the application on her pad. He demanded details we didn't have for plans we hadn't made to break into and out of a building we hadn't seen. He countered all of Michelle's ideas with ideas of his own—ideas which put him in the line of fire, and us out of it.

Michelle quickly grew frustrated. "God, Matt, I wish I'd ignored your suggestion to leave a message for Daddy. He's driving me up the wall."

"Are his suggestions any good?"

Michelle sighed, "Yes, of course, they are. This is Daddy we're talking about, after all. But a lot of them involve us sitting around and waiting for him and his team to get in here and help."

"Is that such a bad idea, hon? You know he'll come in heavily armed and well-prepared," I said. "I love you with every fiber of my being, Michelle, but you know Jonas is better at this sort of stuff than you are."

"But he's not on the scene and Foster doesn't know him from Adam. Foster is willing to trust us to rescue him and his future adopted daughter—what was her name?"

"Evie."

"Yeah, Evie. Anyway, he'll trust us but I don't think he'll trust Daddy. And this late in the game, I'm not willing to risk it." Michelle's pad buzzed as yet another message from her father showed up. "Geez, he just won't give up."

"Have you tried to compromise?"

"Um, not exactly."

"Hon, we're going into the great unknown here. Perhaps, you should tell your father everything we know—including a bit about those stories of Psi Corps' depredations that we hope Foster will tell to the press—and let him come in behind us. If we get trapped or caught, maybe he can do something to help. If nothing else, he can try to get out with Foster and Evie."

"You know Daddy's not just going to leave us in Psi Corps' clutches," Michelle said with a shrug, "but he'll also assign a team to make sure Foster and Evie get away safely."

For the next twenty minutes, Michelle sent everything we knew to her father. I was surprised it took her that long. Maybe we knew more than we thought we did. In the end, father and daughter came to an arrangement neither one of them particularly liked but that both of them could accept. With that contentious bit of negotiation out of the way, Michelle and I returned to the tunnels and continued on our way toward Psi Corps' headquarters.

"While you and Jonas were having your little... discussion... I dug up what is publicly available about Psi Corps' headquarters. The office opens to the public at nine, which leaves us about six and a half hours before the place is crawling with employees and whoever else goes to Psi Corps but isn't an employee."

"Did you find an office directory, babe?"

"Yep, and I actually paid attention to what it said. Specifically, all of the publicly accessible offices occupy the six floors that are above ground."

"So you think all of the psychics assigned to headquarters are in underground rooms?"

"It makes sense," I said. "Why wouldn't Psi Corps keep their most valuable assets underground where they are easier to both control and protect?"

"What do you think the chances are we can get into those underground rooms from these tunnels?" Michelle asked.

"Somewhere between 'no chance in hell' and zero."

"Yeah, that's about what I figured."

While we talked and walked, we checked every door we came to looking for stairs going up. We found another staircase behind the fifth door we'd passed since returning to the tunnels. We ascended until our pads got a signal. Michelle immediately checked her message drops.

"Oh, thank God," she said. "We've got a message from Foster!"

"What does his message say?" I asked.

"Hang on," Michelle muttered before typing a brief reply. Then she looked up and said, "He wants us to stay here until he responds."

I cast a nervous glance up and down the stairs. "Why?"

"Probably so we can plan our next moves as quickly as possible."

"You don't think it's so he can send Psi Corps security to pick us up?"

Michelle shrugged, "I don't think so. Why go to all that trouble when he could have had us last night in the basement of that building? Foster knew exactly where we were before coming down the stairs. If he just wanted to capture us, that was the perfect time. I can think of half-a-dozen ways he could have taken us without putting anyone at risk."

With all the training her father gave me, I could, too. "If you're satisfied, that's enough for me."

"Satisfied? Not a chance, but without directions from Foster we're searching for a needle in a haystack."

"You know, I heard the expression hundreds of us times but, until we moved to Ark's Landing, I had never even seen a needle. Or a haystack, for that matter." Michelle gave me an incredulous, what-are-you-talking-about look. Shrugging, I said, "Sometimes, my mind coughs up strange thoughts during moments of stress."

"I love my psycho husband. I love my psycho husband," Michelle murmured, almost as though she was reciting a prayer.

"I think you mean psychic, hon."

Michelle arched an eyebrow and gave me a haughty look. "If I *meant* psychic, I'd have *said* psychic."

"Wow, Michelle, were you channeling your inner Jayna with that look?"

"Of course not, babe. My comment was far too clever to come from an vacuum-head like Jayna."

I shook my head in mock sorrow. "I hate to tell you, Michelle, but the comment wasn't all that clever."

Michelle flashed a vicious smile. "And yet it's *still* too clever for the likes of the school bitch."

"You might want to save that Jayna-induced aggression for Psi Corps, hon." I matched Michelle's grin. "Also, remind me to include this scene when I write my autobiography."

Michelle's pad buzzed gently.

"It's Foster. I'm going to concentrate on my message exchange with him," Michelle said. "I'll fill you in when I'm done."

"Gotcha."

While I waited for her to finalize plans with Foster, I pulled up all of the publicly available maps of the area and studied the layout. We were at a disadvantage because Psi Corps knew the grounds and we didn't. I didn't have time to level the playing field in that respect, but I could reduce the disparity until we rendezvoused with Foster. Once we had him, I hoped that situation would even out fast.

It took Foster and Michelle fifteen minutes to finalize their plans. By then, I had memorized the grounds of the Cairo Catastrophe Memorial and knew where to find doors into most of the buildings.

"I've got a message from Daddy. Let me answer his questions and then we'll be ready to roll," Michelle said when I looked up. She peered at my pad. "Good idea studying the layout, babe. Find Hardin Hall, figure out the safest route there, and see if you can find a little courtyard surrounded by bushes."

I did as instructed while Michelle typed quickly on her pad. By the time she turned her attention back to me, I knew where to go and how to get there.

"Is this a good place to leave the tunnels, Matt?"

"As good as any. Are you getting tired of being underground?"

Michelle led the way upstairs. "Yeah, and Foster says we'll run into guards if we stay down there much longer."

At the top of the stairs, Michelle pulled the thermal dampening cloth out of her backpack. We slid arms around each other and wrapped the cloth around us. Our heads weren't covered, but any guard checking an infrared scan would see a couple of small heat sources, something he could dismiss as small animals, rather than two people. After a quick kiss for luck, we slipped through a door and into the Memorial's grounds.

We took a roundabout path to Hardin Hall, sticking to shadows as much as possible and hurrying across open ground when we had to cross it. If anyone did see us on an IR scan, I realized our behavior would actually reinforce the idea that we were a couple of animals. In the end, either no one checked the scanners or they got the impression we wanted. Half an hour after leaving the stairs, we crawled under a row of bushes and into the small courtyard next to Hardin Hall.

I started toward the only door joining Hardin with the courtyard but Michelle caught my arm. With a shake of her head, she pointed toward a dark corner where the building and bushes met. We settled in and covered ourselves with the thermal dampening cloth.

Michelle placed her lips against my ear and breathed, "Foster will come get us as soon as possible. We just wait here until then."

While I'm always happy to cuddle with my wife, the waiting was nerve wracking. I was very relieved when I heard the door open after only ten minutes. We both held still, waiting for Foster to announce himself. It was a good thing we did because the first voice belonged to a woman.

"See? I told you this place was perfect."

"You're sure no one will notice we're gone?" a man asked.

"Definitely," the woman purred. "I've been walking rounds in this place for years and no one ever checked up on me."

"And no one else knows about this place, Shiela?"

"I wouldn't go that far, Barry, but no one ever comes here at three-thirty in the morning. Relax, baby, we can do it two or three times and no one will ever know." Shiela suddenly giggled, "I'm getting paid while getting laid!"

Barry's voice lost its nervousness. "Mmmm. I guess that makes you a prostitute."

"And you must be a gigolo!" Shiela's tone of voice went sultry, "Looking for a good time, spacer? Come on over to my dark corner and prepare to be amazed."

We heard footsteps in the grass. The horny couple was going to be amazed, all right, because they were headed right for Michelle and me.

As the footsteps drew nearer, I felt Michelle tense for action. We could probably take the two guards—especially since they had no idea we were here—but could we do it before one of them shouted for help or raised some alarm? If either of them did that, we were screwed.

Praying Psi Corps couldn't afford to hire psychic nulls for menial guard positions and that their watch-psychics were concentrating their attention well beyond the walls of the Cairo Catastrophe Memorial, I gently broadcast disinterest to the amorous pair of guards. I couldn't deter them from doing the deed nor did I want to. Okay, I really didn't want to listen to them go at it two or three times, but as long as they did it somewhere besides our corner I would be satisfied.

"Why are we going into this dark corner?" the guard called Barry asked.

"I...don't know," Shiela responded.

"We guys are big on visualizing and..." Barry chuckled, "...I'll see you better if we stay out in the light."

Shiela giggled. "Well aren't you the smooth one? Okay, honey, let's do it in the light."

The footsteps started again, this time heading away from us. A few seconds later, we heard the unmistakable sounds of clothes being removed. Michelle and I didn't relax until nervous chatter and laughter turned to gasps and moans.

Michelle placed her lips against my ear and breathed, "Don't get any ideas from listening to them."

"Don't worry, hon, listening to those two does not exactly put me in the mood."

"Good. Did you have anything to do with their decision not to use this corner?"

"Yeah."

Michelle kissed my cheek. "Good job, babe."

After that, we just sat there listening to the other couple and hoping they'd be quick about it and leave. We had no such luck. After the first time, they talked for a little bit and then went at it again. Then they talked for a little bit and... Well, you get the idea. By the time the couple began putting on their clothes, we knew way more about them than we wanted to know. Finally, after nearly an hour, the couple left the courtyard, still giggling and chatting.

"I need a shower after listening to all of that," Michelle said with a shudder. "I hope we don't sound that insipid when we're making love."

"We probably do, just like most couples in the galaxy. Please tell me you're not going to worry about that, next time."

Michelle leaned into me. "I won't, as long as you do your part and keep me distracted."

"I'll do my best, hon."

"You'd better," Michelle growled softly. "Now, do you want to try to take a nap while we wait for Foster?"

"I'm too keyed up to sleep. How about you?"

"Same here."

We huddled together under the thermal dampening cloth for nearly another hour before we heard the door into the courtyard open again. Michelle raised her blaster and checked the setting. Reminded by her example, I did the same. Both guns were set to stun.

Someone stepped onto the grass and the door clicked shut behind them. "Matt? Michelle? It's me, Harry Foster."

Michelle carefully peeked out from under the cloth to verify the man's identity. "It's him."

She threw off the cloth and stood, her blaster leveled on the other man. "I assume you're alone?"

Foster held his hands out, showing he was unarmed. "Yes. You can put the gun away, Michelle. If I wanted to capture you, I could have done it last night, when you were trapped in that basement, or I could have shown up here with a team of guards. I understand you want to be cautious, but it's much too late to decide you don't trust me."

"Yeah, but old habits die hard. What now?"

"Now, we get badges for the two of you and a change of clothes. Then, we'll see if we can get past the guards and into Evie's room."

We followed Foster into the building, through an obviously unused room, and out into a hallway. Foster didn't stop and listen at the door before stepping through it, which surprised Michelle.

In a stage whisper, she asked, "Shouldn't you be a little more careful? What if there had been a guard out here?"

"There's nothing important in this building," Foster said. "Guards never come here."

"Tell that to the pair of guards who had a tryst in the courtyard an hour ago," Michelle said.

Foster stopped so suddenly Michelle actually ran into him. He spun about and looked at us with wide eyes. "Oh my God! What did you do with them?"

"We did our best to ignore them," Michelle said.

"You didn't kill them?"

"Why does everyone assume we're a pair of bloodthirsty murderers?" Michelle asked. "Of course we didn't kill them. Why would we do that? They screwed—several times—and then they left. Matt made sure they stayed away from our corner."

Foster's eyebrows rose. "How did he do that?"

"Why don't we discuss that while we walk?" Michelle asked, waving for Foster to get moving again. "You're sure there aren't any guards in this building?"

"Less sure than I was a minute ago, but unless there's another pair of guards making a rendezvous in that courtyard we should be safe."

"Great. 'Should be safe' are not words to inspire confidence in me. But we're on your territory, so I guess I don't have any choice but to trust your knowledge." Michelle waggled a finger in my direction. "Matt, tell him how you dissuaded those guards from using our corner."

Foster was fascinated by my description of this facet of my ability. He began digging for details as soon as I finished telling him about it.

Michelle rolled her eyes. "Amateurs. There will be plenty of time to talk about this, after we're safe. Right now, let's concentrate on getting Evie and getting out."

"Right. You're right," Foster said. "Sorry, it's just...I've never heard of anything like that before."

"Yeah, we get a lot of that where Matt's concerned," Michelle said.

"But you love me, anyway, hon," I said.

"I wouldn't be here if I didn't, babe." Michelle turned back to Foster, "So, exactly what is your plan?"

"We're going to get a pair of maintenance coveralls for each of you and I'm going to take a couple of badges for you. We'll pick ones with pictures that look as much like you as possible. As long as the guards don't look too closely or decide to scan the badges, we can get inside the precog dormitory."

"Why would you leave Evie to get maintenance people? Don't they come around on their own?"

"They do, but the precogs can be very high-strung. The littlest things, even imagined things, can throw them off. It's not uncommon for a precog to complain about a smell that's keeping them from dreaming properly. I had Evie complaining loudly about that just before I left to find you."

Michelle nodded. "Not bad. How much cleaning equipment do these people usually bring with them?"

"A scrubber drone. A sweeper drone. Air fresheners. Standard stuff."

"I suppose she has a trash disintegrator in her room?" Michelle asked.

"No, she doesn't. Precogs like to doodle and Psi Corps likes to examine their doodles. They've learned of some very interesting predictions just by examining trash from a precog's room."

"Perfect!" Michelle said. "Just tell me the guards at the door are not psychic nulls, and I think I know how we can get Evie out of there."

BREAKING OUT

F oster shrugged at Michelle, "No, the guards for the precog dormitory aren't psychic nulls. We nulls are pretty rare, so Psi Corps doesn't waste us guarding psychics who can't affect a person's mind. They only assigned me to a precog because of my daughter. Why does this matter?"

"Are you seriously asking that, Foster?" Michelle asked. "Matt just finished telling you how he can turn attention away from himself by broadcasting indifference."

"You know I can't make both of us effectively invisible, hon," I said. "I failed every time we tried that."

"You don't need to go to that extreme, babe. As long as you can make the guards feel apathetic, they'll probably just wave us through without scanning our badges. Then you do the same thing when we leave."

"Oh, I get it!" Foster said. "Say, that's pretty clever."

"No offense, Foster, but you'd make a lousy spy," Michelle said.

"No offense taken. Why do you think I went to so much trouble to get in touch with you two?"

"It's clever, hon, but how will this help us get Evie out? There's no way I can make the guards so apathetic they'll just let one of their psychics wander out the door."

"That's why I asked about the trash, babe. We just get a trash container big enough for Evie to get into, and then cover her in a layer of trash. As long as you keep the guards from digging through the trash, we should be fine."

A thought crossed my mind. "It might be easier for me to just reach inside the guards and pull out any curiosity they're feeling."

"You can remove emotions as well as broadcast them?" Foster asked.

"Uh, yeah."

"Wow, you really hit the empathic jackpot. No wonder Psi Corps wants you so badly. I'd love to study you, myself!"

"I'd appreciate it if you wouldn't sound quite so enthusiastic about imprisoning my husband and using him as a test subject for the rest of his life," Michelle snapped. "Do you talk this way around Evie?"

"No, of course not. It was a thoughtless comment and I apologize," Foster muttered. "I guess I'm more nervous than I realized or I wouldn't be saying stupid things like that."

"I understand," I said, "but you've got to put aside your nerves or you might blow the whole operation by saying the wrong thing at the wrong time. I wish I could just block those feelings for you, but-"

"I'm a psychic null." Foster took a deep breath and released it slowly. "I'll try to be more careful from now on. And mentioning being careful, we've got to go out into the main courtyard to reach the dormitory building. Just stick by me and act like you belong here."

"That ought to be easy enough," Michelle said. "We've had so many people tell us this is exactly where we belong that I practically feel like we're part of the Psi Corps family."

On that wry note, we followed Foster out of the building. It was still way too early for many Psi Corps employees to be out and about, but we did see a few of them from a distance. No one showed any more curiosity about us than we showed about them.

In less than five minutes, Foster took us down a short flight of stairs and through a basement door.

"This is the entrance used by the cleaning crews," Foster said. "Their lockers and equipment aren't far, now."

"Will anyone be down here at this time?" Michelle asked.

"They shouldn't be, but maybe I should go in first, just in case."

Michelle and I slipped into a dark room and waited while Foster scouted ahead. Several minutes later, he returned with a cleaning cart floating behind him. He led it into our room and pulled a couple of coveralls from the trash bag.

"Someone was moving around in the front room, so I just grabbed what I thought we'd need," he said in a low voice. "I guessed at your sizes, but coveralls never fit well, anyway. No one will give it a second thought."

We pulled the clothing on and, as expected, the fit was baggy. The legs for Michelle's coveralls brushed the floor, so I knelt and rolled them up a few centimeters. Then Foster handed us the badges.

"The cart is keyed to your badge, Matt. It will stay about a meter behind you."

"Got it," I said as I clipped the badge to a front pocket.

Michelle checked her badge and frowned. "This woman doesn't look a thing like me. She's got brown eyes and brunette hair, for God's sake!"

"Sorry, but that was the only badge with a young woman's picture," Foster said. "Besides, if anyone looks that closely at you, we're probably screwed anyway."

"That's a good point." Michelle put her blaster into one of the coverall's voluminous pockets, made sure I did the same, and then put the extremely expensive backpack in the trash bag. "Okay, let's get this over with."

We passed a few people on our way to the nearest elevator. None of them did more than glance at us and give the universal nod of acknowledgment. No one looked at our badges or questioned why we were following Foster.

To our dismay, someone was in the elevator when it reached the basement. Michelle and I ignored the man and moved to the back corner. The man barely noticed us but he spoke to Foster.

"You going down to the dorm, Harry?"

"I am." After the other man punched a button, Foster added, "Thanks, Pete."

"No problem." He jerked a thumb at Michelle and me. "Is Evie having an OCD night?"

"Yes," Foster sighed. "Bad enough that I went in search of a crew rather than just wait for one to work us into their schedule."

"Better you than me, mate."

"Your sympathy is touching."

Pete laughed as the elevator stopped. He gave a half-wave as he exited. "See you later."

Once the doors closed, Foster slumped against the wall. "Nicely done, Matt."

"All I did was keep a low-level emotional scan going on Pete. He wasn't even a little curious about us, so I left him alone."

The elevator stopped on our floor and, as before, Michelle and I followed Foster into a short hallway. It ended at the guard station. A couple of bored-looking women watched us as we approached. I didn't feel any curiosity stirring, but this time, I wasn't taking any chances. I directed my empathic ability at them and broadcast a continuous stream of low-level apathy.

The guards' eyes were dull and about as uncurious as we could hope for. Since we were with someone they recognized, I was confident we could just breeze past them. Apparently, Foster was less certain.

"It took me longer than I thought it would to find a cleaning crew," he said, his voice tight with nerves. Foster gave a nervous laugh. "You know how it is—there's never a crew around when you need one."

To my dismay, the guards' eyes focused on Foster. Dammit, the man was going to blow all of our careful planning by acting completely out of character! Michelle knew it, too.

"Sorry, sir," she said in a matter-of-fact tone of voice. "We've got a lot to do today and really need to get back to doing it. So, if you could take us to your precog's room...?"

At the same time, I increased the power I was using on the guards.

Foster took Michelle's hint. Nodding over his shoulder at her, he walked past the guard station and opened the door. At the same time, the guards' eyes lost their focus and they settled back in their seats.

After the door shut behind us, Michelle whispered, "You almost blew it back there, Foster! Just act naturally and don't speak unless you have to."

"I'm sorry," Foster mumbled. "I've never been this nervous before."

"If you want to get out of here, you have to find a way to control yourself."

"I'll do my best."

We went through another door and suddenly there were lots of people wandering around. Of course, they all knew Foster and didn't care to know us.

"It's about time you got back," one woman snapped. "Evie won't shut up about whatever it is she thinks she can smell."

"Sorry about that, Barb. I got back as soon as I could. I'll get her quiet as fast as possible."

"You'd better. She's already woken up three other precogs, including Doug, and you know he won't go back to sleep as long as Evie is unhappy."

Foster turned left down another hallway while Barb kept going straight. He gave her a reassuring wave before turning away from the woman.

"Barb is such a pain in the ass," he said. "Her Doug does this sort of thing at least once a week and I don't complain. But let Evie do it once a month and Barb still gets all pissy."

Foster stopped at a door and knocked lightly.

"Evie? I've got the cleaning crew."

He opened the door and we followed him into Evie's dorm room.

Evie, dark-skinned and with a shy smile, sat on the bed. She was dressed like a typical teenage girl and had her feet drawn up and her arms wrapped around her legs. The girl's chin rested on one knee as her eyes darted back and forth between Michelle and me.

Her room wasn't more than four meters by four meters and it reminded me of Cassie's room back on Piscain Station. Hand-drawn artwork dotted the walls. It hung above the bed, chairs, a desk, and a dresser. Unlike the artwork in Cassie's room, Evie's drawings were of Foster, a woman I assumed was his wife, and a girl who had to be their daughter. Sometimes Evie included herself, though not often and never when the image's setting was outdoors.

As the door slid shut, Michelle said, "What's this about a bad smell?"

Evie's eyebrows drew down in confusion and she said in a stage whisper, "We just made that up. Didn't Dad tell you?"

Dad? Obviously, both Foster and Evie thought of each other as family even without official adoption papers. It reminded me of Zav and the four psychics he raised for so many years and gave me a twinge of homesickness.

"Yes, Evie. I said that for the benefit if anyone who might be passing by in the hallway."

"Oh! That was a good idea, Michelle."

"Thank you." Michelle pulled out some cleaning drones and turned them on. "I'm doing this so it sounds like we're cleaning up in here. It will also help cover the sounds of us hiding you in the trash bag."

"What?" Evie's eyes darted nervously to Foster.

"Don't worry, Evie," I said. "It's Michelle's idea to have you in the trash bag. We'll put some paper trash in there to hide you and then just take you right past the guards. They'll never even know you're in there."

Evie eyed the trash bag nervously. She'd fit in it, but it would be tight. If she suffered from claustrophobia...

I sat down on the bed next to her. "Are you scared of enclosed spaces?"

"No, that would be silly," Evie protested. "I...just don't like them very much... Okay, I don't like them at all. But that doesn't mean they scare me."

"I know what you mean. I don't like heights, only they really do scare me. They scare me so much I almost got Michelle and me caught by space pirates rather than step across a big, deep open space. It wasn't more than a meter wide, but it terrified me."

"What happened?" the girl asked.

"Michelle helped me get past my fear—just like I'm going to help you with yours."

"How are you going to do that?"

Michelle sat down on the other side of Evie. "Matt is going to just take your fear away."

The girl's eyes opened wide. "He can do that?"

Michelle nodded. "He did it for me once when we were both outside of our ship in space. That's what I'm really afraid of. Anyway, one second I was scared half to death and the next, poof, the fear was gone."

Evie's eyes turned back to me. "Show me."

"Evie, this isn't the time-" Foster began.

"It's fine," I said. "I'm going to have to do this soon, anyway."

At the moment, Evie was just very nervous. I felt that most of it had to do with the danger and excitement of our planned escape, but her claustrophobia was mixed in with the rest. I psychically reached inside the girl, enveloped those emotions, and gently pulled them out of her. I stuffed the emotions into a corner of my mind and walled them off.

Evie's mouth fell open in surprise before quickly forming a bright smile. "Wow! That is amazing."

"Yeah, that's my husband," Michelle said as she stood. "Now, let's get you into the trash bag. Foster, can you help me lower her into it? Matt, can you start gathering the drawings off the walls? We can use them to cover her."

Five minutes later, Evie was curled up inside the trash bag and covered in all of her drawings and everything else in the room that she'd written or doodled on. Michelle and I gathered up the cleaning drones and packed them back on the cleaning cart. At the same time, Foster stuffed clothes and pillows under the bed covers, making it look as if Evie was in the bed.

Michelle gave the room a quick sweep. "Okay, is everyone ready to go?"

I nodded and Evie gave a muffled acknowledgment. Foster shook his head.

"I've got to stay here—at least for a few minutes. It will look odd if I go with the cleaning crew when everyone expects me to be in here getting Evie to go to sleep."

Fear stabbed through Evie when she heard that. I understood her reaction but knew she had to stay calm. Once again, I reached inside of the girl and pulled roiling emotions out of her.

"How long until you can follow us?" I asked.

"Not long—ten to fifteen minutes. You two can just take Evie back to the stairs you used to come up from the tunnels and I'll meet you there as soon as possible."

Michelle was already busy composing a message to Jonas before Foster stopped speaking. "I'm telling Daddy where to meet us and to go ahead and get your wife and daughter."

"Thank you." Glancing at the trash bag, Foster lowered his voice and added, "If anything happens to me-"

"We'll take care of all three of them," Michelle said, her voice also pitched low.

Foster gave a brief nod. He opened the door for us and, in a raised voice, said, "That's got it. Sorry I had to pull you away from your other work."

"It's all part of the job, sir," I said.

"Turn off the light on your way out, please."

Michelle nodded and hit the light switch. The room darkened

behind us as Foster shut the door. We headed back the way we came, only attracting the attention of Barb.

She strode past us on her way to the room across from Evie's and, just loud enough to ensure we heard her, muttered, "It's about time."

We didn't acknowledge her comment, and she didn't expect us to. The rest of the brief trip to the elevator passed without incident. I broadcast apathy at the two guards when we left the dormitory, and kept broadcasting while we waited for the elevator.

Fortunately, we didn't have long to wait. Unfortunately, the elevator wasn't empty. We heard two men speaking before the door opened. Michelle and I exchanged worried glances when we both recognized one of the voices. It belonged to John Thomas, the former director of the Piscain Station Psi Corps office—a man who would easily recognize both of us.

Michelle moved to the right side of the hallway, lounged against the wall, and put her hand into the pocket holding her blaster. With the cart following me, I went to the opposite wall and did the same thing. We both tugged the bills of our caps lower and studied the floor.

The elevator stopped and the door slid open. Thomas and a second man we didn't recognize strode from the elevator. They conversed in low tones and only gave us a quick glance as they headed for the precog dormitory. I knew Thomas was a psychic null but ran a quick scan on his companion. I wasn't surprised that I couldn't read him, either.

As soon as the two men were clear of the elevator doors, Michelle and I pushed off from the walls and entered the elevator. Neither of us took our eyes off Thomas's back as we watched for any kind of reaction. We didn't see anything out of the ordinary and, with great relief, I punched the button for the basement.

Nothing happened. The doors remained open. The button I selected didn't light up.

Looking back down the hall, the two guards were no longer relaxing in their seats. One of them concentrated intently on a control panel while the other stared at us. Former director John and his companion were not quite running, but they were walking very fast away from us.

"Well, damn," Michelle said as she pulled out her blaster.

"Yeah, it seems like we can't catch a break this time around," I said as I drew my own blaster.

"They're armed!" the guard watching us shouted as she reached for her own gun.

At the guard's shout, the two men began running. At the same time, the guard working with the control panel jumped to her feet and grabbed for her gun.

My eyes flicked to the power setting as I brought my gun up to fire. I already knew it was set to stun, but Jonas trained me to always check before shooting a firearm. He also trained Michelle and me how to select targets. I was to Michelle's right, so I aimed for the guard on the right. I knew she would fire at the guard on the left for the same reason.

Our first shots missed and we flattened ourselves against the side walls of the elevator. With my free hand, I pulled the cart against the wall so Evie would also be out of the line of fire. The girl's fear spiked as blaster bolts splashed against the back wall of the elevator. I wanted to remove her fear, but couldn't spare the concentration necessary to do that.

The two men crashed through the doors into the dormitory and shouted for help. At the same time, the two guards ducked behind the low wall of their cubicle, giving them much better cover than we had. At least, Michelle and I were better shots, so the guards had no time to aim properly. Of course, we couldn't hit the guards, either.

"Can you put the fear of God into those women?" Michelle asked.

"I guess the time for subtlety has passed," I said. "I'm on it."

With gunfire just outside the dormitory and two Psi Corps officials shouting for help inside the dormitory, there were plenty of emotions for me to draw upon. Fear was prevalent, but there was also lots of alarm and concern. There was a surprising amount of elation, too. Apparently, Foster wasn't the only one no longer enamored with Psi Corps. Ignoring the elation for the moment, I absorbed all of the fear and other negative emotions. Then, I blasted it all back at the two guards hiding behind their cubicle wall. Screaming in abject terror, the guards collapsed to the floor.

"Stay with Evie," Michelle said as she ran toward the guard station. "And call Foster and tell him to get his ass out here."

Grabbing my pad, I entered Foster's code. I watched Michelle hurdle the low cubicle wall and stun the two guards at close range. She bent over the control panel and was studying it when Foster answered.

"What the hell is going on out there?"

"Some bad luck. Someone who knew us came out of the elevator and obviously recognized us," I said. "You need to get out here, now."

"I'm expected to stay with my precog. If I'm out in the hallway, anyone who sees me will know something is up."

"Everyone already knows something is up, Foster. So get moving. Run, do not walk."

"Oh, yeah. I guess that's true. Okay, I'm on my way."

"One more thing—identify yourself as you come through the doors, otherwise Michelle might shoot you."

"Uh...right," he said before signing off.

"He's on his way," I called to Michelle.

"Good. Um, do you mind switching places with me? I can't figure out these controls. Besides, I need to call Daddy."

Leaving my badge with the cart, which was programmed to follow it, I sprinted down the hall toward the guard station while Michelle ran back to the elevator. She was already keying her father's code as we passed each other. Michelle took up a firing position inside the elevator as I vaulted into the guard station.

Jonas must have answered his call, because the next thing my wife said was, "Hi Daddy, things aren't going as smoothly on our end as we hoped."

I tuned out Michelle's conversation with her father and concentrated on the control panel. The thing was ancient—probably older than me—and not very intuitive. I tapped through several menus without finding the controls to the elevator. Then, I noticed an icon for voice control.

I tapped the icon and said, "Cancel elevator override."

The message 'VERIFY CANCEL OVERRIDE' displayed on the screen.

"Verified. Cancel override," I said.

The doors to the dormitory burst open accompanied by the shout, "It's me! Foster! Don't shoot!"

Seeing me at the guard station, Foster stopped and asked, "What are you doing in there?"

"Don't worry about him," Michelle called. "Just get down here!"

Foster didn't argue or even waste time responding, he just ran for the elevator. Meanwhile, the control panel displayed another message—'PASSWORD?'.

Crap. There was no way I could guess a password or slice the controls fast enough to ensure our getaway. Then I remembered something I learned from the guy who taught me how to slice systems. Most people—even guards—do not take network security seriously. They write down their password and keep it nearby in case they forget it.

I pulled open the drawers and looked for something with a single word scrawled on it. Nothing. I ran my hand along the top and the back of each drawer. Again, nothing.

"Daddy says we need to go to the roof for pickup, Matt," Michelle said. She paused for a few seconds and then added, "Preferably today, babe."

"Cute, hon," I said. "I'm doing my best."

I grabbed the screen and looked behind it. Still nothing. Had I stumbled across the one pair of security conscious guards in the entire Terran Federation government? At that thought, my eyes involuntarily flicked to the unconscious guards on the floor.

One of the guards' badges had flipped over when they

collapsed. Something was scrawled on the back of the badge. I snatched it and quickly read what was written on it.

"This job sucks."

The message 'PASSWORD ACCEPTED. OVERRIDE CANCELED' displayed.

Stepping back from the control panel, I flipped my blaster to full power and fired three quick shots into it. Switching the gun back to stun, I hopped over the cubicle wall.

"We're all clear, hon," I said and sprinted for the elevator.

I'd covered half the distance when I heard the dormitory doors open again. Trusting Michelle to cover me, I hugged the right wall and kept running. But, instead of the expected sound of blaster fire, I heard a woman's voice.

"Foster? What are you doing?"

"Take Doug and go back to his room, Barb," Foster said. "This doesn't concern you."

"You're escaping, aren't you?"

Foster gave a pained look down the hall. "If you call for help, Barb, this woman will stun you both."

"I won't call for help," she said. "Foster...Harry, please take us with you!"

Foster's eyes widened in surprise at Barb's request. His mouth opened and closed a couple of times as if it was anticipating words his brain wasn't sending. Papers tumbled out of the trash bag as Evie rose, eyes bright with trepidation, excitement, and curiosity. Michelle's worried eyes flicked back and forth between Foster and Barb before settling on me.

"We don't have time for a discussion," she said. "It's your call, babe. Make sure it's the right one."

I knew that was Michelle's way of suggesting I perform a scan on Barb and Doug—and I was way ahead of her. Doug, a boy just entering puberty, was easy. His mind was a jumble of emotions— fear directed behind him, hope directed ahead of him, and a strong desire to go with Evie—but it held no deception. Barb's mind was also a jumble of emotions and they were far more complex than

Doug's simple ones. Anticipation battled with fear battled with deception battled with desire directed toward...me?

While I puzzled on that, Michelle said, "Now would be a good time to make up your mind, Matt."

"Right, hon. Of course, they can come. We don't leave behind any *psychic* who wants out."

Michelle's eyes narrowed when I stressed the word 'psychic' and she gave an almost imperceptible nod. Then she waved her hand at Barb and Doug, "Come on!"

Doug burst into a run but Barb took measured, if quick, steps. When the boy dashed past me, I looked at Barb and said, "The elevator leaves when I get to it."

Annoyance briefly overwhelmed Barb's other emotions as I turned and jogged after Doug. I heard her pace quicken and then turn into a run. When she reached me, Barb's annoyance faded as quickly as it arose. Nervous anticipation rose in its place.

I glanced at the woman, a false smile on my lips, and let my eyes roam over her as if I was checking her out. Barb was attractive enough that I knew she must get her share of lascivious looks from interested men. The knowing smile she gave me as my gaze traveled down the length of her body told me I was right.

We were only a couple of meters from the elevator when I noticed that her right jacket pocket hung considerably lower than the left pocket. *That* was why my eyes roamed over Barb, not the sexual attraction the woman assumed. Too late, Barb realized what I was doing. Her hand darted for the pocket but I was way ahead of her.

I spun and swept Barb's feet out from under her. She hit the floor hard and her breath went out with a whoosh. I dropped onto her, my knee in the small of her back, and caught her right hand. Pulling her hand away from the pocket, I reached into it and pulled out a stun grenade.

"Really, Barb?" Michelle said. "Did John give that to you? Didn't he warn you who you were facing?"

I felt confusion and fear take over Barb's mind as she fought to breathe. Rolling her over, I looked into her eyes and said, "He didn't tell you, did he?"

I stood and entered the elevator, leaving Barb gasping on the floor. Her eyes tracked me, though, and Barb's confusion shined in them. She really didn't recognize me. Either Psi Corps kept its people in the dark or else Barb just didn't pay attention to anything going on around her.

Foster solved that little mystery when he said, "Barb has always been self-centered. I doubt she gave the department alerts more than a cursory glance."

"Well, Barb," I said, "let me end the mystery. Your good buddy John sent you—an unshielded, normal person—to catch me, the infamous Matt Connaught. John knows I'd attack unshielded guards on sight. I guess he hoped you could use Doug to distract me long enough for you to set off this grenade and stun all of us."

"Tell John he loses, again. When you wake up, that is," Michelle said. She shot Barb as the elevator doors slid shut. Turning to Doug, who was helping Evie out of the trash bag, she added, "Don't worry, Doug. It's set to stun. She'll be okay."

Doug looked thoughtful for a second and then asked, "Does getting stunned hurt?"

"I'm afraid so."

"Good," Doug and Evie said at the same time.

Michelle's eyebrows rose, as did mine.

"Barb was a bit of a..." Foster began.

"Bitch," Doug said.

"Asshole," Evie said.

The two kids dissolved into a fit of giggles.

"What have I told you about using such language, young lady?" Foster said, trying for a stern tone and failing miserably.

"Sorry, Dad," Evie said through her laughter, "but you know it's true."

Foster shrugged, "I can't argue with you there, kiddo."

The elevator reached the top floor of Hardin Hall. Blasters leveled, Michelle and I scanned the corridor as the door opened.

Finding it clear, we all piled out. At Michelle's suggest, I stuck my maintenance badge on the edge of one of the doors. The cart dutifully hovered right next to it. When the elevator doors began closing, they bumped into the cart and sprang open again. The trick wouldn't stop the guards from pursuing us, but it might slow them down a bit.

"Do you have any idea where we can find stairs to the roof?" Michelle asked Foster.

"I think they're just part of the regular staircase," he said, pointing to a door a few meters down the hall.

Foster was right. From far below, we heard voices and the sounds of many feet pounding up the stairs after us.

"Time to go, kids," Michelle said and charged up toward the roof.

The rest of us followed, with me bringing up the rear. I ran through the door at the top of the stairs and onto the roof. Michelle was out in the open, scanning the sky in all directions and waving her arms. High in the air, lights flashed from just outside of the Memorial grounds, and two aircars zoomed in low over the roofs of nearby buildings.

We heard shouts from nearby buildings, and one of the cars peeled off in that direction, blaster fire spitting from its windows. The second aircar dropped onto the roof, a door flew open, and Jonas leapt out.

"Get in, quick!" he said.

"We've got one more passenger than expected," Michelle said, guiding Evie and Doug into the back seat.

Foster jumped in, followed by me.

"We've got room for him, pumpkin."

First Michelle, and then Jonas, dove into the aircar. It rose from the roof before the last door closed, and roared off into the night sky.

THE MIDNIGHT MIRACLE

The second aircar followed in our wake, all the while spraying covering fire at Psi Corps' guards. In seconds, we were beyond the range of small arms fire.

"Simpson, monitor comm traffic for pursuit orders!" Jonas commanded.

"Already on it, sir," one of the men in the front responded.

"Good," Jonas said. "Guerrero, what's on the scanner?"

"Nothing yet, sir," another man said. "I'll- Wait! I've got six aircars lifting off from the Memorial."

Simpson added, "They're calling on local and federal law enforcement for help stopping us. They report we are heavily armed and have at least one powerful rogue psychic. Psi Corps also wants us taken alive, if possible."

"Sir," Guerrero said, "the scanner has identified eighteen law enforcement vehicles responding to Psi Corps' call...Make that twenty-three, sir."

"Jonas, did you disable the overrides so Cairo air control can't take over the cars?" I asked.

My father-in-law gave me a pained expression. "Really, sir, you shouldn't even have to ask."

"Daddy, you'd have asked Matt the same question, if your positions were reversed."

"We now have thirty-three aircars closing on our position, sir," Guerrero said. "ETA for the first vehicles is twenty-eight seconds."

"Have your driver switch places with me, Jonas," I said. "I've got a lot of experience with-"

"Not this time, sir. If I have to call on your psychic abilities, I want you giving it your full attention."

"He's right, babe." Michelle took my hand in both of hers. "Also, the time for stealth is long passed. You should absorb as much emotion as you possibly can right now. We may not have time for you to...load your mind...later."

I sighed and nodded. "You're right, hon."

To this point in our rescue and escape, I'd only used my empathic power at close range so the psychics inside Psi Corps wouldn't notice me working right under their noses. Now, I needed every emotion I could draw upon if there was any hope of us getting away from all of the aircars coming after us.

"Take us up, Morton," I heard Jonas order the driver. "Maybe we can avoid our pursuers by going over them."

"No, Daddy," Michelle countered, "that takes us farther from Matt's source of emotions. Have Morton go lower."

"That will give Psi Corps and their allies the higher position, pumpkin," Jonas objected. "From there, they can force us down."

"They'll probably do that, anyway, Daddy. There are just too many cars coming after us. Matt's ability is our only real chance of getting away from them."

Foster, his face pale with fear, sighed, "If only you hadn't been recognized, we-"

Michelle said, "Unexpected things happen, Foster. We deal with them as best we can—which is what we're doing now."

"That's my girl," Jonas agreed, the ghost of a smile flitting across his face. "You heard my daughter, Morton, take us lower."

During this exchange, I stretched my mind out and into the city below. I found the whole range of human emotions—love and hate, joy and fear, satisfaction and misery—and I drew them all to me. My mind filled with the feelings from thousands of people and still I absorbed them. Thousands more emotions packed into my brain and my empathic ability somehow stored them so I could draw upon them later.

When I felt I could absorb no more, I remembered what awaited Michelle if we didn't escape. I thought of Foster, his family, and Evie. I thought of Doug, running away with his friend to an unknown future. I thought of Cassie and Rob and not being there for their wedding. I thought of the children Michelle and I would have, if we could only escape from Psi Corps and get home to Ark's Landing. And I made myself absorb more emotions, packing them so tightly I barely kept them in check.

"Sir?" It was Simpson. "Psi Corps just issued a warning that the rogue psychic is preparing for a massive attack."

"Matt's not trying to hide himself anymore," Michelle said. "Their psychics can't have missed the effects he's having on the populace."

Simpson added, "Now, Psi Corps is warning of something they call a category ten psychic incident."

"What the hell does that mean?" Jonas growled.

Foster, his voice quavering, said, "The original Cairo Catastrophe was a category ten."

"God above," Michelle said, "they've given up on capturing us. The Cairo cops will blast us out of the sky rather than risk a repeat of the Catastrophe."

"But Matt won't do something like that," Evie insisted. "I've dreamed about him a few times and I know he's not a monster."

I considered the power I held in my mind and what would happen if I blasted it out with my full strength. Nothing short of that would ensure I incapacitated everyone who was chasing us. But our pursuers were scattered all around us and moving at high speed. I didn't have the skill to target just them. Hell, I didn't know if that kind of pinpoint accuracy was even possible with so many minds to target and all of them in motion. With the power I held pent up in my head, I couldn't do anything but blast the emotions out in all directions—and at all of the people living in Cairo.

I could already feel my own worry for my family and friends working its way through the stored emotions and changing them. My own fear for the people of Cairo combined with the worry and further tainted the positive emotions I'd absorbed. Love turned to hate. Hope faded into despair. Joy soured into fear.

Having seen the Memorial hologram, I didn't have to imagine what these emotions would do to the unprotected minds of the citizens of Cairo. I knew exactly what would happen.

And I knew I couldn't go through with the attack. I couldn't blast away the sanity of thousands, maybe millions, of people. Nothing that might happen to me was worth that kind of horror.

"Land the car and let me out," I said. "I'm going to surrender."

Everyone looked at me except Morton, the driver. He was busy flying the car at high speed through the maze of Cairo streets and somehow managing to stay ahead of the mass of pursuing cars.

"No!" several people cried at once.

Michelle took my head between her hands and turned me to face her.

"What is the matter with you, Matt?" Even in the low light, I saw tears glistening in her eyes. "After all we've been through to be free of Psi Corps, why suddenly give up? You've used your power on lots of people before. Why is it suddenly such a problem, now?"

"Because I've absorbed too many emotions. They're packed so tightly inside my mind, it's all I can do to hold them there." I ran a hand through her soft, blonde hair. "Worse, my fear for you and everyone else in this car is...I don't know exactly how to describe it. My own emotions are...changing...the emotions I absorbed. Emotions like joy and love are turning into misery and hate."

"Fascinating," Foster muttered. "At least one theory concerning the Catastrophe holds-"

"Shut up!" Michelle snapped. "Matt needs our help, not stupid theories."

"I don't think you can help, hon," I said. "And if you don't get far, far away from me, you might end up at ground zero when my mind can't hold those emotions anymore. I've got to turn myself over to Psi Corps while I can still control everything inside my head. They've spent centuries studying psychic powers. If anyone can help me, it's them."

"Can't you just let the emotions leak out slowly?" Michelle asked. "That should be okay, right?"

"It might start out okay," I said, "but I think it will be like a leak in a dike. It will start off small but quickly build into a torrent. Then...it's the Cairo Catastrophe all over again. I'm sorry, hon, but-"

Michelle suddenly swung one leg over me and moved onto my lap. Straddling me, her arms wrapped around my neck, she said, "You say your negative emotions are...curdling...the stored emotions?"

"Yes, and that's-"

"Well, if it works in one direction, I don't see any reason why it won't work in the other."

Pressing her body against me, Michelle kissed me. Her kiss was so unexpected that I didn't respond to it. Michelle pulled her head back just enough so she could speak. When she did, her warm breath blew across my face like the winds of hope.

"Matthew Connaught, you had damned well better return my kiss or you will spend the next month sleeping on the couch!" She shook my head just enough to make sure she had my attention. "Is that clear, babe?"

"Loud and clear," I said.

Michelle's mouth covered mine again and this time I responded. Putting one hand behind her head and the other in the small of her back, I opened my mouth and pulled Michelle to me. Our mouths and tongues hungrily explored each other. I stroked Michelle's hair while my other hand worked under her shirt and gently rubbed the smooth skin of her back.

Michelle's kisses ranged over my face and toward one ear. Her tongue flicked over the ear and, when she whispered, her breath tickled it.

"Read me now."

"But what if I lose control?"

"You won't, babe. Now, read me!"

I scanned Michelle. Her mental shield was down, as I knew it would be. With extreme care, I opened myself to her emotions. It was just a pinhole of an opening, but Michelle's emotions streamed through it.

Love.

Trust.

Joy.

Tenderness.

Desire.

Longing.

Peace.

Wonder.

They all squeezed through the tiny opening I gave to them. Gently, they widened the opening until everything I meant to her poured through in a flood of beautiful emotions. Throwing caution to the wind, I opened myself fully to her mind. My own feelings for Michelle merged with Michelle's feelings for me, something we had only managed before when making love. As one, our feelings surged against the mass of stored emotions roiling inside my head.

Love engulfed hate and erased it.

Trust washed away fear.

Joy burned away misery.

Tenderness soothed anger.

Desire replaced loneliness.

With each passing second, more and more of the roiling emotions calmed and were transformed. Once begun, the change gained momentum and spread inexorably through my mind. I have no idea how long Michelle and I were emotionally joined, but we changed every emotion inside of me.

Somehow finding the power to speak, Michelle said, "Morton, put the car on autopilot."

"But–" Morton began.

"Do it!" Jonas ordered. "Destination, the GenCo offices."

"Autopilot engaged," Morton said, "but we're sitting ducks."

Bringing her lips to my ear again, Michelle whispered, "Let the emotions go, Matt. They can't hurt anyone, now."

With a sense of profound relief, I shoved the mass of emotions from my mind. They blew out of my head in a fraction of a second. I would have collapsed from relief and exhaustion if Michelle hadn't been holding me up.

As I purged the emotions, the others in the car gasped as their minds caught a tiny fraction of what I'd held in check.

Evie smiled and whispered, "I told you Matt wasn't a monster."

Foster said, "I felt that. Just a little bit, but I felt it."

Jonas reached out and hugged Michelle and me. "Thank you for making my baby girl so happy, Matt."

I laughed, "Thank you for making your baby girl, Jonas."

Overwhelmed by the released emotions, our pursuers forgot about little things like flying their cars. Automatic safety systems kicked in, smoothly landing all of them.

Our own car flew itself to the GenCo office building and landed on the roof. We were still a long way from home, but, for the moment, we were safe.

Supported by Michelle, I stumbled into the rooftop elevator. She guided me to one corner and let me lean against the wall as the others filed in.

"Look at them, Matt," she whispered. "It's amazing."

My bleary eyes wouldn't focus properly, leaving me squinting at our fellow passengers. "What's amazing, hon?"

"Can't you see it, babe? They're practically glowing with happiness."

"They are?"

"We are, Mr. Connaught," Evie said as she wrapped her arms around Foster and leaned against him. "I don't know about the others, but I'm happier than I've been since I met Dad and the rest of the family."

Foster hugged the girl and kissed the top of her head. "This is the first time in my life I've found myself wishing I wasn't a null. I guess I'll just have to settle for that tiny taste I got when you did… whatever it was you did."

"See, Matt?" Michelle said. "You did that!"

Pulling Michelle as close as possible, I said, "*We* did that, hon. Without you…I don't even want to think about that."

The elevator door opened. The others stood aside, letting Michelle and me exit first. We hadn't taken three steps into the hallway when a dark blur burst out of a nearby door and barreled into us. A small arm went around each of us and a small head burrowed into our chests.

From the doorway, a woman wearing a guard's uniform said, "I'm sorry, sir. I couldn't stop her."

"I'm glad you couldn't," I said to the guard. "Hello, Raneem."

"I was so afraid you were going to get caught!" she said. "And then I was so happy and I didn't know why except I figured out it had to be you and then I was even happier because the happiness meant you got away."

Michelle laughed and returned Raneem's hug, "Remember to breathe, Raneem. Also, it's really hard to walk like this, and we're blocking the elevator."

"Oh, yeah." Raneem looked around me and into the elevator. "Sorry."

Taking my hand, our young friend began pulling me down the hall. "Are you hungry? They've got all sorts of food here and me and my friends-"

"My friends and me," Michelle corrected before she could stop herself.

Jonas laughed, "Wait until I tell your mother about this. She'll be so proud of you, pumpkin."

"*Anyway*," Raneem continued, "the people here let my friends and me eat all we wanted. They even gave us cake, and the guards even call me 'Miss Raneem,' like I'm someone special."

"You are someone special. You always were," I told her. "But what I really need is a place to get some sleep."

The guard took that as her cue, "Security Chief Young warned us you might be tired, sir. We've had the penthouse suite prepared for you. The, ah, children who accompanied Miss Raneem are in three of the rooms. They're a bit boisterous. Should we move them to other rooms?"

"No, thank you," Michelle responded. "Matt is so tired I doubt he'll even notice. So am I, for that matter."

"I'll take them there," Jonas said to the guard. "You can go on about your normal duties. Alert me to anything out of the ordinary, no matter how slight."

The guard all but saluted, "Yes, Security Chief Young."

"There's no need to be so formal, Miss Jenkins. A simple 'Mr. Young' will suffice," Jonas said.

He led us to an elevator that required a special code to open. A short ride later, Michelle and I found ourselves wading through a gaggle of boys and girls, all about the same age as Raneem. Our young friend finally released her hold on us and led the way through the little crowd.

"Get out of the way, everybody. Matt's tired, and so is Michelle. They're going to bed and we're all going to be really quiet so they can sleep."

The kids parted, and Michelle and I stumbled into the master suite. A huge, incredibly inviting bed filled one corner. Someone shut the door behind us, while Michelle helped me get undressed. I crawled into bed and felt Michelle snuggle up next to me before I fell into a deep sleep.

I surfaced from the depths of sleep slowly. The first thing I noticed was something gentle and warm blowing across my chest. Then I realized a comfortable weight covered half of my body, bringing more warmth with it. At the last, before consciousness fully returned, I felt the sensuous tickle of fine hair falling down around my neck.

My eyes fluttered open, squinting at the light reflecting off Michelle's golden blonde hair. She had one arm under my pillow and the other draped over me. I kissed the top of her head and wrapped both arms around her. She propped her chin on my chest and smiled languidly at me.

"Hi, sleepyhead," she said.

Michelle's voice was more relaxed than I'd heard since before the attack on our anniversary. A quick empathic scan showed the same thing—her shield was down and I couldn't find any trace of anxiety.

"Hi, yourself," I murmured. "From your tone of voice and emotional state, can I assume Psi Corps hasn't got the GenCo building surrounded?"

"Correct. After what happened-"

I pulled Michelle up until her mouth met my lips, and silenced her explanation with a kiss. She returned it with a fervor that I appreciated with every fiber of my being.

"Explanations can wait," I told her.

Michelle smiled seductively, "Wait for what, babe?"

"For what comes after your amazing bit of public foreplay in the backseat of the aircar."

Softly scraping her fingernails over my chest, Michelle lowered her mouth to my neck. "I was hoping that's what you meant."

Our emotions joined far more quickly and thoroughly than they'd ever done before. We shared every sensation, gasping and arching backs in unison. Then our bodies joined and we truly were as one.

I have no idea how long our lovemaking lasted, nor do I care. For the duration, my whole universe began and ended with Michelle. Finally, physically spent, we floated together in an emotional afterglow that slowly faded away until we were, once again, back in the real world.

"That was..." Michelle began. "I don't have any words to

describe it, babe."

"I know what you mean, hon." I kissed her once more, snatching a final few seconds of intimacy. "If you want to tell me about the fallout from our emotional outburst, early this morning, I think I can pay attention to it, now."

"Do you want the short version?"

"Sure."

"The newsies are calling your emotional blast-"

"*Our* emotional blast."

"You're the one with the psychic power, Matt. I just-"

"You 'just' saved the lives and sanity of untold thousands of people. I was absolutely lost until you came to my rescue." I caught Michelle's gaze in mine. "I'm not kidding, Michelle. You're the one who figured out how to avert the catastrophe. I just enjoyed everything you did to change those stored emotions. After that, releasing them was easy."

To my astonishment, Michelle actually blushed and lowered her eyes. "You're giving me too much credit, babe. I was terrified of losing you and was grasping at straws. Thank God, the straw I grabbed worked."

"I still say you're selling yourself short, but I can also tell you don't want me to go on about it. That's husband instincts, by the way, and has nothing to do with psychic abilities. So, what are the newsies calling *our* emotional blast."

Michelle looked at me again, a smile tugging at the corners of her mouth, and said, "The Midnight Miracle."

"Midnight?" I said, rolling my eyes. "It was closer to five in the morning."

"Alliteration rules the news cycle in these situations, Matt. After all, you can't have a Cairo Catastrophe and then a Five AM Miracle. Don't you have any poetry in your soul?"

"You heard the poems I wrote back in school, hon. I sucked at it, then, and I suck at it now. Still, I suppose it's a good thing that the newsies are giving the event a positive spin."

"They don't have any choice, Matt." Michelle's face lit up and her eyes sparkled as she continued, "That emotional blast stopped a shootout between police and a gang of criminals, caused hundreds of other criminals to simply turn themselves in, convinced at least a dozen people contemplating suicide that life was worth living, and put everyone in Cairo into incredibly good moods."

"You're joking, right?"

"No, babe, I'm not. It's getting world-wide play on the vids. Psi Corps has gone silent, ignoring questions about the Miracle, but everyone else is talking about it. Daddy has been in conference with GenCo marketing reps working out the best way to explain what you-"

"*We!*"

"What we did."

"Won't Psi Corps just refute our story, once we release it, and take the credit?" I asked.

"Maybe, but they'll only do that if they're desperate or incapable of advance planning. If Psi Corps takes responsibility for the Midnight Miracle, we'll challenge them to do it again, though on a smaller scale. Since the Miracle Man," I opened my mouth to interrupt again, so Michelle quickly added, "and Woman aren't part of Psi Corps, they won't be able to do that."

"But you think we will?"

"We'll restrict it to just a few people—enough to convince the newsies that we're telling the truth—but why not?" A troubled look came into her eyes. "Um, you—I mean, we—can do it again, right?"

"I don't see why not, but I think we should try it again before we make any announcements." I let my eyes roam down the length of Michelle's naked body. "I even know how we can fill my mind with nothing but joyful emotions."

"Well," Michelle mused, "it *is* for a good cause."

She opened her mind and body to me and, once again, we were one.

Much later, we found out the Midnight Miracle was repeatable.

CONFRONTING THE ENEMY

Michelle and I emerged from our room into a swirling mass of laughing children and one amused woman. Raneem ran up and gave us each a big hug. In quick succession, the rest of the kids did the same.

One of the girls pretended to swoon, saying, "Read me now!"

The rest of the girls took up the cry and soon the floor was littered with giggling girls.

"Have you been telling our story to all of your friends, young lady?" Michelle asked Raneem, smiling to ensure Raneem knew Michelle wasn't upset.

"Well, we had to have *some* way to pass the time while we waited for you and Matt to wake up." The little girl flashed her dazzling smile. "Hey, did you know Matt can do that miracle thing even when he's asleep? He sent happy waves at us just before we heard you two get up."

Michelle looked at me, her eyes twinkling. "I *thought* I felt something like that a while back."

The woman, struggling hard to contain laughter, said, "Mrs. Connaught, your father asked that I bring the two of you to him when you emerged."

"You aren't up here to keep an eye on the kids?" Michelle asked.

"No, ma'am, though having me around did give their current minder time to take a break."

"Thank you, uh...I'm sorry, I don't know your name."

"Elaine Ware, ma'am," the woman said, leading us to the door. "I'm part of the local GenCo security team."

"I hope we didn't keep you waiting very long," I said as we exited the penthouse.

"Your father-in-law warned me that you and Mrs. Connaught tend to...sleep...quite a lot after you get out of a difficult situation." Elaine's cheeks colored slightly as she used the obvious euphemism. "But the children kept me entertained. It also meant I was there for your most recent happy wave."

We entered the elevator and it descended rapidly.

"Is that what people are calling this ability of mine?" I asked. "The 'happy wave' sounds sort of silly to me."

"It won't to anyone who's experienced it, sir," Elaine said.

"Besides, it beats *your* name for it, babe," Michelle said.

"What does he call it?" Elaine asked.

"A positive emotional blast. I mean, seriously?"

"I think Mrs. Connaught is right, sir. I'd stick with the happy wave, if I were you."

I was saved the indignity of a response when the elevator stopped and the door opened.

Elaine led us down a hallway, through a few twists and turns, and then out into the building's lobby. It looked far different than I expected.

A strange banner hung on the far wall and two huge versions of it dangled from the ceiling four stories above us. The banners were dark blue, with a ring of silver stars encircling a silver spaceship. The ship looked familiar, though it took me a few seconds to figure out why. Even then, Michelle beat me to it.

"It's the *Ark 2*," she said in a low voice.

"Yeah," I said. "Do you have any idea what's going on, Elaine?"

"I think explanations are best left to Security Chief Young," she replied as Jonas approached.

"Thank you, Elaine," Jonas said. "I hope your wait wasn't too boring."

"Not at all sir. The children were most entertaining."

"I hope the children didn't keep these two from getting some sleep."

Elaine's mouth slid into a slight smirk. "Based on the happy wave I experienced thirty minutes ago, I'd say Mr. and Mrs. Connaught are very well...rested."

Jonas flashed a knowing smile. "What did I tell you?"

"Daddy!" Michelle said, her own cheeks reddening slightly. "I'd rather not discuss our...sleeping habits...in public."

"Then I suggest you keep your happy waves just between the two of you, pumpkin."

"That," Michelle said archly, "was simply us making sure Matt could replicate his initial success."

Jonas cocked one eyebrow and said, "Of course."

"Hey, I've got an idea—let's change the subject." I waved my arm toward the banners. "What's all of this for?"

"It's standard procedure for a planet to display their flag in their consulate offices, sir," Jonas said.

"Consulate offices?" Michelle and I asked at the same time.

"You are standing in the lobby of the Ark's Landing Consulate in Cairo," Jonas replied. Looking at me, he added, "It was your father's idea."

"Because a consulate is sovereign territory," I said. "Psi Corps can't do anything to us in here because it's outside of the Terran Federation's jurisdiction!"

"Damn, that is good!" Michelle said. "So, who's the Ark's Landing Consul?"

"Um, you are, pumpkin." When Michelle opened her mouth to speak, Jonas quickly added, "It's just temporary, only until the planetary council can appoint a permanent consul."

"Why me?"

"It had to be you or Matt. If either of you was captured, we could have used the associated diplomatic immunity to have you released. Apparently, the council thought Matt would be too controversial, so they chose you."

"Then why in God's name didn't you use our diplomatic immunity to protect us from the cops and Psi Corps last night?" Michelle's eyes blazed so brightly her father actually took a step back.

"The messenger drone carrying your appointment arrived an hour after we got back here. Besides, even if the appointment *was* official last night, it would only have freed the two of you. It wouldn't have worked for Harry Foster, Evie, or Doug." Jonas met Michelle's gaze. "Even if you'd thought you would just waltz out of Psi Corps using diplomatic immunity, we both know you'd have done everything possible to complete the rescue."

"Like father, like daughter," I said.

Michelle crossed her arms and gave me a flat stare. "You got a problem with that, babe?"

"Nope. I knew what I was getting into when I married you." Grinning, I added, "I hope the Honorable Consul Mrs. Connaught finds that answer to her liking."

"She does," Michelle nodded, her normal smile returning. "So, Daddy, what are my official duties?"

"You're holding a press conference, tomorrow morning, at nine. Matt will be at your side," Jonas told us. "Oh, and you have final approval on all appeals for sanctuary."

"You mean the Foster family, Evie, and Doug? Consider them approved. Do I have to sign anything?""

"Yes, but that can wait. There's a reason the press conference is so early in the morning," Jonas said. "Psi Corps is challenging the legitimacy of this consulate and your appointment to the office. Further, they claim you kidnapped three Psi Corps employees and are holding them against their will."

Michelle and I looked at Jonas in astonishment. She found her voice, first.

"How in God's name can Psi Corps make such a ridiculous claim?" she demanded. "That's just stupid! I mean, we can just bring all three of them out to the press conference and let them tell everyone the truth."

"In response, Psi Corps will trot out half-a-dozen telepaths who will swear Evie and Doug are under duress and lying to protect themselves or loved ones. They can't read Harry Foster, but will insist he's obviously facing the same threats," Jonas countered. "That's what Harry says they'll do, anyway. I've had a team researching similar situations over the last hundred years, and their findings match what Harry told me."

"What could we possibly threaten them with that's worse than going back to Psi Corps?" Michelle asked.

A pained expression passed over Jonas's face. "Harry thinks they'll use Matt's attack on someone named Toma, as the threat. After all, it incapacitated a psychic null. What could it do to an unprotected mind? Worse, Matt can attack from a distance, so even if we publicly tell our refugees they're free to go, Psi Corps can claim they're too scared of Matt to actually leave."

"But anyone with half a brain will know Psi Corps is lying," Michelle insisted.

"Probably, but they've got a lot more power inside the Federation than we'll ever have," Jonas replied. "Not even the newsies will go against Psi Corps, unless we can give them a story too compelling to ignore."

"Ask Foster—hm... I suppose should I start calling him Harry, shouldn't I?" I said. When Jonas shrugged in response, I continued, "Ask Harry for the story about the teenage precog who fed incorrect information to Psi Corps, letting a whole family of rogue psychics evade capture. Form a team to research the fallout from the precog's deception. Put everyone you can on the team and, with my personal authorization, use every GenCo resource available—including as much money as you need to get this done *fast*. Maybe *that* will give us the compelling story the newsies want."

"I like that, Matt!" Michelle agreed enthusiastically. "But,

Daddy, use the same methods to get hold of Toma's medical report. We have it on good authority that he's recovering, but we need to know his exact condition, in case we have to respond to Psi Corps accusations."

Jonas nodded and turned to go. He stopped and looked at Michelle and me. "Have I told the two of you just how proud I am of you?"

Michelle reached up and kissed her father on the cheek. "We had a really good teacher."

Without another word, Jonas hurried off.

"He's really worried, isn't he?" I asked.

"Yes, but he won't let that stop him. Come on, babe; you and I need to have a strategy session. We can't limit our options to that story about the precog and glib responses to Psi Corps' accusations."

"Shouldn't we include some of the others, hon?"

"No. If Psi Corps brings a bunch of telepaths to the press conference, we can't have them reading our plans from unprotected minds. I can shield myself and your empathic ability will scramble their attempts to read you."

"Harry's a psychic null," I said. "They couldn't read him."

"I know, but we should let him spend time with his family. Besides, he can do more helping Daddy and the research teams than anywhere else."

For the next several hours, Michelle and I holed up in an empty conference room. We had dinner brought in, and only interrupted our planning when someone needed our input. Once, our 'input' involved giving Raneem hugs and kisses goodnight, something we did happily. By the time we turned in, we had a few more ideas to use against Psi Corps.

We were up early, reviewing our plans and the results of the research. The information was as good as we could hope for, given our short deadline. It had considerably more substance than simple conspiracy theories, but also fell somewhat shy of being unarguable truth. Still, all it took was one enterprising newsie taking it seriously to give the story some traction and give us our chance we needed.

When we finished with the review, Jonas asked, "What did you and Matt come up with, pumpkin?"

"Please don't take this the wrong way, Daddy, but we're not going to tell you," Michelle said.

I waited for Jonas to go ballistic and order his daughter to fill him in. Instead, he folded his arms, looked at Michelle in a thoughtful manner and asked, "Can I assume you have a good reason for that?"

"Of course," she replied, telling him the same thing she told me the day before.

When Michelle wrapped up her explanation, Jonas smiled, "Textbook security protocol. That's my girl!"

We went to the lobby to await the newsies and Psi Corps' representative. While Michelle discussed protocol plans with some of the GenCo employees on loan to the Ark's Landing Consulate, Jonas inspected the security preparations. Left to myself, I spoke with our refugees and did my best to calm their nerves. Doug was particularly nervous.

"What's got you so worried, Doug?" I asked.

"What if they take me back?" he asked, in return. "They'll punish me for running off like this!"

"We're not going to let that happen."

"What if you can't stop it, sir? They're Psi Corps; they can do anything they want!"

"Not here, they can't, Doug. Not unless they want to create an interstellar diplomatic incident."

"They won't care. They're going to-"

"Do you want me to remove that bundle of nerves, Doug? It'll make you feel better."

"You can really do that, sir?" At my nod, he said, "Then, yeah, please take it out."

I gently extended my ability into the boy's mind, wrapped it around his collection of fears, and pulled them out. Never one to waste emotions, I stored them in case trouble arose.

"Oh, wow! That's amazing. Thanks, sir."

"Why don't you just call me Matt? Every time you say 'sir' I have to stop myself from looking for my father."

I left a more relaxed Doug talking with Evie, Evie's sister-to-be, Sarah, and Mrs. Foster, and walked over to where Michelle was finishing up her protocol conference. "How does everything look, Madam Consul?"

"The proper form of address is Mrs. Connaught, Consul General of Ark's Landing, babe."

"Oh. I hope you won't mind if I just stick with 'Michelle' or 'hon' instead of all that official crap? It could really distract me during our more...intimate...moments together."

Barely containing a grin, Michelle sniffed, "It violates proper protocol, but I suppose I can allow you a certain level of familiarity with me."

Before I could think of a suitable response, a convoy of identical, black aircars dropped down in front of the building. Each one bore the Psi Corps shield on its side. Doors popped open and armed guards leapt out. They, in turn, opened each aircar's rear door. A stream of Psi Corps officials, handlers, and psychics exited and marched toward the lobby doors. Leading the way was John Thomas, the former director of Psi Corps' Piscain Station office, and the man who sent Barb after us with a stun grenade.

As Thomas neared the door, an aide or flunky or whatever dashed ahead of him and activated the sensor. The doors slid smoothly aside just before Thomas strode through them. Three paces into the lobby, he stopped and looked around as though he owned the place. The remaining aides and flunkies split into two groups, one forming against the inside of the transparent lobby entrance and the other lining up just outside of the same barrier.

Ever the graceful host, I extended my right hand and said, "Welcome to the Ark's Landing Consulate, John."

He flashed a perfunctory smile, ignored my proffered hand, and replied, "Thank you, Matthew. Though during these official proceedings I'll thank you to refer to me as Assistant Director Thomas."

"Well, if we're going to be formal about it, you'll refer to me as Mr. Connaught. And Michelle is Mrs. Connaught—or, better still, Madam Consul General—to you."

"Of course."

Looking over Thomas's shoulder, I said, "You're more than welcome to bring the rest of your minions inside. I'm sure they'll be more comfortable out of the heat."

"Those are my telepaths and their handlers, Mr. Connaught. They're on hand to ensure the veracity of everything said during this...I'm tempted to say 'travesty' but will curb my acerbic tongue and call it a press conference."

"How generous of you, Assistant Director Thomas. We welcome telepathic verification, provided its honesty is not constrained by you."

"Why don't you wait for the newsies to arrive before beginning your performance, Mr. Connaught?"

"If you insist," I nodded, refusing to let them irritate me. "Back to my original invitation, the telepaths and their handlers are welcome within the consulate. Unlike many planets, Ark's Landing does not fear psychics."

"Do you take me for a fool, Mr. Connaught? My telepaths will remain outside of Ark's Landing's sovereign territory. I can't have some of my most valuable assets begging Mrs. Connaught for asylum—especially before a pack of newsies."

That had been my plan, of course, though I hadn't thought a control freak like Thomas would actually fall for it. Offering a thin smile, I said, "You can't blame a man for trying. Now, if you'll excuse me?"

I rejoined Michelle, who was discussing security considerations with her father. I stood politely until they both paused for breath.

"Is there a data pad I can use?" I asked, keeping my voice low. "I need to look something up."

"Sure, Matt," Michelle said. "You can use the one on the lectern. Just don't lose my notes."

I gave her a pained expression. "Remember who you're talking to, hon."

She offered me an apologetic smile. "I'm sorry, babe. I'm just nervous about the press conference. I've never been a planetary consul, before."

"Do you want me to reach in and pull out that bundle of nerves?"

"I'd have to lower my mental shield, and I'm certain John brought some psychics with him."

"He did. Half of the people lined up just outside of the lobby are telepaths. Oh, and he insists on being called Assistant Director Thomas during official proceedings. I told him to refer to you as 'Madam Consul General,' so call him on it, if he doesn't."

I accessed the data pad, being careful to preserve Michelle's notes, and spent several minutes digging into the local GenCo office archives. The office data manager kept the information in good order, so it only took me a few minutes to find what I was looking for. I noted the information and then cleared my research from the screen. By then, the newsies were setting up to cover the event.

She looked up when I approached. "Did you find what you needed, Matt?"

"Yes. I left a message for you on the pad. Use it anytime you think it will help, or when I give you a signal."

"That's very mysterious, babe."

"I know, but you'll understand when you read my note." I looked over at Thomas. "How impatient do you think he will be?"

Apparently, he was simply waiting for us to turn our attention on him. He walked out into the middle of the lobby and, in a loud voice, said, "If I could have everyone's attention, please?"

The newsies already had their cams on Thomas, as if they knew he was going to try taking over the news conference. Either his reputation preceded him or the newsies were tipped off. It didn't matter, since we expected a power play from whoever Psi Corps sent to the event.

"Assistant Director Thomas, this is my press conference." Michelle kept her tone even. "You'll be given ample opportunity to respond once I finish speaking."

"Why are you afraid of letting me speak first, *young* woman? Pardon me, I meant to say Mrs. Connaught, Consul General for the Ark's Landing colony."

Thomas looked into the cams and shrugged. He could easily claim the gesture was part of his apology. Viewers would probably assume he was questioning Michelle's age, Ark's Landing's foolishness for appointing her as their consul, or both. Judging by the way his eyes watched Michelle, I was certain he also hoped to provoke her temper.

She offered him a bland smile. "I could ask you the same question, Mr. Thomas."

Michelle's response prompted a frown—quickly cleared—from Thomas. At a guess, he hoped she would go on the defensive. Had she done so, he could have kept her reacting to his arguments rather than presenting her own case. With that option gone, Thomas tried a different tack.

"I'd like to see the Psi Corps employees you kidnapped early yesterday morning. I am concerned for their well-being and for that of their families." Thomas gave us a stern look. "I'll warn you now, neither Psi Corps nor the Terran Federation government accedes to extortion."

Michelle raised her eyebrows in surprise. "I thought Psi Corps was part of the Terran Federation government."

"It is."

Michelle gave a signal and Foster began leading his family toward her. "Then why did you name them both in your warning? Furthermore, why did you put Psi Corps first? Is it because you believe the Federation exists to serve Psi Corps, rather than the other way around?"

"Absolutely not."

"Well, that *is* a relief." Michelle smiled, as Foster and his family joined her at the lectern. "Ah, here's that Psi Corps employee and his family. As you can plainly see, they're all in excellent health."

"Is this some kind of joke? Where are the other two you took from Psi Corps last night?"

"You only asked to see the employees, Mr. Thomas."

"So?"

"Mr. Foster is the only employee who came with us."

"Lies! You also took two teenage precogs. A girl named Evie, and a boy named Doug. We have it all on vid."

"I never said Evie and Doug didn't come with us."

"Then why haven't you brought them before me?"

"Because they're not employees, Mr. Thomas. Employees get paid." Michelle's tone sharpened to match her words, "Evie and Doug are slaves—or they were, before we liberated them."

"That's preposterous! I demand you retract that absurd statement."

It was Michelle's turn to shrug, "Show us employment records, salary and tax receipts, and a bank balance—right now—and I'll give your request serious consideration."

"That sort of information is confidential and cannot be displayed without the proper authorization."

Michelle jerked a thumb over her shoulder. "Evie and Doug are out of your sight, but they're here. I'm sure they'd happily give you all the authorization you need."

"They're minors and are not legally allowed to give such authorization."

"How very convenient for you, Mr. Thomas."

"My hands are tied, Mrs. Connaught. It is, after all, the law."

"That's true. Do you know what else is the law, Mr. Thomas? Anyone—even a minor—may legally resign from his, or her, job.

I'll happily concede Evie and Doug are employees if you allow them to resign, should they wish."

Thomas's face reddened and several expressions of displeasure flashed across it. "Mrs. Connaught, you're not fooling anyone with your semantic arguments. We can return to this fascinating discussion once we've settled the *real* issue here."

"And what is that issue, Mr. Thomas?"

"How long are you and Ark's Landing going to shelter the lawbreaker, Matthew Connaught?"

"Mr. Connaught is no longer a citizen of the Federation. As such, he is not bound by their laws concerning psychics."

"I'm not referring to psychic laws." Thomas struck a dramatic pose, pointing an accusatory finger at me. "That man murdered a feeble-minded psychic woman I all but raised. He did it right before my eyes, and in the coldest of blood. And the laws against murder, Mrs. Connaught, apply to everyone—even your husband!"

"I don't believe you understand the concept of diplomatic immunity, Mr. Thomas," Michelle said.

"How unexpected," Thomas said, his tone dripping with sarcasm. "Rather than respond to my charges, Mrs. Connaught hides behind diplomatic immunity."

"I'm just—"

"Hiding behind diplomatic immunity. We all recognize what you're doing and no one who truly knows you is surprised."

I laid a hand on Michelle's shoulder and turned her toward me. In a low voice, I said, "I'll take care of this. Why don't you go read the note I left for you at the lectern?"

"Are you sure, Matt?"

"I can handle myself, hon. Don't worry."

With a brief nod, Michelle turned and walked back toward the lectern. Thomas watched her for a second, then turned toward the newsies. He spread his arms in mock astonishment, implying Michelle was simply ignoring his charges.

"There's no need for such theatrics, Assistant Director

Thomas," I said. "You have accused me of a crime, and I am going to respond to your charges."

"Ah, so you're finally going to stop hiding behind your wife's skirts?" Thomas asked.

"I won't dignify that asinine question with an answer." I shook my head, as if disappointed Thomas. "I will, however, respond to your charges that I committed cold-blooded murder."

"I can't imagine that response will be very long," Thomas said. "Something along the lines of, 'Yes, I did it' is about all you can say."

"Come now, Mr. Thomas, you know there were extenuating circumstances."

"Murder is murder, Mr. Connaught. There is nothing else to say."

"Trite, but true. On the other hand, under Federation law, self-defense—or the defense of one's family—is not murder. I acted in self-defense after you threatened Michelle's life. I believe your exact words were, 'Once Sadie feeds on a mind, she can always find it again. This young man can't keep her out forever. When he drops his guard, that young woman is as good as dead.' You followed that with promises that only you could control Sadie and Michelle would be safe only for as long as I did everything you asked."

"I categorically deny saying any such thing."

"Of course you do. I'll bet you even made sure any vid recordings of the scene were wiped. But, there were about three dozen witnesses."

"As if we would believe a bunch of psychics who abandoned their posts and went with you to Ark's Landing."

"Isn't that why you brought your telepaths?" I asked. "Though, there is also the question of how we can trust people over whom you hold such power."

"While I know the telepaths will be completely truthful, I also know they cannot read an empath—you—or a psychic null—me. Which brings us back to our impasse."

"You're forgetting that we have a third witness present. After all, how could Sadie feed on Michelle's mind, or you threaten her, if she wasn't there?" I raised an eyebrow in question, "You are willing to admit she was present?"

"Mrs. Connaught has a quite effective psychic shield," Thomas said. "I'm afraid that my telepaths cannot read her."

"Now, that is curious," I said. "How could you know Michelle has a mental shield? Could it be, that your telepaths have already tried to read her? That's against the law, isn't it?"

"That is irrelevant to the question at hand," Thomas said, his tone supercilious.

"From the way the newsies are tapping away at their pads, I think you're the only person in the room who believes that. But, I'm willing to let it go so that we can get on to more important matters." I looked over my shoulder at Michelle. "Are you ready and willing to drop your mental shield?"

Michelle inclined her head. "I am."

I turned back to Thomas, "Are your telepaths ready?"

Thomas turned to an aide and jerked his head toward the telepaths lined up just outside of the lobby. The aide hurried to the door and spoke quietly to one of the handlers outside. He returned to Thomas's side and nodded once.

"My telepaths are ready. Mrs. Connaught, please drop your mental shield."

Michelle took a deep breath and released it slowly. "All right, my shield is down."

As I'd anticipated, Thomas was so certain of his authority that he never turned around to look at his telepaths. He just stood there, hands behind his back and a triumphant look on his face as he watched me. All of his aides—or minions, or whatever you want to call them—followed his lead. They didn't even turn around when the lobby door slid open, apparently assuming one of the handlers was bringing the results to them. It was only when a scuffle broke out between a telepath trying to enter the lobby and a handler trying to drag him away from the door, that any of them turned around.

All six of the telepaths were pushing to free themselves from their handlers and enter the lobby.

"Get them to the aircars—now!" Thomas snarled.

"You do not issue orders in my consulate," Michelle snapped. "Furthermore, you may not forcibly remove people from the sovereign territory of Ark's Landing without my permission."

"They are not on your sovereign territory, Mrs. Connaught," Thomas replied. "So, this does not concern you."

"The consulate grounds extend twenty meters beyond the lobby, Mr. Thomas." Michelle gave him a patronizing smile and said, "May I suggest you restrict your comments to matters about which you have some knowledge?"

Michelle looked at Jonas and waved him towards the commotion. Her father pointed to several members of his security staff and they waded into the scuffle. After forcibly separating the handlers from the telepaths, Jonas turned back to his daughter.

"Mrs. Connaught, what would you like me to do with these people?" he asked.

"Find out what was going on, please."

Jonas didn't even have to ask. As soon as Michelle finished speaking, one of the telepaths, a woman on the far end of middle-aged, said, "Our handlers wouldn't let us tell the truth."

"Well, that is most shocking." Michelle looked at Thomas, "Are the handlers acting under your orders, Mr. Thomas?"

"Certainly not, and I object to any such accusation!"

"I'm very relieved to hear that, Mr. Thomas," Michelle said. "You will, no doubt, have no objection to letting the telepaths tell us what they found when they read my mind?"

Thomas looked as though he had just swallowed a mouthful of bugs. He managed a weak and insincere smile. Apparently, unwilling to trust his voice, he nodded to Michelle.

The telepath who spoke earlier took that as her cue. "Everything happened just the way Mr. Connaught said it did. Also, everyone in Psi Corps knew about Sadie. She terrified-"

Thomas waved a hand in dismissal, "I don't think we need to hear anything else. My telepaths and I will be leaving."

"You're more than welcome to leave," Michelle informed him. "But, the telepaths may remain until they are ready to leave. Unless you think of them more as property than people, Mr. Thomas. And, even if you do, they won't leave until they are ready."

Michelle turned from Mr. Thomas to the telepaths. "Are you ready to leave or is there anything else you would like to say?"

The woman who spoke earlier said, "Madam Consul General, the six of us request asylum from the Ark's Landing."

Behind her, the other five telepaths all nodded vigorously, showing their support for the request.

Thomas's face reddened and he shouted at Michelle, "You have no right-"

Michelle's voice cut across his like a whip, "I have every right. Just as the telepaths have every right to request asylum from a repressive government that holds them as slaves. Unlike the Terran Federation, Ark's Landing respects the rights of all people—including psychics."

Off to one side, virtually forgotten, the newsies frantically tapped away at their data pads and checked their vid feeds. Several more cams rose into the air above them and focused on both Michelle and Thomas. They caught Michelle's triumphant smile and Thomas's impotent fury. They also caught Michelle's compassionate expression when she turned her attention to the six telepaths and Thomas's hateful glare when he did the same.

Smiling alarmingly, Michelle declared, "After careful consideration of Ark's Landing's previous stance on the issue of psychics' rights, I grant asylum to these six telepaths."

She looked at Jonas, and said, "Security Chief Young, please escort these refugees into the consulate. Also, assign a detail to ensure Mr. Thomas and the rest of his delegation find their way out of the consulate and off of its grounds."

Finally, she turned her attention to the newsies. "We have more information to share with you, if you would be willing to stay a little longer? Mr. Foster has a story he is most eager to tell you. We can, of course, give you time to file what you have so far with your news agencies."

Strangely enough, no one ever got around to asking me about the Midnight Miracle.

VICTORY

We escorted the newsies to a large conference room and gave them time to file the part of the story they already had. Then, Michelle introduced Foster while her aides passed out data pads filled with all of the information our research teams had unearthed about the unfortunate precog and his late sister. While Foster recounted that story, couching his own life as a precog handler in the same context, Michelle and I retreated to a corner and watched the proceedings.

"What do you think, Matt?" Michelle asked. "Do they believe Foster?"

"I assume you're not asking me to read them without their permission?" At Michelle's nod, I said, "The newsies are paying attention to what he's saying. Plus, we've got lots of research supporting his story. The evidence is circumstantial, but it's also believable. If any of these newsies have dealt with Psi Corps in the past, I think they'll give Foster's story a fair listen."

"That's my feeling, too," Michelle said. "By the way, finding out how far the consulate grounds extended was really clever. It never even occurred to me to check."

"I only thought of it after Thomas lined his telepaths up just outside the door. Nobody gives much thought to it, but buildings are never constructed to fill an entire lot. I just made sure our property line extended beyond the lobby doors. You and the telepaths did all the rest."

We sat in a comfortable silence watching Foster respond to questions from the newsies. After much convincing, he even introduced Evie and his family. The four of them answered personal interest questions, the typical sort of thing newsies ask to round out their stories. Michelle and I returned to face the newsies when they were finished with the Fosters and their soon-to-be adopted daughter.

The senior-most newsie finally turned to us. "You have given us quite a fascinating story, Mr. and Mrs. Connaught. But we originally came here to find out about the Midnight Miracle. I think it's past time for us to do that."

"Please be assured we have not been avoiding that subject," Michelle said. "We felt the events of the last two hours were dramatic enough that we didn't want to derail the unfolding story. If you don't have any further questions about recent events, we are more than ready to discuss the Midnight Miracle."

The same newsie turned her attention to me and asked, "Are you the psychic responsible for the Midnight Miracle?"

Nodding, I said, "I am."

"By all reports, you're the most powerful empath since the unfortunate soul responsible for the Cairo Catastrophe. How can the people of the Terran Federation trust a man with such power?"

"They don't have to, ma'am. I live on Ark's Landing."

"And yet, you're standing right here with me on Earth. Given the ease of interstellar travel—especially for someone of your wealth—I believe my question is still relevant."

"That's a reasonable point." I took a moment to order my thoughts and then said, "I want nothing more than to be allowed to live out my life in peace. I do not want to spend that life looking over my shoulder, wondering when the next Psi Corps attack will take place. I do not want to spend that life worrying that Psi Corps will capture me and Michelle and then use her to force me to do their bidding. I do not want to spend my life worrying that Psi Corps will kidnap my future children, in the hopes they will have psychic abilities. I do not want to spend that life as a slave to the Terran Federation and their fear of psychics."

"That's a very impassioned response, Mr. Connaught, but it doesn't answer my question."

"I am not a threat to the people of Earth. I am not a threat to the people of the Terran Federation. I never have been, and I never will be. Everything I have done since Michelle and I went on the run from Draconis, months ago, has been in response to attacks by the Terran Federation on me. If the Terran Federation will stop attacking me, I will happily leave the Terran Federation alone."

"You keep saying Terran Federation. Don't you mean Psi Corps?"

"I believe Michelle went over that subject with Assistant Director Thomas, in the lobby. However, just to make sure there is no confusion, I'll go over it again. Psi Corps is a department of the Terran Federation government. It operates under Terran Federation law. It enforces Terran Federation law with respect to psychics. Anything done by Psi Corps is done *by* the Terran Federation and *for* the Terran Federation.

"You fine, upstanding, *free* citizens of the Terran Federation may recoil from the word 'slave' but I cannot think of a more appropriate name for the psychics controlled by Psi Corps. If this offends your sensibilities, I suggest you all get off your collective asses and do something about it. You could start by freeing all of the psychics, repealing the psychic impressment laws, and eliminating Psi Corps. Until you're willing to do that, the Terran Federation is no better than the lowest frontier slave trader."

"Really, sir? Aren't you being a bit melodramatic?"

"Have you ever asked a psychic how they feel about Psi Corps and the psychic impressment laws?" The newsie shook her head and I continued, "Next time you want to know what it's like to be the target of such laws, I suggest you ask the slave, and not the master."

The newsie had the grace to look uncomfortably thoughtful, as did her colleagues around the conference table. After a moment of silence, one of the younger newsies waved for my attention.

"You have given us much to think about, Mr. Connaught, but one problem still remains."

"And that is?" I asked.

"What do we do with all the psychics?"

"You could try letting them live in peace while providing training in the control of their psychic abilities. Psi Corps already does part of that, so the basic ideas should be pretty easy to implement. Think of it as public education for psychics."

"But what about the Federation citizens who are uncomfortable with the idea of psychics walking freely among them?"

"Doesn't the Terran Federation pride itself in its tolerance of those who are different from the norm? If the population is incapable of overcoming such bigotry, then you may send all of the Terran Federation psychics to Ark's Landing. We will happily welcome them."

"Even if one of those psychics is more powerful than you are?"

"Yes. I fear governments far more than I fear any psychic." I looked around the conference table, making eye contact with every newsie there. Then I said, "It is time for the Terran Federation to end this experiment with slavery. It is time to extend full rights to *all* citizens. No, slaves are not citizens, so let me amend that. It is time to extend full rights to all *human beings*. It is time for the Federation to stop living in fear and start living in peace. It is time to dismantle the machinery of oppression that threatens anyone with the misfortune to be born psychic."

Having said my piece, I turned and left the conference room.

To my surprise, my harsh words for the Terran Federation, Psi Corps, and the psychic impressment laws dominated the news cycle. The stories opened with the Midnight Miracle but centered on me and my call to stop enslaving psychics.

Over the next several days, those opposed to my call built elaborate straw versions of me and my arguments. Time after time, I was forced to comment on ridiculous claims.

"No, I didn't say psychics were superior to non-psychics nor did I claim psychics should become mankind's rulers. For God's sake, my wife is non-psychic and I assure you I'm not stupid enough to try ruling *her*!"

That one drew a laugh, which was the idea. No one ever convinced the mass of humanity of anything using only logic and facts. Make your point. Sugar-coat it with humor, though, and you can open minds. Besides, responding seriously to such a stupid claim just legitimizes the stupidity.

"I never claimed the Terran Federation owes psychics anything beyond the right to live their lives as they see fit. Psychics are just as human as non-psychics. We want to live and love just like everyone else, bounded by the same laws as our non-psychic fellow citizens. In other words, psychics want the same freedom enjoyed by everyone around them."

I won't repeat everything else I said nor go into the details of every response, but the ongoing debate kept us hopping at the Ark's Landing Consulate.

We got our first big break five days after the Midnight Miracle. By then, the story and its ensuing controversy had spread across most of the Terran Federation. Debates raged on every planet, but it was my original home planet of Draconis that went beyond mere debate.

Michelle and I were relaxing in the penthouse, enjoying a lull in the parade of newsies and politicians demanding time with us. I sat on the sofa, Michelle's head cradled in my lap, absently running my hand through her soft hair. Minutes before, her eyes had drifted shut and her expression softened as she slid into a much-needed nap.

I was annoyed beyond reason when I heard loud shouts coming

from the hallway. I silently cursed the shouter as Michelle's eyes fluttered open. Then, the penthouse door slid open and Jonas charged into the room.

"Matt! Michelle!" he shouted. "Oh my God, you're not going to believe this!"

Sitting up and rubbing at her eyes, Michelle said, "Daddy?"

"It's Draconis, pumpkin! *Draconis!*"

I'd never seen Jonas this excited before, in my life. Hell, I'd never seen even Jonas excited, before. Ever. Not even after I used my empathic ability to find and rescue Michelle from the space outside of Pegasus Station had he shown excitement. He was thankful, yes, and his eyes glistened as he'd embraced the daughter he'd feared lost forever, but he wasn't excited.

"What's wrong, Jonas?" I asked.

"Wrong? *Nothing* is wrong, son!"

Michelle and I exchanged worried glances. Jonas had been my head of security for nine years and my father-in-law for just over a year. In that time, he had never once called me 'son'.

"You're not making any sense, Daddy."

"I'm sorry, Michelle. It's just..." He took a deep breath, released it, and, in a much calmer voice said, "A messenger drone from the planetary government of Draconis just arrived. It was specifically directed to the Ark's Landing Consulate, though it says identical ones were sent to the Prime Minister of the Terran Federation, Earth's planetary government, and every major news service on the planet." Jonas took another deep breath, smiled broadly, and said, "The planetary government of Draconis has officially suspended enforcement of the psychic impressment laws, and will begin processing psychics out of Psi Corps' Draconis office tomorrow morning."

Michelle's hands flew to her face and her eyes blinked rapidly. Then, she threw her arms around me and kissed me. For once, I returned her kiss on autopilot as my mind tried to come to grips with the news.

Jonas was just standing there, grinning at us, when the door slid aside and Harry Foster charged into the room.

"There's more news!" he said, his face a mask of excitement. "Earth's planetary government has called an emergency session to debate the psychic impressment laws. Speculation is that they'll follow Draconis' lead."

"There's a long way to go, but with the two richest and most populous planets in the Federation taking the lead, the rest will follow quickly enough," Jonas said. "You two have done it—you've changed the galaxy!"

He came over and gave both of us a hug. "Have I told you just how proud I am of the two of you?"

Michelle smiled, "Not since breakfast, Daddy."

The day after the drone from Draconis arrived, I planned a visit to the hospital where Toma, the psychic null whose shield I'd so thoroughly blasted, was recovering. Jonas stopped me, advising against a personal visit by Michelle or me. He went in our place, acting as an official representative of Ark's Landing.

Toma was recovering, and showed every sign of regaining his natural shield. He did not have the slightest interest in reconciliation with anyone from Ark's Landing, least of all me. Jonas didn't press the point and was back at the Consulate in less than an hour.

Five days later, we—including the six telepaths, the Fosters, Doug, Raneem, and her friends—boarded a ship for the return trip to Ark's Landing. By then, sixty-three Federation worlds, following the path blazed by Draconis and Earth, had suspended the laws. Seeing the writing on the wall, the Federation Prime Minister called an emergency session of the Federation Parliament to debate the laws, Psi Corps, and the future of psychics throughout the Federation. Planetary representatives were still arriving when our ship lifted off.

We got the official word two days later, during our transit through the Piscain Hub. The Federation Parliament had officially repealed the impressment laws and begun the long process of dismantling Psi Corps and introducing psychics back into Federation society.

After toasting our victory, I looked at my wife. "I still can't believe how quickly it all happened. We went from nowhere to a full repeal in, what, a week and a half?"

Michelle kissed me lightly on the lips. "Sometimes, all it takes is one impassioned voice to ignite a population."

I smiled and gave her a kiss in return. "I think you mean *two* impassioned voice, hon."

A day later, we landed on Ark's Landing, where we were welcomed by at least half of the city's population. Arm-in-arm, Michelle and I waved to the crowd.

I smiled broadly, pulling Michelle tightly against me. "It's good to be home again."

The next few weeks passed in a blur, as we found adoptive homes for Raneem's friends and Doug. We didn't have to look far for someone to adopt Raneem, though. Jonas and Magda invited her into our family. Like Cassie before her, Raneem leapt at the chance.

The Fosters officially adopted Evie and began their new lives as a family of four. Gene and Mark—Cassie's 'psychic brothers'—spent so much time visiting the two girls that I'm sure Harry felt like he had a family of six.

One sunny morning, a couple of months after our return, something extraordinary happened. As Michelle and I made love, merged in mind and body, we felt a tiny spark join in our emotional union.

Startled, Michelle stopped moving and looked down at me. "Oh my God, who is that?"

A sudden realization came to me. "Hon, I think that's Nora."

"Nora? Does that mean-?"

"You're going to be a momma."

"And you're going to be a daddy." Slowly, lovingly, Michelle began moving again. "Life is about to get very interesting for us, babe."

"Oh, good," I said, pulling Michelle into a long kiss. "I hate boredom."

YOU MIGHT ALSO ENJOY...

If you enjoyed *The Fugitive Snare*, you might enjoy *The Counterfeit Captain*, the first book in the Captain Nancy Martin series.

Please consider posting a brief review of
The Fugitive Snare.
Reader recommendations are the best advertising.

ABOUT THE AUTHOR

Growing up, Henry worked at the usual range of menial jobs before ending up in software development. In between the menial jobs and the IT jobs, he achieved some small fame as the writer and co-creator of the small press comic book titles Southern Knights and X-Thieves. In 2006, Henry also took up the mantle of professional storyteller. He performs regularly throughout the state of North Carolina and has recently released his first book of children's stories.

Henry has been a fan of science fiction for as long as he can remember. He has loved space opera and planetary romance since the beginning, that is why his science fiction novels end up in those subgenres.

Henry currently lives in Raleigh, NC, with his wife, son, two cats, and lots of imaginary friends all clamoring to tell him of their adventures.

www.henryvogelwrites.com

ALSO BY HENRY VOGEL

Science Fiction Novels

The Lost Planet

Fortune's Fool

The Scales of Sin & Sorrow

Scout's Honor

Scout's Oath

Scout's Duty

Scout's Law

Scout's Training

Hart for Adventure

The Fugitive Heir

The Fugitive Pair

The Fugitive Snare

The Counterfeit Captain

The Undercover Captain

The Recognition Run

The Recognition Rejection

The Recognition Revelation

Illustrated Children's Book

I'm in Charge! and Other Stories